ENEMY MINE

THE SEDONA FILES: BOOK 6

CHRISTINE POPE

DARK VALENTINE PRESS

ENEMY MINE

ISBN: 978-0692724972

Copyright © 2016 by Christine Pope.

Revised version copyright © 2019

Published by Dark Valentine Press

Cover design by Lou Harper

Book formatting by Indie Author Services

CHAPTER ONE

THE STRANGER'S HAND FELT HUMAN IN MINE, WARM, strong. But he wasn't human. At least not entirely.

I didn't know what he was. I didn't even know his name. But his fingers clasped mine tightly as the communications center in the alien base disappeared in a flare of brilliant yellow light. I caught the briefest flash of the despairing look in my friend Callista's eyes, the panic on the faces of her parents, a strange resignation emanating from Raphael, Callista's soul-bonded lover.

Then they were all gone, and I found myself standing on a floor of dark polished metal, walls of the same substance close by on either side. It was a corridor, probably on the Reptilians' spaceship, judging by the blocky, unadorned architecture, very similar to what I'd seen in their underground base outside Sedona. At least, I assumed they'd brought me to their ship and not another base, although the prescience that had told me to step forward and take the green-skinned man's hand seemed to have deserted me for the moment, and all I had to rely on was the usual five senses.

The stranger hadn't deserted me, though. He still held my hand, and even though I didn't know him, knew nothing of how he'd come to be here with a race of malevolent aliens, I couldn't help being somehow reassured by his touch. At least it felt normal, an anchor of something real in a sea of strangeness. I clung to him as I tried to push back my fear.

This was your decision, I told myself. *You knew this was where you needed to go.*

For some reason, though, that inner reminder didn't reassure me at all.

Also gathered around us in the hallway were the Reptilians we'd encountered in the communications center at their former base. They stared at me with their strange red eyes, but I couldn't begin to decipher their expressions. How could I, when the only things they shared in common with a human face were a pair of eyes and a mouth? Their noses were only two slits in the center of their faces, and their mouths not much more than that, a lipless gash.

The leader, the one with the pale golden skin, who called himself Lir Shalan, bent toward the

young man holding my hand and murmured something in the Reptilian language, but of course, I
couldn't understand anything he said. Nor could I
pick up any of his thoughts or even his emotions.
Usually, I didn't experience that kind of difficulty—
my real problem was keeping other people's mental
babble out of my head—but he was an alien, and
there must have been something about my ability to
read minds and sometimes see bits and pieces of
possible futures that just didn't translate when it
came to dealing with the unfamiliar architecture of
his brain.

The stranger who held my hand replied in the
same tongue, and Lir Shalan gave what looked like a
satisfied nod before he made a brusque gesture with
one hand. He headed off down the corridor, the rest
of his team or entourage or whoever they were
following only a few paces behind. The heavy boots
they wore clanged off the metal floor, but within a
moment the sound had faded, and I was left alone
with the green-skinned man.

He offered me a hesitant smile. His teeth were
straight and white, and looked very human. Really,
he seemed almost completely human, if you could
ignore the pale sage tint to his skin and the deep ruby
color of his irises. The Reptilians' eyes were that
shade, but their pupils were slits, whereas the
stranger's were round and black, like those of any
human.

"Come with me," he said, and his voice sounded normal enough, too, warm and not overly deep, and with an accent as American as my own. "Your name is Taryn Oliver, correct?"

"Y-yes," I replied, startled that he knew who I was. But then, he must have known something about me, or why else would he have leaned forward and had that brief but intense exchange with Lir Shalan back in the communications center? I was almost positive it was in that moment he'd suggested it would make more sense for them to take me instead of Callista.

"I am Lir Gideon," he offered. "This ship is called —" He hesitated, as if he'd intended to say something else, then went on, "Come to think of it, the human mouth has difficulties with the Reptilian language."

"You seem to manage all right," I said, my voice a little shakier than I would have liked. Yes, I'd come here of my own free will, had confidently told Callista that I was ready to have an adventure of my own, but now, standing on the deck of an alien ship, I was beginning to feel some of that confidence deserting me. And while my mind boiled with questions, instead I'd taken refuge in that slightly sarcastic comment, mostly because I wasn't sure how I was supposed to react to him.

"Well, I've had my whole life to practice." Then his shoulders lifted slightly, as if dismissing the topic.

I realized then how tall he was, how broad under the heavy robes he wore. "Anyway, this ship is the *Eclipse*. Let me take you to the place where you will be staying."

He began to lead me down the corridor, which appeared very different from the way Callista had described Raphael's Pleiadian-built ship. That vessel, apparently, had been quite beautiful, with colored lights serving as the ship's signs, and furnishings that seemed almost organic rather than manufactured. In contrast, the Reptilian ship was dimly lit, all square angles and hard, cold surfaces. Doorways with rectangular panels set into the walls next to them were spaced along the hall at regular intervals, but Lir Gideon passed them all by without pausing.

As we walked, I mustered enough courage to ask, "Are you taking me to a lab or something?"

My question must have startled him, because he stopped almost mid-stride, then stared down at me, black brows lifting against his pale green skin. "A lab? Why would you think that?"

"Well—" I didn't want to offend him, but it seemed like a standard enough thing to ask. After all, the Reptilians were pretty well known for performing all kinds of experiments on humans, most of them extremely unpleasant. I didn't know why I would be treated any differently. After an awkward pause, I went on, "Your people had the captured female astronauts in a lab, and—"

"Oh, no," he cut in. "This situation is not like that at all. You are an honored guest, Taryn Oliver."

"Just Taryn," I said, actually managing to smile up at him. His revelation that I was a guest and not the human equivalent of a lab rat had relieved me more than I wanted to admit. Well, assuming he was telling the truth. I couldn't read any more from him than I could from his leader. "We don't use both names in casual conversation."

"Is that what we are having?"

Well, I didn't know how casual I felt, but it did seem a lot easier to talk to him than I'd thought. Maybe that was because, from the surreptitious glances I'd stolen at him as we walked along, he didn't seem all that much older than I was. Maybe twenty-four or twenty-five, while I wouldn't be twenty-two for a few more months, but still. Close enough to seem relatable.

Except that he was a hybrid, or...something. I still hadn't quite puzzled that out. The only hybrids I'd met—like Logan and Grace, who was half-hybrid— looked just like regular humans. Extremely attractive humans, but still.

And Lir Gideon...he actually was good-looking as well, once you got past the odd coloring. His hair was thick and black, just slightly wavy, and something about the high cheekbones and strong nose and full, wide mouth made me think of portraits I'd seen of Renaissance courtiers. Except for the green skin and red eyes, he didn't look as if he would have been out of place at the court of the Medicis.

But there was my imagination getting the better of me again. The man who walked next to me definitely was no Medici. I really didn't know what he was.

"I suppose it's a conversation," I said, in answer to his question. "As for casual…." All I could do was lift my shoulders.

Another smile, this one not nearly as hesitant as the last one he'd offered me. "Well, I can understand why you might feel a bit strange. But here we are."

He placed his palm against a panel embedded in the wall. As with all the others, it was placed next to a door. This door slid open at his touch. Inside was a chamber just as dimly lit as the hallway we'd traversed to get there, but by that point, I'd become accustomed to the reddish-tinged semidarkness. The Reptilians' eyes must have been more light-sensitive than human eyes.

I didn't have much choice but to follow him inside. The room was not overly large, maybe a little bigger than my bedroom back at the house where I'd grown up. I didn't know exactly what I'd been expecting, except this didn't seem to match my fears of labs filled with horrible surgical equipment, or possibly some kind of jail cell.

Even in the dim lighting I could see there was a table with a square metal chair sitting in front of it, and up against the windowless far wall was an odd backless kind of sofa with a metal table placed before it. Directly opposite the wall with its table and chair was a sort of cubbyhole with a rectangular opening. As I squinted into the gloom, I realized there seemed to be some kind of padded surface inside that cubbyhole, or whatever it was. The bed?

The question must have been plain on my face, because Lir Gideon said, "That is where we—I mean, that is where you will sleep. You see?"

Without answering right away, I went over to the cubbyhole and peered in. Sure enough, the entire surface within was raised about three feet off the floor, and held a kind of mattress, really just a pad about four inches thick and covered with a heavy, soft fabric whose nap felt surprisingly soft against my fingertips.

I knew nothing about the Reptilians' home world or how they'd evolved, but if they were anything like the reptiles on Earth, then it made sense that they'd want a dark, warm, burrow-y sort of place to sleep.

"It's—it's very nice," I said, then added lamely, "Thank you."

"You are welcome." He stood there for a moment, seeming to watch me, although it was hard to tell for sure in that gloomy lighting. "I suppose this must seem very strange to you."

There was an understatement. I didn't sense any kind of menace from him, but at the same time, I had to wonder why he'd wanted me here at all. The Reptilians were well known—among UFO circles, at least—for their rapaciousness, and yet if that sort of thing was his intention, why was he just standing there and looking at me in that calm, quiet way?

"It is," I said frankly. "I suppose I don't understand why I'm here."

Even in the dim light, I could see his eyebrows lift. "I thought you stepped in to save your friend."

"Not really. It seemed to me that you both decided you didn't want Callista, but wanted me instead. Or did I misread what you were saying to each other back at the base?"

A pause. He shifted slightly, and I stiffened, but he'd only moved over to the chair so he could rest one hand on its back. "No, that's an accurate assessment of our exchange." He stopped again, the ruby eyes unreadable under his straight black brows. "Unlike her, you are completely human, correct?"

"Yes." Callista Jones might have been three-quarters Pleiadian and Grace Rinehart half-hybrid, but I wasn't anything except your ordinary run-of-the-mill human. Well, except for being psychic, but even the powers that had been with me almost since I could remember appeared to have deserted me for the moment. "Nothing but *homo sapiens* in my DNA."

"And yet you have powers that most humans do not possess."

I wondered how he knew that. Then again, how did the Reptilians know anything? Some kind of strange surveillance system that no one, not my mother and father, not the Rineharts, not even

Callista's Pleiadian parents, had really been able to figure out. True, the Reptilians were supposed to have been banished from the area for the past twenty-five years, ever since Callista's mother Kirsten drove them out of Sedona, but it seemed obvious enough to me that they'd still been keeping some sort of watch.

"I flip a few Tarot cards at the shops in Uptown," I said, my tone careless.

"It's much more than that. I was watching you, back at the communications center at the base. I saw it in your eyes. Recognition. Resignation."

The room was not cold—in fact, it was slightly warmer than what I found comfortable, a concession to the Reptilians' physiology, no doubt—but a shiver went down my spine then. I'd felt Lir Gideon's gaze on me during that encounter. At the time, I'd been desperately attempting to keep Callista and her parents and Raphael from noticing anything strange about my reaction, but Gideon had obviously seen something.

Because for weeks before that confrontation at the base, I'd been having dreams and flashes, sure signs that something huge and unavoidable was approaching. At first, I hadn't been able to discern anything except an overwhelming sensation of dread, but as time wore on, I began to catch glimpses of *them*. The Reptilians, that is. I didn't say anything to my parents. There was nothing they could have done. I'd known this encounter was approaching with the inexorable power of the tide. It had been inevitable.

What I hadn't seen was Lir Gideon. Not that he was precisely a surprise, more that the presence of the Reptilians had somehow cloaked him until the time came for me to see him in person. And then when I had stood there in the communications center, silent as I watched Callista try to bargain for her lover Raphael's life, I'd seen this strange man, not quite human, not quite alien, felt his gaze on me, and I'd known this was what the dreams and visions had been drawing me toward.

Why, I couldn't say for sure. I supposed time would have to tell me that. For now, I'd just have to remember that everything happened for a reason, even if I couldn't see what that reason was.

"You're very observant," I said, hating that the shaky edge was back in my voice. "No one else seemed to notice."

"They were focused on other things."

Had he watched me then the way he watched me now? I could feel the weight of his gaze on me, and I didn't know what to do about it. Ever since my psychic powers had awakened, I'd done my very best not to go into a person's mind unless they explicitly invited me—unless they were broadcasting so strongly I had no way of avoiding their thoughts —but right then, I wished I could see even just a little of what Lir Gideon was thinking.

"You knew," he went on. "I saw that you knew.

You had come along with your friend and her parents because you knew in the end it was your presence there that would be the most important."

"I don't know about that. Callista had to be there to do what she could to get Raphael back. That was all her decision."

And then I saw it—a twitch of the muscle in Lir Gideon's cheek. If I hadn't been watching him so closely, and if my eyes hadn't adjusted to the light as much as they had, I know I would never have seen it. But that telltale was enough.

"And you knew, too, didn't you?" I asked.

"Knew what?"

His pronunciation and inflections were almost perfect. He must have spent a lot of time listening to our various broadcasts and internet videos to get it that close to normal. But something in his voice just then had shifted subtly, and I knew the innocent act was just that—an act. The shift in his voice had coincided with that faint muscle twitch, both of them telling me he must be trying to hide something.

"You knew that I'd seen something, and so you knew I would come along with Callista and her parents. That's really why you took Raphael. Your boss Lir Shalan only wanted him as bait."

A faint narrowing of his eyes when I mentioned Lir Shalan. But otherwise, Lir Gideon didn't react, except to give the faintest of shrugs. "It is true that the person you refer to as Raphael wasn't that impor-tant to us. Or rather, we knew we had to step carefully there, as he is an agent of the Assembly, and there could have been repercussions if he was harmed."

"But it was okay to take me."

Face impassive, he asked, "Have you been harmed?"

No, of course I hadn't. And it wasn't as if I'd been dragged here against my will. I'd put my hand in Lir Gideon's, had let him lead me away as that baleful yellow light glared all around us. At the same time, I couldn't quite puzzle out exactly what was going on. All right, so I had strong psychic powers. I'd understand better if I'd been hauled off to some lab to be dissected. Instead, I was standing here in the Reptilian equivalent of an anonymous hotel room, having a mostly civilized conversation with a man who didn't seem to be human or Reptilian, or like any of the aliens Callista had described seeing or meeting when she went before the Assembly on the far-off world of Penalta.

"No, I haven't been harmed," I said at last. *Not yet, anyway,* I added mentally.

"Nor will you be. You are our guest, Taryn. I know you have little reason to believe me or trust what I have said to you, but we do not offer hospitality lightly. If you are here with us, you are safe."

How very noble. Nothing I'd heard so far about the Reptilians seemed to indicate that they followed any sort of code, but I had to admit that all the information I'd been provided so far had come from somewhat biased sources. As for the abductions the aliens had been conducting over the years, well, I decided it was probably better to ask about that later on. Lir Gideon's tone was even enough, but I thought I could hear an edge of tension to it, as if he was just waiting for me to ask exactly the wrong question and trying to decide what he should do if I did.

"Well, I feel better now," I said. The words hadn't come out quite as sarcastically as they might have if someone like Grace was saying them, but neither were they entirely neutral.

Lir Gideon affected not to notice. "I'm pleased to hear that. You should make yourself comfortable here. Are you hungry? Thirsty? Do you wish to rest?"

Considering I'd gotten out of bed to go meet Callista and her parents not even three hours earlier, it wasn't quite time for me to go to sleep, as tempting as that might sound. I could crawl into that cubbyhole and try to pretend certain parts of this day had never happened.

"Not hungry, or tired," I replied. "But some water would be nice."

As I spoke, I wondered if I could even trust any of the water I'd be given on this ship. After all, I had no idea what the Reptilians considered clean, or healthy. There was always the possibility I'd end up poisoned just because they didn't know enough about human physiology to provide me with the right things to eat and drink.

If he noted my misgivings, Lir Shalan gave no

sign. He went over to the wall on the other side of the table, where there was another of those flat panels, although bigger than the biometric scanner he'd used to gain access to the room.

Which made me realize he could come and go here any time he liked. Including when I was asleep. Could come in here and—

And what? I couldn't ignore the Reptilians' history; it was the sort of thing my parents would never discuss openly in front of me, but I knew that the aliens weren't exactly saints when it came to how they behaved with human women.

Anyway, whatever he was, Lir Gideon definitely wasn't a Reptilian. Actually, in this light, it was a lot more difficult to see the pale green hue of his skin, or the deep red of his eyes. He almost looked like a normal human man, except for those high-necked robes he was wearing.

"This panel will provide whatever you need," he said, and I forced myself to concentrate on what he was saying. It would be stupid to miss out on his instructions for using the food replicator or what-ever it was just because I was busy manufacturing worst-case scenarios in my head. "It does under-stand some basic English words, so you can ask for water, or food, and it will supply those things for you."

"Will it get me a cheeseburger?" I asked, just to see how he would react.

To my surprise, he actually smiled. "It won't be

quite the same, and won't have the bread component—"

"The bun."

He nodded. "Yes, that. But I think you might be surprised. Come and try it for yourself. It will need to learn your voice patterns."

Wondering how in the world all this could possibly work, I stepped away from the cubbyhole's entrance, where I'd been standing all this time, and went over to the food synthesizer panel. In doing so, I had to pass quite close to Lir Gideon, who didn't seem inclined to move out of my way. In fact, the sleeve of my jacket brushed against his robes, and I felt a strange shiver pass over me. Not revulsion. I'd held his hand earlier, and been glad of it. No, this felt more like my body reacting when my brain didn't know quite what to do.

He didn't seem to notice, however, so I put on what I hoped was an expression of mild curiosity as I faced the panel embedded in the wall. "What do I have to do?"

"Speak your request. Slowly, so it will not have to work as hard to understand you."

I had a feeling that if it had been Callista standing here, she would have done something snarky like order a double dirty martini and a plate of nachos. But I couldn't bring myself to do that. For one thing, I didn't like martinis very much, and another, I didn't want to confuse the synthesizer unit.

So I said, "A cheeseburger and some water, please."

Lir Gideon shifted slightly, possibly from amusement. "You don't need to say 'please.'"

No, I supposed a food synthesizer wouldn't care about the niceties, especially a machine designed by the Reptilians. However, it didn't appear that I'd confused it too much, because approximately ten seconds later, a blue light flared in the panel, and a plastic door slid out of the way. Sitting inside the recess it revealed was a square metal plate, and on top of that plate was a fairly respectable-looking burger patty with a slice of yellow cheese on top. Off to one side was a square plastic cup, presumably filled with water.

I hesitated, unsure whether it was safe to reach inside and retrieve the plate.

"Go on," Lir Gideon said, his voice tinged with amusement. "It won't hurt you."

So I picked up the plate, which was slightly warm to the touch, along with the cup. Its surface was cool against my fingers. I looked inside and saw clear liquid. It definitely looked like water.

Then again, so did vodka. And formaldehyde.

"Would you like me to drink from it first, to show that it's safe?"

He wore a half-smile that did interesting things to his full mouth. I tore my gaze away and said, "No, I'm sure it's fine," then lifted the cup to my lips.

It did taste like water—nicely chilled high-end

mineral water, not something from a tap. My estimation of the Reptilians went up slightly.

The burger, though…without the bun, I wasn't sure how to eat it without making a mess.

"The utensil is attached to the bottom of the plate," Lir Gideon said.

I went over to the table and set down the cup of water so I could feel the underside of the plate. Sure enough, there was a square-edged implement that looked like some high-priced European designer had come up with his version of a spork. It seemed to be attached magnetically, because I felt a slight resistance as I pulled it away.

Thus armed with my spork, I didn't have much reason not to try the burger. I told myself that the water had tasted fine, so the manufactured meat and cheese should be okay, too.

Even so, I hesitated for a long moment, spork poised over the patty as it lay in the middle of the plate. I could feel Lir Gideon watching me, and didn't dare look up to see whether he was smiling outright this time.

Well, if I'd been brave enough to reach out and put my hand in his, then I should also have the courage to take a bite of the burger. I pulled in a breath, then used the edge of the spork to cut off a small piece of meat and cheese, and placed it in my mouth.

Suddenly, it was summer, and I was at one of the Rineharts' backyard barbecues, enjoying a burger after spending the afternoon wandering along the banks of Oak Creek. This replicated patty I was eating tasted just as if it had come straight off the grill, with that wonderful mixture of slight charring and a complicated combination of spices rubbed on the surface to wake up the ground beef.

"So?" Lir Gideon asked.

"That's amazing," I replied, once I had finished chewing. "It doesn't taste like it came out of a machine at all. How in the world can one of your food synthesizers duplicate Earth food like that?"

It had seemed like an innocuous enough question, but something in his expression clouded. "It had input from one of your people."

Oh. It wasn't too difficult for me to figure out why the Reptilians would have had a human captive around to help them program their food synthesizers. An awkward silence fell, and suddenly, I didn't have much of an appetite for the rest of the burger, even though it had tasted marvelous only a moment earlier.

But I forced myself to nod, then take a few more bites before I set the plate with its half-eaten patty down on the table. Lir Gideon seemed content to watch me as I did so, not offering anything else by way of conversation, or providing any further explanations. While I wasn't the sort of person who felt the need to fill up awkward silences by forcing myself to talk, I thought I should try to say something.

"So," I began, desperately trying to think of a

topic that seemed somewhat neutral, "is 'Lir' some form of address in your language, like 'Mr.' or 'Ms.' are in English? I noticed that both you and Lir Shalan were referred to that way."

"No," Gideon replied. "'Lir' is a surname." He paused for a second, then went on, "We share it because he is my father."

CHAPTER TWO

FOR THE LONGEST MOMENT, I COULD ONLY STARE AT him. I'd guessed Gideon wasn't human, at least not completely, but I'd never imagined that a Reptilian like Lir Shalan could actually be his father. I blinked, trying to sort through my roiling thoughts. "So...he used his DNA and human DNA to create you?"

It seemed like a safe enough question. After all, the Reptilians were well known for their propensity to play with genetics the way a master mixologist might whip up a new cocktail.

Another of those hesitations. "Not exactly." Gideon's gaze flickered from me to the little sitting area with its hard, backless couch and flat metal table. "Perhaps you would like to sit down."

In general, if someone suggests that it might be a good idea for you to sit, then you'd better do as they say. I retrieved the cup of water and then went to the sofa and perched on one end, just in case he intended to sit down as well. At least that way, we would have as much space between us as possible.

He didn't sit, however. He remained standing, making me feel quite small as he loomed there in his long, dark robes. But I tried not to show my uneasiness, and instead took a sip of water as I waited.

When he spoke, his tone was quiet and calm, revealing little of what he himself might think of the current topic of conversation. "My mother was as human as you are, Taryn. And I was conceived and born just like any other human. No one created me in a laboratory. I am not a hybrid, at least not in the way you have come to think of hybrids, as the result of genetic manipulation by our scientists."

That revelation hit me almost like a physical blow. Because if Gideon truly had been conceived in the same way that humans had for hundreds of thousands of years—if you left out those undergoing fertility treatments, that is—then that meant Lir Shalan had been with a human woman, had....

I made my mind stop there. Yes, I'd heard the rumors and the stories, but that was all they had been...up until now. But there Gideon stood, saying that he was the product of one of those unions. Even with all the rumors I'd heard, however, no one had ever been able to provide definitive evidence that the women who'd been abducted and sexually assaulted by aliens had produced half-alien offspring. They claimed they had, but those children's DNA had been tested and had come back completely normal.

With his green skin and red eyes, Gideon probably didn't have anything close to "normal" DNA.

"You are surprised," he said.

Shocked was probably a better word. Or flabbergasted. I drank some more water to cover my amazement, then asked, "Are there others like you?"

He didn't answer right away, but instead came over and sat down on the sofa next to me. His proximity made me feel that much more off balance. It wasn't any one thing, but just his general presence, the way his robe flowed over the edge of the couch and brushed against my leg, the way that this close, I could see the strange ruby glint of his eyes, even though they were framed in a fringe of thick black lashes that would make most women jealous.

"Exactly like me? No. Unlike true hybridization, which is controlled in a laboratory and produces the same result every time, these sorts of pairings are... unpredictable. The results are rarely similar."

"But there are others who were born in a similar way."

"A few."

Right then, even though it was probably only around ten o'clock in the morning, I thought I could use something to drink that was a lot stronger than water. And I didn't even drink very much; I couldn't, because keeping out of other people's minds required a good deal of mental control, and control was a difficult thing to manage when you were on your third martini.

My brain didn't want to accept what he'd just told me. Lir Shalan, the leader of the Reptilians charged with occupying my world, had been with a human woman and had a son by her. A son who now sat next to me. Because he was half alien, his looks could be misleading, but in appearance he only seemed a few years older than I. Which seemed to indicate that he had to have been born not all that long after Kirsten Jones drove the Reptilians out of Sedona.

"Who is she?" I asked. "Your mother, I mean."

Gideon's entire body seemed to tense. That is, I could see how his shoulders lifted slightly, the way the muscles along his jaw tightened. "She was a woman who was taken from Sedona as the base was being evacuated."

I couldn't miss the "was" in his reply. So she was probably dead. I didn't dare ask, though. "Taken? You mean abducted?"

"Yes." He pushed himself off the sofa and went over to the food synthesizer. "Water," he said.

Once again, the blue light flashed, and the door slid open to reveal a cup identical to the one I held. He took it out and drank some of its contents, then turned back toward me. Some of the tension seemed to have left his face, and I guessed he had gone to fetch the water to give himself some time to decide how best to continue the conversation.

He didn't sit back down, but again stood a foot or so away from the couch, staring down at me. "She was a visitor to Sedona. She wanted to be there for the solstice, you see, and so was out at the Boynton Canyon vortex that night."

I nodded. My hometown got thousands of tourists every year, some who came only to hike and gawk at the amazing red rock formations, while others wanted to tap into Sedona's unique energies. A lot of people dismissed the ideas of the vortexes and the powers associated with them as complete woo-woo, but I knew better. A power like no other on earth—maybe in the entire galaxy—was concentrated there. It was that power which had allowed my own mother to blast the aliens from their base while desperately attempting to save my father, and it was that same power—amplified by Kirsten Jones's half-Pleiadian abilities—which had driven them out completely a quarter-century earlier.

So I could see why someone would hike out to Boynton to be there when the earth turned from dark to light, and the power of the solstice united with the vortex energies. I didn't know if I would have the courage to do something like that, simply because that fateful solstice had taken place at something like four o'clock in the morning, and blundering around Sedona's wilderness areas in pitch darkness was not generally a wise thing to do.

Especially if it put you in the path of a group of alien refugees fleeing the destruction of their base.

"So he took her?" I asked, trying very hard not to think of what a horrifying experience that must have been, and to keep my tone neutral.

"She was brought to him. He was not at the base, you see, but here on his ship. Not this exact ship—this one is much newer—but he has been stationed in this system, and overseeing your planet, for many years."

Did I dare ask about Reptilian life expectancy? I knew the Pleiadians, like Martin Jones and Kirsten's father Gabriel and Callista's soulmate Raphael, lived for thousands of years. But I had no idea how long Reptilians lived. Longer than humans, I guessed, just because Gideon's explanation seemed to indicate that Lir Shalan had been in charge here for more than a quarter-century, and probably much longer than that.

"*Droit de seigneur,*" I murmured, and Gideon's black brows pulled together.

"Excuse me?"

So his English was flawless, but clearly, he didn't understand French. I didn't really know why I'd thought he would, only that I didn't have a very good idea of what the Reptilians did and didn't know about my world. But I supposed if Gideon's mother was American, and Lir Shalan had been over-seeing a base in northern Arizona, then it made sense they'd only know English, or possibly Spanish as well.

I hesitated, wondering whether I'd offend him with my explanation of the French phrase. Then again, I wasn't the one whose father had stolen a woman from her world, just because his people had thought she might be useful. But since I'd mentioned the phrase, I didn't see any way to avoid telling him what it meant. "It was an old custom in medieval France—and England, once it had been invaded by the Normans. It just meant that the lord of the manor had the right to a woman on her wedding night, rather than the man she'd married. It's not applicable in this case, really. I guess it popped into my mind because of how you said your mother was given to the person in charge, instead of being taken by one of the people who found her."

During that rather lame explanation—although I wasn't sure I could even call it that—Gideon's frown hadn't disappeared, had deepened, if anything. But then he nodded slightly. "I can see how you might think that. My father was in command, and so he did have first right to any…." He stopped there, as if unsure how to put it.

"Spoils of war?" I suggested.

"I suppose so." From the carefully neutral tone of his voice, I guessed he didn't much like that phrase being applied to the woman who'd given birth to him.

Something in his reaction heartened me a little. Gideon seemed to be doing his best to remain as cool and factual as possible, even when speaking of his mother, but I got the impression he was bothered by talking about her in such a way. And if he could have that kind of response, then it seemed to me there must be a good deal more to him that was human besides his appearance.

Or he could also be putting on an act, behaving in a way calculated to put me off my guard. I really had no idea, because I didn't know him, and I couldn't seem to penetrate his thoughts. Whether that barrier existed because of his Reptilian heritage, I wasn't sure. I'd never encountered a Reptilian before I saw Lir Shalan and his henchmen back at the ruined base. Aliens in and of themselves didn't seem to be an issue, since I'd had to put up my own mental barriers to avoid being blasted by Callista whenever she was having a particularly bad day. But the Reptilians appeared to be an entirely different story.

Even without my peculiar gift giving me hints, I had the feeling that Gideon was wishing he hadn't brought up the topic of his mother. I didn't know what to ask—or rather, I had so many things I wanted to ask him, I didn't know where to start. Inquiring whether he had any siblings didn't seem like a very good idea, and I guessed that any questions as to the nature of the Reptilians' plans for me would also be ignored.

Why he'd told me that Lir Shalan was his father, I didn't know. Maybe to impress me with his importance? No, that didn't feel right. That little fact had come out when he was explaining why part of his name was the same as that of the alien leader. I wondered then if his mother had named him Gideon, or whether it was a Reptilian name that just happened to have an earthly analogue.

What I asked, though, was the question that seemed to matter most right then. "Why me?"

He didn't blink, or even look away, but in an odd way, it appeared as if his focus had shifted, that he was trying to avoid eye contact. Why? Maybe he hadn't yet realized that I couldn't read his mind. Anyhow, my abilities didn't work that way. I didn't have to be looking someone in the eye to pick up on their thoughts, although that sort of contact did help.

"You're special. You possess interesting talents," he replied.

Well, true enough. But so did my mother, and so did Kirsten and Callista, Martin and Raphael. Or was I more interesting to the Reptilians because I was human and still possessed psychic abilities?

That explanation seemed plausible enough, although the deeper implications of why they'd chosen me began to sink in a second or two later. Did they want me for their breeding experiments? If I were really lucky, all I'd have to do was give up some DNA for them to play with, but what if they wanted something more from me than that?

I went cold again, despite the warmth of the room and the jacket I was wearing. However, I didn't want Gideon to see how much his reply had unsettled me. Thank God the Reptilians weren't what you could call psychic, despite their surveillance tactics.

"Well, thanks," I said in a careless tone that I

doubted would have fooled anyone, let alone the half-Reptilian man who stood only a foot or so away. "My parents think I'm special, too."

Since I'd almost finished my water anyway, I set the cup down on the flat piece of metal that served as a table and got to my feet. Carefully not looking at Gideon, I sent a quick glance around the room. "So where are you taking me? Back to your world?"

"No, we haven't gone anywhere at all."

"Excuse me?"

"Come."

He held out a hand. I wasn't sure if I wanted to take it, especially after those revelations about his parentage. What if Lir Shalan had decided I would be the perfect mate for his son? I certainly didn't want to encourage that line of thought, and taking Gideon's hand might seem that I was being friendly with him. But then, I'd already blown it if I was going to be standoffish. After all, I'd held his hand when he first brought me here.

There was also the distinct possibility he just didn't know all that much about human interactions, and only wanted to take me by the hand because that was the easiest way to guide me to wherever it was he wanted to take me.

So I let out a small breath, and once again laid my hand in his. Those strong fingers didn't feel any less human, even though I now knew that half his parentage was Reptilian.

"This way," he said, leading me out of the room that apparently was to be mine.

We didn't head back the way we had come, instead going farther down the corridor and then to a bank of elevators. Like the rest of the ship, they were made of metal, and didn't seem all that different from elevators you'd find back on Earth. Well, except that they seemed to be turbocharged; Gideon pressed the index finger of his free hand against the panel to the right of the door, and we shot up so quickly that I almost lost my balance.

But he tightened his grip on my hand, keeping me from stumbling. I wished I could pull away, and then scolded myself for being uncharitable. Whatever he —and the rest of the Reptilians—were up to, in that moment, he'd prevented me from taking a nasty spill. I could be grateful for that small moment of courtesy, even if he'd only done so in order to keep the future mother of his children from doing a face plant on the floor of the elevator.

When the doors opened, we emerged into a hallway identical to the one where my borrowed room was located. Here, though, I could see other crew members moving through the corridor, and had to force myself not to stare at their alien faces.

They didn't seem to be bothered by the same scruples, unfortunately; their flat reddish gazes appeared to follow me as Gideon guided me along. He had to have noticed their scrutiny, but he did nothing to acknowledge it, or them, for that matter.

Did they resent him because of his half-human blood? Or was he accorded a certain amount of deference as the son of their leader?

Yet another thing I didn't know, and a topic I probably wouldn't want to bring up. Even with all my not-staring, I'd noted that the aliens on this level wore dark gray jumpsuits with some sort of metal insignia fastened to their high collars, very different from the sweeping robes Gideon had on—the same type of garments all the Reptilians in Lir Shalan's entourage had worn. Maybe they were the elite, while the ones I saw now were more like worker bees.

My questions fell away, however, as the corridor opened up into a sort of observation deck, one that stretched a good ten yards to either side of us. Directly in front was a wall of glass—well, probably not glass, but some sort of transparent material holding back the vacuum of space.

Because I could see now that we were in orbit above the Earth, a beautiful blue-green disk so close it felt as if I could reach out and touch it. We were just passing over the shadowy line that marked the coming of night. To mostly open ocean, I realized as I peered out at the view, although I thought I recognized the continent of Australia about to pass directly below us.

"It's beautiful," I breathed.

Gideon let go of my hand so he could wrap his fingers around the metal railing directly in front of us. It hit him roughly at waist level, although it was higher than that on me. Clearly, the Reptilians as a race were taller on average than humans.

"This is what I meant when I told you that we really hadn't gone anywhere at all," he said. "There is your world, not so very far away."

He was right; it didn't feel far. But since I had no way of getting off this ship, that huge blue-green orb filling the window—or view screen, or whatever it was—might as well have been light-years away.

"Why haven't you left?"

The red eyes flickered over toward me. "Because we have matters to attend to here."

That didn't sound good. "What kind of matters?" I asked, not bothering to keep the suspicion out of my voice.

But Gideon only shrugged and returned his attention to the view of Earth beneath us. "We did your people a service in returning their astronauts to them. It's only natural that your leaders would wish to speak with my father and the others involved in that rescue."

On the surface, that reason sounded fine and noble...except I knew that Lir Shalan and his people hadn't "rescued" those astronauts at all. No, they'd had them imprisoned on the Reptilian base on Mars, and no doubt all of them would have suffered a variety of gruesome fates if they hadn't been set free by Raphael and Callista and her parents. The astronauts had been sent safely on their way afterward, their ship's programming altered so they could return to Earth even without following their originally set course.

Unfortunately, the Reptilians had decided to roll the dice, and step in and pretend to rescue the Mars mission's team, thus earning them the world's gratitude...and, I feared, giving them carte blanche to do pretty much whatever they wanted.

I didn't reply at first, mostly because angering Gideon by flinging those truths in his face wouldn't do me any good. So far, he'd been civil to me, even friendly. While I didn't want to be here, better to do so in his company than that of his fearsome father or any of the other members of Lir Shalan's team. Starting an argument didn't seem like a very wise idea.

Besides, I honestly couldn't tell if he was being disingenuous or whether he truly didn't have any idea what a liar and manipulator his father was. Yes, Gideon had been there on Penalta when Callista was brought in front of the Assembly to defend her actions at the Mars base, actions that had resulted in the death of a Reptilian soldier. But she'd told all of us that Gideon hadn't spoken at all, hadn't done anything except observe. I supposed it was possible that his father had kept him out of his plans, and so he didn't know that those astronauts hadn't been rescued at all, had only been used as pawns in Lir Shalan's endless games of planetary chess.

"And once they're done with their business?" I

asked, both fearing the answer and wanting to know what my eventual fate would be. If I was going to be hauled away to Alpha Draconis to live my life in exile among the Reptilians, I figured I'd better start steeling myself to that possibility now. My stomach tightened with dread, though, and I wondered how I could ever survive on a world so far from everyone and everything I loved.

"Oh, I think it will take some time," Gideon replied evasively.

So he wasn't going to give me any real information. I didn't know why I'd expected anything different. He might have looked far more human in appearance than Reptilian, but it seemed clear enough to me right then that he'd been raised to be his father's son. Being polite or even friendly to me was only a means to an end.

And I didn't really want to think about what that end might be.

CHAPTER THREE

AFTER LINGERING ON THE OBSERVATION DECK FOR A FEW more minutes, Gideon led me back to my room. The discarded hamburger patty looked very forlorn on its metal plate, but he went to it and carried it over to a slot that opened in the wall when he waved a hand in front of it.

"Disposal unit," he said briefly. Then he stepped over to the door I'd noted earlier and pressed his hand on the panel next to it. "Rest facilities."

I didn't want to go any closer. There was something far too intimate about having Gideon look on while I took a tour of the bathroom. "Thanks. I'll take a look when I need it."

His brows drew together once again, but then his expression cleared. "Of course. Your people are somewhat private about such things. If you do have any questions—"

"I'll manage," I broke in. "Thanks."

Another of those awkward little pauses descended. His gaze flickered toward the "rest" room, and back over to me. "If you will be comfortable here for a while, I must go speak with my father."

"I'll be fine," I assured him as he left, although I had a feeling I'd actually be anything but. Bad enough that I was marooned here on an alien spaceship, with no chance of getting away. What made it worse—foolish as it seemed—was that I hadn't caught a glimpse of anything in the place that looked like a computer or a television or an entertainment console. How in the world was I supposed to keep myself entertained in this windowless box of a room?

I thought longingly of the phone I'd left behind in the Joneses' SUV, a phone packed with games and books and a couple of movies I'd downloaded but hadn't had a chance to watch yet. The contents of that phone could have kept me occupied for at least a week, probably more...assuming I could figure out a way to charge it.

Of course, the thought of being trapped in here for a week only made my brain hurt that much more. What had I been thinking when I reached out and took Gideon's hand?

The quick and easy answer was that I hadn't been thinking at all. I'd more or less acted on instinct, had allowed the visions to guide me. Now those visions had faded away, and yet here I was. Anger flickered in me. What good were those visions if all they'd done was lead me to an alien ship, only to abandon me?

The door had closed behind Gideon. I went and laid my hand on the panel next to it, just as I'd seen him do, but it didn't open. Not that I'd really expected it to. He hadn't called me a prisoner, but that's exactly what I was. Tears started in my eyes, and I forced myself to blink them away. Crying wouldn't solve anything. I had to be strong, no matter what happened.

If only this room had a window, even a single teeny porthole that would let me see the world I'd come from. Maybe then I wouldn't feel so alone, although I ached to think of what my parents must be going through at the moment, realizing that their daughter was a captive of the hated Reptilians. How had Martin and Kirsten even broken the news to them? *Sorry, she just bolted past us before we could stop her....*

I doubted my parents would believe there was nothing the Joneses could have done. But it was the truth. I'd known I had to step in. Right then, my instincts had taken over.

Only now those same instincts appeared to have deserted me.

Since there wasn't much else for me to do, I went over to the cubbyhole/bed, and, after unlacing my hiking boots and kicking them off, I climbed in. The flat padded surface was surprisingly comfortable, despite how thin it appeared.

It was far too early to sleep, but that hadn't been my intention in coming in here. I'd thought that maybe I could focus, meditate, see if my strange inner eye could flare back into life. I needed it now more than ever before.

I'd read about isolation tanks, but I'd never experienced one. They were a fad of an earlier time, although I'd heard that several people in Sedona still owned them. Whether they used them or not, I had no idea, but I didn't have time to worry about that now. The cubbyhole where I now sat could serve a similar purpose, even if it wasn't quite the same. Some of the dim reddish light from the main part of the room did penetrate in here, and I thought I could hear a very low, almost subsonic background hum that probably came from the ship itself. Maybe the life-support systems.

Otherwise, though, the space was dark and warm and quiet, excellent conditions for achieving the sort of meditative state I required. My mother had always outright stated that she stank at meditating, but I'd taken classes in Sedona, learning how to either increase my concentration or let things drop away, depending on what I needed at the time. Mostly it was a matter of learning how to shift my focus, the perfect tool for staying out of people's heads unless specifically invited in.

In this particular case, though, I didn't want to stay out. I wanted to get in.

Because Reptilians were built on a larger scale than most humans—especially young women in their early twenties—I had plenty of space to cross my legs in the lotus position and lay my hands on my knees, palms upward. Because the light was so dim, I didn't bother to shut my eyes. I only did that when I was trying to focus inward.

Now, though, I needed to send my consciousness outward, to see if I could learn anything useful.

Some people called it astral projection. I never really thought of it that way, just as another skill in my toolbox. It was also something I'd never discussed with anyone, not even my mother; the first time it had happened, I'd thought I was just having a particularly vivid dream. But things I had overheard while in that state turned out to have occurred at the very moment I'd experienced them for myself, and that was when I realized I couldn't just see into people's minds, or receive strange snippets of the future, but could actually have my conscious self move out into the world independent of my body.

I didn't do it very often. The sensation was too unnerving, as if I could actually feel my consciousness separate itself from my physical form with an audible *pop*. But I couldn't think of too many things more unsettling than being held prisoner on an alien spaceship, so I was willing to take the risk right then. If I could leave this room, even in an incorporeal state, I'd at least have shown that I had some control over my situation.

There was that odd sensation, like a rubber band that's been stretched too tight suddenly snapping in two. And then I was moving out of my little cubby-hole of a bed, slipping through the door as if it didn't exist. To my astral self, it didn't.

Growing up hiking the trails around Sedona had taught me to keep track of my surroundings. A big Reptilian ship wasn't that different. My mind had subconsciously tracked the route here, and I went back that way, drifting along the corridor, keeping an eye out for anything that might be useful. I didn't see much, though. This level or deck or whatever it was seemed strangely deserted. For all I knew, this was an area kept aside for guests, like ambassadors or envoys or something like that.

Down the elevator shaft, not bothering to wait for an actual car this time. The shaft looked strange to me, its sides curiously bare. There wasn't any sign of the sort of infrastructure needed in terrestrial eleva-tors—no cables or conduits or anything like that. Possibly, the whole thing worked off magnetic energy.

It was the sort of thing my brother Michael might know, and I experienced a sharp, hurtful pang then at the thought that I might never see him again. He'd been preoccupied the last few years, focused on getting his doctorate, but as I was growing up, he'd always been my hero and protector, ready to step in to shield me from the inevitable teasing. Callista had never experienced any of that, because she was so damn beautiful that most of her oddities were given a pass. And Kelsey, Callista's cousin, was human and normal and girl-next-door gorgeous, so no one gave her too much crap about hanging out with what some kids at school referred to as "the UFO weirdos."

But I'd been kind of an odd-looking kid, skinny and with way too much curly hair, thanks to my mother, and so I was the one the bullies inevitably wanted to pick on. Michael, three years older, was big enough to scare most of them off, thus making him my knight in shining armor ever afterward. I didn't want to think about never seeing him again.

Actually, I couldn't allow myself to think about it, because focusing on anything except what I was doing right then would be a surefire way to fling my consciousness directly back into my body. I had to be calm, yet focused.

The elevator shaft ended, and I found myself drifting through the wall and into yet another of those seemingly endless corridors. I wondered then how big the ship really was, and how many levels it had. Certainly, it was orders of magnitude larger than the craft that had taken Earth's astronauts to Mars. From the little I'd been able to tell as Gideon guided me around the *Eclipse*, this starship felt almost like a small city. Did it carry troops in proportion to its size?

Probably better not to go there just yet. Besides, thinking of Gideon seemed to draw me toward him. I could hear his voice, and yet I couldn't understand anything of what he was saying, since he was speaking in the Reptilian tongue, its syllables strange and sibilant. Answering him was Lir Shalan—or at least, that's who I thought it must be, since his deeper accents sounded strangely familiar.

In my current disembodied state, it would be easy enough to find out. I'd learned from earlier trips outside my body that I was completely invisible, that I didn't even give off a ghostly shimmer when I traveled on the astral plane. The voices of Gideon and Lir Shalan drew me to them down the corridor, and within a second or two, I was inside the room where they were holding their conversation.

It was far more opulent than the one where Gideon had left me, and a great deal larger. *Captain's quarters,* I thought, taking in the darkly upholstered furniture, the odd sculptures of beaten metal on the walls, the strange waterfall of pulsing light in one corner.

The two of them stood in the center of the room, however, ignoring the angular couches to either side of them. I found myself studying them both, attempting to see if I could find any similarities in their features, even though Lir Shalan was so obviously alien. But I could find nothing, except possibly the sharp angles of his high cheekbones, softened but still visible in his son.

The alien leader appeared angry; his red eyes flashed fire, and while he wasn't waving his hands around, from time to time he would make an odd, stabbing gesture with his left hand, as if to punctuate a point. During this onslaught, Gideon stood there calmly enough. From time to time, when his father paused for breath, Gideon would say something, his tone far calmer.

I would have given a great deal to know just what the hell they were talking about. It appeared as if Lir Shalan thought Gideon had done something wrong, although I had no idea what that could have possibly been.

And then I felt it—just a strange little flicker of emotion, come and gone so quickly that I barely had a chance to reach out and touch it before it disappeared. Worry? No, that didn't feel quite right. Sadness wasn't right, either.

Then it came again.

Guilt.

Definitely coming from Gideon. Guilt over what, I wasn't sure. Because he had failed his father somehow?

And then a flash, not of an emotion, but more like an image that had sprung from his mind.

An image of me, shimmering, almost unrecognizable.

I gasped, and my concentration wavered for a second. Unfortunately, that one flicker was all it took. With an almost physical bump, I fell back into my body. At once, I was aware of the stiffness in my legs, and I carefully unfolded them from the lotus position, running my hands over my jeans-clad thighs to loosen things up a bit. How long had I been wandering the corridors of the ship in my astral state?

No way to know for sure, since I hadn't been wearing a watch when I came here with Gideon.

Gideon.

That flash—it had shocked me more than I wanted to admit. It was never easy to see yourself as others saw you. In this case, though, I didn't know what to think.

Obviously, I hadn't had much of a chance to look at myself in a mirror since I'd gotten here. If asked, though, I probably would have replied that my hair was a mess and the tinted lip balm I'd been wearing earlier that morning was long gone.

In Gideon's eyes, though, I'd been a goddess, someone I didn't even recognize, with a mane of long curls he wanted to bury his face in, skin he wanted to caress, lips he wanted to—

It was insane. He'd been raised among Reptilians, so why would he even be applying human standards of beauty to me?

Yes, I thought then, *but he had a human mother. She must have taught him something before she died.*

A shiver went through me. I didn't want him looking at me like that. He might have appeared mostly human, but Lir Shalan's blood—whatever color that might be—also ran in his veins.

I pushed myself out of the cubby/bed and went to the restroom, thinking it was time for me to get some cold water on my face. If there was even a sink. God only knew what kind of bathroom facilities Reptilians required.

To my relief, jutting from one wall was a square, sink-like receptacle made of steel or something that looked just like it. A wave of my hand to the left, and cold water came out of a pipe in the wall. To my right, and it was warm—instantly warm, unlike the water at my parents' house, where it seemed as if you always had to waste a good bit before it got to be the temperature you wanted.

Taking a breath, I bent and gathered some cold water in both my hands, then splashed it up against my cheeks. I didn't have to worry about ruining my makeup because I wasn't wearing any. The water did feel good, seeming to bring me back to myself.

There wasn't a mirror, just a blank wall of more steel above the sink. I could vaguely see my reflection in it, but not enough to catch any real detail. Just as well, because I probably looked like hell, Lir Gideon's inner concept of me to the contrary.

I had to wonder where that had come from. Maybe he had only a hazy idea of what human women were supposed to look like, and that was why he'd immediately slotted me in as his ideal. He had no true frame of reference, except a mother who'd died...when? I didn't know, but something told me it had been some time ago, when he was fairly young.

As for the argument, well, it was quite possible that Lir Shalan had been taking his son to task for not immediately forcing himself on me and getting the third generation of Lirs underway. The joke would have been on them, though, because I'd been getting once-yearly birth control shots ever since I turned eighteen. Wishful thinking more than anything else, though, because somehow I'd managed to still be a virgin at almost twenty-two. I tried to brush any self-recrimination aside, though, knowing I had far bigger things to worry about than why I was old enough to drink but still not emotionally ready to get in the sack with a guy.

Okay, think logically. There were hormones you could take to reverse the shots. Maybe the Reptilians had gotten their hands on them, maybe not. If that was the case, then I really would be out of luck. Anyway, since I didn't have a black belt in judo or training in krav maga, I doubted I could have fought off Gideon if he'd been inclined to follow in his father's footsteps.

So far, he'd acted like a perfect gentleman toward me, but if Lir Shalan continued to apply pressure....

A strange squeal assaulted my ears, and I started, for a second thinking there must be something wrong with the plumbing. But then it came again, and I realized it must be the Reptilian equivalent of a doorbell, since it was coming from that direction.

I didn't see any towels, so I wiped my damp hands on my jeans and hurried over to the door. This time when I placed my palm on the panel, the door hissed open, disappearing into the wall.

Outside in the corridor stood Gideon. His expression was far grimmer than when I had last seen him, but he appeared to gather himself as soon as he saw me, and even managed to smile. "I've brought some things for you."

"You have?" It didn't seem wise to be gazing up into his face, not after the way I'd caught him imagining me, so I looked downward. In his hands he held a black plastic case, about the size of a laptop bag.

"You came to us as you are, and so I thought it would help if you had some different clothing to change into."

"What's wrong with this?" I asked, looking down at my jeans and the denim shirt I wore over a tank top. I also realized that I was padding around in my sock feet, since I'd taken off my hiking boots before getting into the cubby/bed. Immediately, I glanced back up and prayed he hadn't noticed. Something about being without my boots felt oddly vulnerable.

"Nothing is wrong with your clothing," he said hastily. "But surely you will begin to tire of wearing the same thing? And at some point those clothes will need to be cleaned."

Those words drove home to me more than anything else that they planned to keep me here for some time. I could feel the nervous tension knotting in my belly, but there wasn't much I could do about it.

"Um, thanks, I guess." Ungracious, I knew, but after catching even that small glimpse of his thoughts —and worrying about what kind of pressure his father might be putting on him—I didn't quite know how to act. "Here, I'll take it."

He handed the case over to me and then looked on, gaze expectant. The message seemed to be that he wanted me to open it immediately so I could see what it contained.

I let out a small sigh, then took it over to the table. The case latched with a set of tabs that released when I pushed my thumbs against them. Inside was what looked like unwieldy wads of dark cloth, all either deep gray or black. When I lifted one of them out, though, I saw that it was a long dress of some sort, probably adapted from one of the Reptilian-style robes, although this garment seemed more fitted, and the neckline, while not particularly low, did have a definite scoop to it.

"They're very nice," I said, since I had to say something. "Do you have a tailoring department on the ship?"

He looked blank for a moment, then shook his head. "No need for that. Everything we wear is repli- cated in much the same way that our food is generated. Our machines take the components and create what we need."

Handy. I wasn't about to ask how those machines had known my measurements. Actually, as I folded the dress I held and laid it on top of its companions, I thought I could tell the garment wasn't all that fitted. It would probably slip right over my head.

"Will you wear it now?" Gideon asked.

The request struck me off guard. Were his half-alien sensibilities offended by my jeans or some-thing? But there was something in his face—not really pleading, more that he hoped I wouldn't argue with him. Why, I wasn't sure. Maybe this was some sort of odd test devised by his father to see how compliant I was.

Well, I could be as accommodating as the next person...up to a point. However, when it came to choosing my battles, I didn't think this one was worth the effort. It couldn't hurt to make them think that I was willing to go along with their wishes. So far, I'd seen absolutely nothing that made me think I'd be able to escape this ship, but my chances had to be better if the Reptilians had the impression that I was cooperating with them.

"Sure," I said. "Just give me a minute."

Something about Gideon's posture appeared to relax slightly as I took the dress and draped it over one arm, then went into the bathroom and shut the door. I looked, but I couldn't detect any sort of locking mechanism. Maybe he planned to come in here while I was half-undressed.

Or maybe I needed to give him a little credit. He'd remained where he was as I entered the bathroom, and even though I still didn't know exactly what his and Lir Shalan's argument had been about, it seemed safe enough for me to believe that Gideon wasn't going to make any unwelcome moves.

Even so, I climbed out of my clothes at lightning speed, then hurriedly tugged the dress over my head. As I'd thought, it was fairly loose-fitting, and probably could have used a belt. But I wasn't here to win any beauty contests. If Gideon wanted me to wear this sack, I wasn't going to argue about it.

The dress was a little lower cut than I'd first thought, though. I tugged it up as best I could and tried to tell myself I wasn't actually showing that much cleavage. Besides, I really wasn't that busty; it was only in the last couple of years that I'd graduated to a C-cup. Things weren't overflowing the way they might have been if I were as "blessed" as, say, Grace Rinehart.

I folded my discarded jeans and T-shirt and set them on the counter, then slipped out of my socks as well. The metal floor was cold against my feet, but for some reason, the thought of wearing thick Carhartt socks and my hiking boots with this flowing dress seemed vaguely ridiculous. If the machines on the ship could produce a dress for me out of thin air, then they could probably manage a pair of flats or something.

Gideon seemed to have already thought of that, because he was holding what looked like two pieces of flat plastic with ankle laces attached. He held them out to me as I approached. "I thought you could use these as well."

I took them from him, trying not to look too dubious. The flimsy footwear didn't seem as if it would do much to support my feet. But when I set the "shoes" on the floor and stepped into them, something sort of marvelous happened. The plastic molded itself to my foot, becoming softer and springier, while the laces wound themselves around my ankles and then tied themselves off.

"That's impressive," I said. "How does that even work? Nanotechnology?"

"Close enough." His gaze was approving, maybe a little too much so. At least he was looking at my face, though, and not at the dismaying amount of skin the neckline of the dress revealed. Then he asked, "Are you hungry? You didn't eat much of that burger."

Nothing in his tone was even close to accusing, but I still felt a little guilty about wasting food like that, even if it had been conjured from its component atoms and no actual cows had died to provide the meal. Until Gideon had asked the question, I hadn't thought much about whether I was hungry or not. Now, though, my stomach seemed to wake up, crying out for something to replace all the energy my body had burned while I was traveling away from it. You wouldn't think that sitting and staying quietly focused like that would count as any real sort of exertion, but in its own way, astral travel was as taxing as if I'd been running uphill for all that time.

"Actually, I am," I admitted, then began to move toward the panel that held the food synthesizer. "I suppose now is as good a time as any to practice with this thing some more."

Gideon's voice stopped me. "I thought you might like to eat someplace other than this chamber."

I didn't know whether I liked the sound of that or not. "You mean like in the ship's mess hall or something?"

"Mess...?" He paused, his head tilted to one side, as if he was trying to process the unfamiliar phrase. "No, the crew does not eat communally, but takes their meals in their own rooms. But I was thinking of my chamber. It is a good deal larger than this one, and might be more comfortable."

Of course it would be. And it would probably have a bigger bed than my borrowed room, too.

I shut that thought down at once. This might be the Reptilian equivalent of asking me to come up and see his etchings...or Gideon might genuinely think it would be more comfortable for me to eat someplace that wasn't quite so cramped.

Nothing ventured, I supposed. I really didn't see the point in refusing him, since I couldn't think of an excuse that didn't sound either rude or paranoid. Besides, going with him to his room would give me a chance to see more of the ship, and more knowledge was always a good thing, even if I might not know exactly what to do with it yet.

So I managed to smile, then said, "That sounds like a good idea," and watched as something in his expression relaxed. Was that a good sign, or….

Too late to refuse now. I held my breath as Gideon opened the door, and prayed I hadn't just made a huge mistake.

CHAPTER FOUR

THOSE ODDLY SQUISHY SHOES DID A GREAT JOB OF making my journey to Gideon's room a comfortable one, or at least as comfortable as a walk through the bowels of an alien ship could be. The skirt of my dress was a little long, so I had to hold it up to avoid tripping, but otherwise it wasn't too much work to follow Gideon as he led me down the corridor and to the elevators once again. This time, though, it seemed as if we just kept going, and going, and I wondered once again how many decks the ship contained, and how many Reptilians were assigned here.

We did pass a number of crew members once we emerged from the elevator, and it was on this upper deck that I got my first glimpse of the "Greys," the aliens that had haunted popular culture for the past seventy-five years. Because of what Martin Jones had told all of us about how they functioned, I now knew that they weren't truly aliens at all, but rather biological robots the Reptilians used to avoid detection by humans. Even so, I had to keep myself from shivering when they passed by, their huge, blank eyes settling on me for just a second or two before moving on to something they considered more interesting.

Their unnerving regard was still better than dealing with the Reptilians themselves. While none of them said anything, I could feel them staring even after Gideon and I had moved ahead. I still wasn't quite sure what his status was here. Yes, his father commanded this ship, apparently, but I didn't know what that meant for Gideon himself. Was he being groomed as the heir apparent? Would the other Reptilians even take orders from someone who was half human?

It seemed like every time I thought of one question, approximately ten more popped up to complicate things.

I couldn't help feeling relieved when Gideon stopped at a door, one that appeared exactly like every other one we'd passed on our way here. He laid his hand on the panel, then said, "Please go in," after the door slipped out of the way and into the wall.

Glad to be out of the hallway and safe from the stares of the Reptilians, I went inside. This apartment —because that was what it seemed to be, far bigger than the room I'd been given to stay in—was furnished much the same as the one I'd seen when I was astral-walking earlier, and at first appeared so identical that I had to stop and take another look around to reassure myself that we were not in Lir Shalan's chambers.

The biggest difference I could see here, though, was that the far wall provided another one of those dizzying views of Earth. Just as on the observation deck, that wall was composed entirely of whatever clear material the Reptilians used to keep out the vacuum and yet remain as clear as plate glass.

"That's incredible," I said, moving toward the enormous window/wall. In that moment, I'd forgotten about my hunger, or my anxiety about being alone here with Gideon. It was enough to see the gibbous blue-green shape of the world where I'd been born, to know that everyone I loved and cared about was down there somewhere.

Worrying about me, probably, but there wasn't much I could do about that. I didn't think Gideon would oblige me by sending a message to let my family know that I was—so far—safe and unharmed.

"It is a good thing to wake up to every day," he agreed. He came farther into the apartment and stopped a few feet away from me. "Or rather, every day we're in orbit. When the *Eclipse* is journeying between the stars, a barrier comes down to protect the window, since the material it's made of is not strong enough to resist the forces of superluminal travel."

Faster than light. I knew both my father and my brother Michael would be flipping out to hear something that had always been declared theoretically impossible discussed so casually, as if Gideon didn't think much more of breaking the light barrier than he would of going faster than seventy-five on the highway.

"That's how you move between the stars?" I asked. "Is it like a warp drive, or do you use mini black holes, or—"

He smiled. No, actually, he *grinned*. The expression was so completely human that I could almost forget the greenish skin, or the deep ruby of his eyes. "You study these things?"

"Well, *I* don't," I replied. "That's really my father's thing...and my brother's. He's getting his doctorate in astronomy." I paused then and gave Gideon a very direct look. "But you probably knew that already."

He didn't glance away, but met my gaze squarely enough. I realized then that making eye contact in such a way probably wasn't a very good idea. The oddest little shiver went through me as I stared at him, and it seemed that we were standing much closer than we really needed to.

His lips parted. I found it hard to focus on anything except his mouth, which was crazy. Yes, it was a nice mouth, and if it had been on someone else, I might have spent at least a little time wondering what it would be like to feel those lips against mine, but not with Gideon. That way lay madness.

He looked away from me so he could gaze down at Earth. We were crossing over North America right then, and I had to keep myself from reaching out and trying to spread my hand over that little corner of the globe called Arizona.

"It is true that we know something of your family, and your associates. How couldn't we? They're responsible for the deaths of many of my people."

The words had been spoken so neutrally that at first I didn't quite grasp what he was saying. Then comprehension rushed in, and I crossed my arms and glared up at him. "Um, last time I checked, those deaths happened because your 'people' were trying to meddle in human affairs. There's a little something called self-defense, you know."

It was hard to believe that the stony face staring down at me was the same one which had worn such a grin of delight only a moment earlier. "Of course you would see it that way."

"What other way is there to see it? My brother is named after a man your people killed!" It was true; my parents had given Michael his name in honor of Michael Lightfoot, who'd died helping to protect Kirsten Jones so she could call on her powers to drive the Reptilians out of Sedona forever.

Only it hadn't been forever. Twenty-five years

was a decent span of time to get some breathing room, but it hadn't been enough.

"Because they had no other choice."

"You keep telling yourself that." I turned away from him, thinking this had been a huge mistake and that I needed to get back to my room before I wasted any more time arguing with him. The smartest thing for me to do would be to spend as little time in his company as possible so we could avoid any further conflicts. He might look far more human than he did Reptilian, but it was clear to me right then that his thought processes were purely alien.

I didn't get very far, though, because I'd only taken a step before his fingers were wrapping around my bicep, pulling me back toward him. Never in my life had anyone put their hand on me without my permission, and I acted without thinking, jerking my arm out of his grip as I snapped, "Don't you touch me!"

He let go, and again I felt one of those same strange flares of guilt before it faded away just as quickly as it had come. His jaw set, but I could see a flicker of doubt in his eyes. "Taryn, I did not mean to do that. I acted without thinking."

That I could believe, especially when I stopped to consider who had raised him. Lir Shalan hadn't wasted a second thought on taking the human woman his underlings had brought to him and using her for his own ends, and so I supposed I should be glad that all Gideon had done was grab me by the arm. It still throbbed where he'd gripped me, though; clearly, he was very strong.

I wouldn't say that it was okay, because it wasn't. But he was watching me, expression troubled, and I knew then that he wouldn't do anything like that again. How exactly I knew, I couldn't say for sure, except Gideon was half human, and therefore not as hopelessly opaque to me as one of the Reptilians might be. I didn't want to pry too much, because even in my current situation, I hated the idea of going into someone's mind without permission. But I wouldn't put up my barriers, either. My best hope of surviving my tenure here—however long that might turn out to be—was to allow those flickers and flashes in so I wouldn't be struggling quite so blindly in the dark.

"Don't do it again," was all I said, but he nodded.

"Would you come with me to the food synthesizer?"

It was an olive branch, one I'd have to take. He was the closest thing to an ally I had in this place. We couldn't be at odds all the time.

"Sure," I said, and somehow managed to smile. "I could do with another burger."

Actually, that meal wasn't as awkward as I feared it would be. We both requested burgers, somewhat to my surprise; I'd sort of figured he would have chosen something from his own home world. In fact, Gideon got creative and asked for some potatoes on the side. They were mashed, not french fries, but I was surprised by how good they tasted, the kind of potatoes where you could tell no one had skimped on the butter.

"I still don't really understand how it works, though," I said, after washing down a bite of burger with some of that sweet mineral water. "How does the synthesizer know what a burger is supposed to taste like, or a mound of mashed potatoes, for that matter?"

He'd been chewing as well, so he had to wait until he was done with his mouthful of potatoes before he could reply. "My mother taught it."

"Your mother?" He'd made an oblique reference earlier to someone training the machine to make human food, but I just hadn't put two and two together.

"Yes. The easiest way to train the synthesizer is to give it an actual sample to analyze. She had my father collect samples of Earth food, and then she fed them all into the processing unit."

I have to admit that my head swam a little at that revelation. From the very little Gideon had said about his mother, I'd just assumed that she'd spent her time locked up and hadn't really interacted with Lir Shalan much, except for the time when her son had been conceived.

"She had him—you mean, she asked him to do something, and he actually did it?"

"Yes," Gideon replied. The ruby-toned eyes glinted at me. "This surprises you?"

"Frankly, yes."

"He could tell her health was suffering because she had a difficult time digesting the food she was provided. The logical thing to do was to give her the things she needed to stay healthy."

"Burgers and mashed potatoes?" I asked. "That's really not a very healthy diet."

"True. But also fruits and vegetables. Processed grains were more difficult for the food synthesizer to manage."

"Which is why the bun-less burger?"

"Precisely."

The question I wanted to ask then was whether Lir Shalan had done these things out of the goodness of his heart, or whether he needed to do whatever was necessary to make sure that Gideon's mother would make a productive little baby factory for him. But I knew Gideon wouldn't give me a straight answer to that kind of inquiry. I didn't know whether he'd answer the question I planned to ask next, but I had to know.

"Do you have any siblings?"

His face took on that closed expression I'd begun to dislike intensely. It meant he was sitting there and weighing what he should or shouldn't say, and deciding how much he thought would be wise to tell me. But then he replied, "No. There were other attempts, but I was the only successful result of that pairing."

Attempts. Did that mean his mother had gotten pregnant multiple times, but had only carried one child successfully to term? Or maybe that Lir Shalan had repeatedly forced himself on her, but she'd only gotten pregnant once?

I couldn't ask Gideon that. He was trying to make himself as closed off as possible, but I knew somehow that he missed his mother, even though she'd been gone for years. As much as I desperately wanted to find out more about exactly what had happened to her, I couldn't ask those sorts of blunt personal questions. Not yet, anyway. Maybe at some point, he'd feel comfortable enough to confide in me, but I wasn't about to hold my breath.

Silence descended as we both returned to our food, but it was a quiet that was anything but easy. A moment or so later, Gideon said, "Your own mother has talents like yours, correct?"

I wanted to point out that I was pretty sure he knew the answer to that question already, since she'd been the one to blast the aliens out of Sedona on the first go-'round. But that kind of reply would only start another argument, and I was trying to be on my best behavior. I might have been prolonging the inevitable, but I was going to do everything in my power to keep Lir Shalan from using me as his next-generation eugenics experiment.

Would that be so bad? a traitorous part of my mind thought at me, visualizing the sensual curves of Gideon's mouth, the strength in those shoulders. Having to be with the alien leader himself was the stuff of nightmares, but his son....

No. No way. If he'd approached me as a friendly alien, like Martin had with Kirsten or Raphael had with Callista, then...maybe. I wouldn't bother to deny that I found Gideon attractive in some ways, despite his strange coloring. But I wouldn't give Lir Shalan the satisfaction of succumbing to his son's charms.

"Sort of like mine," I said, then sipped my water. "We're both clairvoyant to some extent, and clairsentient as well. That means knowing things without knowing how we know them."

"That must be unsettling."

He sounded almost sympathetic, but I told myself he was probably trying to act as if he understood in order to soften me up. Wasn't going to happen, though. "But I'm more of a pure psychic than she is."

"You read minds."

It wasn't a question. "Yes. The talent isn't infallible, of course, and I don't go into other people's thoughts without their permission."

He'd been holding a cup of water, but set it down then. "So can you read my mind?"

"No." Well, that was only a partial lie. I really couldn't directly read his thoughts, even if I could pick up traces of his emotions from time to time. "I only seem to be able to do it with other humans."

I couldn't tell if the barb about "other humans" had sunk in. He gave a nod, then said, "Interesting that you're more powerful than your mother. Where else do you think the gift might have come from?"

Gift. That was how my mother always referred to it, although there were days when I thought it was far more of a curse. I'd lost count of all the times I'd wished I was as blessedly normal and popular as Kelsey Rinehart.

I shrugged. "My father says his great-great-grand-mother was reputed to have the second sight—which is a folksy way of saying psychic powers, I suppose. But he also says no one in his family took those rumors too seriously. He never knew her, of course, since she died long before he was born. So I don't really know if it's just a family legend, or whether I might have inherited something from that side of the family as well."

Gideon was quiet then, apparently musing over what I had just told him. Did the possibility that I'd inherited not just one, but two psychic strains make me more or less desirable as breeding stock? I didn't know.

If that was even the reason why I'd been brought here. I still had the impression that something else was going on, but unless I was suddenly able to start delving into his mind, I doubted I'd ever find out.

"Was it difficult?" he asked then, out of the blue.

"Was what difficult?"

"Possessing these powers when no one else around you—except your mother—did?"

I might have mentioned that Kirsten and Callista and Martin had their own sets of powers, but I could tell that wasn't what Gideon had asked. To him, they didn't really count, because they were extraterrestrial in origin. But I—I was an anomaly, a human with powers she really shouldn't have had.

His expression was curious, one eyebrow lifted slightly as he waited for my answer. Honestly, I didn't know what to tell him. I doubted he wanted a recitation of my problems of feeling like an outcast. Yes, I'd had Michael to defend me, and Callista and Kelsey had been my friends, but that was about it. Even in a place like Sedona, a lot of girls really didn't want to hang out with someone who supposedly could read minds. I'd had one really good friend in high school besides Callista and Kelsey, Lisette Marquez, but she'd gotten a full scholarship to Stanford and was gone, never to return. How could I blame her for that? If I'd had the chance to escape to California, I probably wouldn't have come back, either.

"A little," I said, figuring I could skirt close to the truth even if I wasn't about to give him the whole sob story about feeling like an outsider for most of my life. "It wasn't as if I talked about it much, but word still got around. My mother already had a reputation as a psychic, although she had her own private practice and didn't work in the shops like I do."

"Why didn't you do as she did, instead of working with the public?" He seemed genuinely curious, head tilted to one side as he watched me.

Damn it. Gideon probably had no idea how appealing he looked when he did that. Once again, I wondered how many of his mannerisms he'd unconsciously picked up from his mother. He definitely didn't act like an alien...at least, not all the time.

I picked up my own cup of water and drank some. "It's an easy way to make good part-time money. I wasn't really ready to settle down with a practice, especially since I was just about to—"

The words broke off then, and I couldn't look at him. I'd been planning to transfer to NAU in August, since there wasn't anything more I could do at the local community college, and both my parents had made it pretty clear that being a full-time psychic without a college degree was not in the cards—no pun intended—when it came to my future.

Now, though? I didn't even know what the next day held for me, but I was pretty sure it didn't involve heading up to NAU to make sure all my transcripts had been received and that I would be ready to go for the next school year.

"What is it?" His tone was gentle—too gentle. I didn't want him to be nice to me. I was already fighting something I didn't quite understand.

"Nothing," I replied. "The part-time work was

good to fit in around my college schedule. Anyway, working at the shops is good practice."

"Oh." Gideon didn't say anything for a moment. He probably could tell I was leaving something out but wasn't going to push it. "So you were treated differently because of your gifts?"

"Of course. That is, no one ever came out and really talked about it, but...." I stopped there. No point in going into that one humiliating incident in my sophomore year of high school when I thought Tyler Lewis, one of the best-looking guys in school and someone who should have been completely out of my league, started to take an interest in me. I'd been over the moon from his attention—until it turned out he was only interested because he'd heard I was a psychic, and he was flunking English and wanted me to get the answers to the class's midterm test so he wouldn't get kicked off the football team.

Of course, I'd refused. And then I'd gone home and cried and cried, while my mother tried to reassure me that it would be better one day, that high school wasn't the whole world. My sixteen-year-old self hadn't believed her. Now I knew that she'd been right, but it didn't seem as if I was going to get my chance to experience that world. No, instead I was being held captive on a Reptilian spaceship.

"Anyway," I went on, knowing that Gideon had noted my hesitation but making sure he wouldn't have the opportunity to ask any more awkward questions, "it was a little tense from time to time, but

I got through it. Comes with the territory. Even with some of the problems they've caused me, I still wouldn't want to *not* have my powers. They're part of who I am."

He was quiet, apparently thinking over what I'd just told him. Once again, I caught a drift of emotion, one that made my breath catch.

Desire.

Not exactly in the sense of him wanting to drag me down the hall and into his bedroom so he could have his wicked way with me, but...need. Wanting to take me in his arms and hold me close, kiss me.

A flush of heat went through my body right then, although I honestly couldn't say whether it had come from Gideon, or whether it was simply me reacting to what I'd just felt drifting outward from his thoughts. I clenched my knees together under the table and told myself I couldn't let him affect me this way. I'd be falling right in with his father's plans, and I wasn't about to give Lir Shalan the satisfaction.

The words were out of my mouth before I could stop them. "Gideon, why am I here?"

A sharp tingle of anxiety then, right before he pushed it back. "You're our honored guest."

"Do you really expect me to believe that?"

"Are we going to have this discussion again?"

"Yes," I said, forcing myself to stare into his eyes, to show him I wasn't about to back down. In this light, I could see the beautiful traceries in his reddish irises, swirls of garnet and ruby, cabernet and merlot.

Before that moment, I hadn't realized how gorgeous those eyes were, alien though they might be.

"All right," he said. He laid his hands flat on the tabletop and met my gaze squarely without blinking. "You are our guest, Taryn, even if you don't want to believe me when I tell you that. But we're also studying you, of course. Your behavior, how your powers might be manifesting."

"They're not manifesting at all," I pointed out, pleased that I'd gotten even that bit of a confession out of him. "Like I told you earlier, my powers don't work at all on Reptilians. I might as well be trying to read the thoughts of that desk over there, or the biometric panels you use to lock your doors."

Did he believe me? Hard to say, because my words hadn't elicited any particular flare of emotion from him. He did study me for a few seconds longer, our gazes still locked, while I tried to stare back at him as guilelessly as possible. Right then, I remembered how Kirsten had once said that the leader of the alien base in Sedona—not Lir Shalan, but a Reptilian who had died when she blasted him and his followers off Courthouse Butte—had managed to invade her thoughts on several occasions. I could only pray that Gideon didn't have similar talents.

But then he shrugged and said, "That's unfortunate," and went to pick up his spork so he could return to his neglected meal. I couldn't let out a sigh of relief, but I also lifted my shoulders, glad that he hadn't detected anything strange in my expression. It didn't seem that he could read my mind, or else he would have known I was covering something up. Maybe Lir Shalan's line didn't possess that particular gift, or maybe it was different when the person a Reptilian was contacting was Pleiadian, rather than straight-up human.

Either way, I couldn't help feeling that I'd just dodged a rather large bullet.

CHAPTER FIVE

I WISHED I COULD SAY THAT THE REPTILIANS HAD changed their minds and had decided to send me home once they realized they wouldn't be able to get any particularly useful information out of me, but of course that wasn't the case. The room I'd been given was more comfortable than a prison cell, but it served basically the same purpose.

Gideon did come to see me once a day, usually so we could share lunch. It seemed that the largest meal on board ship was the one served at midday, and so that was the time when he would come to fetch me and take me to his suite. Each time, I wondered if he was going to try anything, but so far he'd been very well-behaved.

Not for lack of trying on his father's part, though. I had plenty of time to spend taking astral walks around the ship, and I did my share of spying on the

Reptilian commander and his son. Their language was still a mystery to me, and Lir Shalan's thoughts equally so, but I could tell things were becoming increasingly strained between the two of them. How long it would take before that particular powder keg blew, I had no idea. I just knew I really didn't want to be around when it happened.

Problem was, there didn't seem to be any way for me to escape. When I wasn't snooping on Gideon and his father, I wandered the corridors of the *Eclipse*, trying to get a better idea of its scale, of how many people—to use the term loosely—were on board. The ship seemed enormous to me, about as big as if someone had taken my favorite shopping mall down in Phoenix and had put propulsion units on it and sent it into space. Strangely, though, the huge vessel didn't appear to have nearly the crew you'd think a ship of that size would need to keep operating. I guessed that a lot of its functions were automated, but still, I couldn't quite figure out how it was all supposed to work.

The Reptilians were a taciturn lot, though. They didn't seem to talk to one another very much, and when they did, it looked to me like they were discussing matters that had to do with the ship's operations and nothing else. As Gideon had said, they didn't take their meals together, but ate alone in their rooms.

And although I couldn't claim to be an expert in Reptilian physiology, it looked to me as if every single one of those crew members was male. Maybe their women looked exactly the same as their men, but I didn't think so. True, one couldn't claim that the aliens were terribly progressive when it came to the way they treated women. Even so, I'd have thought you'd catch a glimpse of at least a woman or two among the thousands who served on the *Eclipse*.

I couldn't ask Gideon, though. So far, I'd managed to keep my out-of-body wanderings a complete secret, and I needed things to stay that way. Although a lot of the intelligence I'd gathered didn't seem all that useful, I was glad that I could at least get out and about, even if it was in an incorporeal form. If Gideon discovered what I was doing…well, I didn't know what would happen. I didn't even know if there was a way to prevent a person from traveling astrally, but I really didn't want to find out.

But, as far as I could tell, he hadn't noticed anything. My days—eight in all so far—had followed the same unvarying schedule. No matter what else was going on, he always showed up for lunch at exactly noon, or what was noon ship-time, anyway. My second day on the *Eclipse,* he'd brought me an older tablet computer, one that had all its personal data carefully erased but which still contained a decent library of movies and TV shows, and an even bigger library of books. Nothing more recent than about five years ago, which told me when the computer's former owner had probably run afoul of the Reptilians, or possibly one of their "Grey" minions. I'd thanked Gideon for the gift and had forced myself not to ask any questions.

Anyway, the tablet had given me a clock that I could follow, so I was able to keep track of the days passing, and to know a little more of what happened when on board the ship. And it was good to have the books and the movies to keep me occupied for those times when I was just too heartsick and tired to summon the mental discipline that would send me into my astral state.

I missed my family. After seeing how Callista had just left the nest in a typically spectacular fashion, I'd been chafing to get out of the house, wondering if maybe I should sublet an apartment for a few months until it was time to transfer to NAU and move to Flagstaff. Circumstances had intervened, however, and I hadn't gotten very far with those plans. Now, though, I just wanted to be back in the house that was the only home I'd ever known, to be able to participate in one of our lively dinnertime conversations about politics and science and books and movies and anything else that had caught our interest that day. To see the crinkles at the corners of my father's eyes as he teased my mother about something, or to hear her goofy laugh as she tried to tell a joke she'd heard from Kara Rinehart earlier that day. All those silly trivial things you didn't realize you missed until you didn't have them anymore.

Needless to say, I did my best to keep my longing for home a secret. Once or twice, I contemplated asking whether I could send a message to my family, just to let everyone know I was all right. But every time the request rose to my lips, I'd look at Gideon, at the firm set of his mouth and the cool expression in his ruby-hued eyes, and I knew there was no point. I had to make him think I was content.

When I was around him, I answered his questions, tried to make sure that I was always matter-of-fact and good-spirited. There were still those awkward moments when I sensed his need for me, or when I found my gaze lingering on his mouth a little longer than was strictly necessary, but I thought I was doing a decent job of holding it together. I didn't want to think about the way I'd keep my eye on the time stamp in the upper corner of my borrowed tablet's screen, counting down the minutes until it was time for him to show up and take me to lunch. That sort of preoccupation—distracting me from reading or watching a show or playing a game—told me I wasn't nearly as detached as I wanted to be.

However, I also wasn't strong enough to tell Gideon that I didn't want to share those meals with him, that since I was a prisoner here, I might as well be treated like one and kept in solitary. I found myself craving his company, wishing we could spend more than that hour or so together each day. And by doing so, I knew I was playing right into Lir Shalan's hands.

I just didn't know what in the world I was supposed to do about it.

Gideon hadn't made a move, though, which of course only contributed to his father's increasing ire. It was almost as if he was sitting back and waiting to see if I would do something first, which I knew wouldn't happen. Not because I didn't want it to— I'd stopped lying to myself on that point a while back —but because I didn't want to think about what the consequences of giving in to that sort of weakness might be.

But then there came the sort of blowout that could only make you grateful no one had ended up dead, or in jail. All right, jail wasn't really a possibility when it came to either Gideon or Lir Shalan. I did know that if our neighbors had ever had the kind of confrontation the alien and his son shared on the twentieth day of my captivity, my father would have been on the phone to the police.

Gideon had seemed edgy that day at lunch, but I hadn't pressed him for an explanation. I could guess well enough. Besides, he wouldn't have told me the truth even if I had asked. Admitting that he was at odds with his father would only have been an admission of weakness.

My curiosity got the better of me, and after our meal, I once again made my way to Lir Shalan's suite. It seemed they always had their confrontations there, as if the alien leader wanted to assert his dominance by having his son come to him, rather than vice versa. And I supposed it worked, in a way; that apartment was pretty intimidating. Also, even though Gideon was quite tall, Lir Shalan had the full height of the Reptilian race on his side, and used it to dominate the situation whenever he could.

He was looming over his son when my astral self slipped through the wall. Gideon—well, with his complexion, he couldn't exactly go pale, but there was something drained and pinched about his face that seemed to be the equivalent of pallor. And I could sense the anger and frustration shooting out from him, almost as brilliant and terrible as a flame.

Lir Shalan's hissing voice grated against my ears, disembodied as I was. If it bothered me that much, I didn't really want to think about what it might be doing to his son. But Gideon shook his head, jaw set, and said something that sounded nearly as cutting.

Back and forth they went. Then, so lightning fast I could barely see it, Lir Shalan's left hand came up and pounded Gideon across the jaw so hard that he stumbled.

He didn't fall, though. He stood his ground, eyes glaring with red fire. A few words in the Reptilians' sibilant tongue, and then he brought one hand against his chest in a sort of mocking salute. The next minute, he stalked out the door.

Lir Shalan remained where he was, ruby eyes almost slits. He muttered something under his breath before going over to a wall and punching it. The metal buckled, and streaks of black blood showed on the shining surface, but the alien leader made his own exit a second or two after that, apparently oblivious to the injury he'd just caused himself. And then the metal appeared to ripple and smooth itself out, erasing every sign of the dent that had been there a few seconds earlier.

Could your heart pound like crazy when you weren't even in your physical body? I'd never thought so before that moment. It was beating wildly, as hard as if I'd just run a marathon. But then I realized that I'd better get back to my room as quickly as I could. By that point, I knew the layout of the ship well enough that it wasn't necessary for my astral form to carefully follow each corridor and use the elevator shaft to get from floor to floor. No, I shot upward, passing through bulkheads and walls as if they didn't exist.

I reentered my body with a sharp *crack*, one I was sure must have been audible to anyone standing nearby. Luckily, I was alone, and so didn't have to worry about giving myself away.

Not a moment too soon, though. I was sitting in my body, gasping and trying to reorient myself, when the squeal of the door chime penetrated the room.

Had Gideon really come here immediately after that confrontation with his father?

Apparently so, because when I opened the door, I saw him standing outside in the corridor, his complexion still that pasty greenish tone—except for a darker splotch on the right side of his face, the exact spot where Lir Shalan had hit him.

"G-Gideon?" I stammered, thinking that it wouldn't seem too out of character for me to be surprised by his sudden appearance. I didn't know exactly what time it was, but lunch had been hours ago.

"Taryn," he replied. His voice was calm. Too calm, probably. "Would you come with me, please?"

I swallowed. I didn't know exactly what he had planned, but I worried it was nothing good. Unfortunately, I couldn't think of how in the world I might refuse.

"Sure, Gideon." There. That had sounded almost normal. After all, I couldn't know anything of what had just passed between him and his father. While it might be strange for him to call on me at a time other than lunch, I couldn't act as if such an occurrence was anything except mildly puzzling. It wasn't as if I hadn't gone with him to his suite on many other occasions.

My compliance didn't seem to have reassured him, though. His mouth was still pressed into a thin line, and he didn't speak as he led me out of my room and along the familiar route to the elevators.

Usually, we would pass some crew members when we reached the level where his suite was located. Today, though, the hallway was deserted. I didn't want to think about what that meant. Maybe nothing at all. Just coincidence.

Right.

Gideon opened the door for me, and I headed into

the apartment as I always did, my destination the spot by the window where I could look down at lost, lovely Earth. He'd always allowed me those few moments to take in the view, to think of the people down there I missed so terribly.

Today, though, he kept pace with me before surging ahead so he could slap his hand down on a control panel to the left of the window. At once, a dark film descended, obscuring Earth and the starfield in which it floated.

"No need to waste time with that," he said coldly.

I looked up at him in surprise and a little fear. I knew I should have been trying to react the way a Taryn who had no idea what was going on would have, but the expression on his face and the tone of his voice frightened me more than I wanted to admit. "Gideon, what's the matter?"

He didn't answer. Instead, he moved away from me and toward the kitchen area where the food synthesizer was located. He didn't give it any commands, however. Still without speaking, he reached up and slid open one of the metal cupboards, drawing out a squat glass bottle nearly filled with amber-colored liquid.

It was no alien liquor, though. Even from where I stood, I could make out the letters on the bottle.

Maker's Mark.

What the hell?

Gideon must have seen the question in my eyes, because he offered me a bitter smile before retrieving a pair of shot glasses from that same cupboard and setting them down on the counter. "A little souvenir from planet Earth," he said. "I'm sure my father knows I have it, but he hasn't bothered to confiscate it."

"I've never seen you drink," I told him, which was nothing more than the truth. "We've only had water together." And, I thought, eyeing the bottle, I guessed that he didn't drink very much. There couldn't have been more than a shot or two missing from its contents.

"Sometimes the occasion calls for something a little stronger." He poured a measure of bourbon into each shot glass. Overfilled them, really; the liquid in one almost ran over the brim, and the other was nearly as full. He took the less-full shot glass and extended it toward me. "Have a drink, Taryn."

I wanted to protest that I didn't like bourbon. Didn't like spirits of any kind, really; they all tasted like medicine to me. Some white wines were okay, but I still could take them or leave them.

But all I had to do was take another look at Gideon's face to know it wouldn't be very smart to argue with him. Willing myself to stay calm, I went over to him and took the shot glass, feeling the stickiness of slopped-over liquor on its sides.

"What are we drinking to?" I asked. I really didn't want to know the answer, but the words had come tumbling out before I could stop them.

"Do we need a reason?"

"I guess not," I admitted.

He lifted his shot glass and bolted the contents neat, as if he did that sort of thing every day. Well, almost. Since I was watching him closely, trying to gauge every reaction, every shift in his expression, I could see the way the muscles in his neck tightened as he swallowed. Probably trying to keep himself from gagging.

I wasn't about to be that reckless. Yes, I didn't see any way out of drinking that crap, but I wasn't going to throw back a shot as if I was playing a game at a frat party. I lifted the shot glass and tried to keep myself from wrinkling my nose at the smell. Then I took one small sip and swallowed as quickly as I could.

That didn't help much. My throat constricted, and I forced the bourbon down, praying I wouldn't spit it right back out again. Somehow, it made it all the way to my stomach without incident, where I could feel it burning away.

Gideon watched me during this whole procedure, expression blank. I'd just swallowed another nasty mouthful when he reached for the bottle and poured himself another shot. That one he tossed back just as quickly as he had the first, and I had to keep myself from wincing. How well could his half-alien physiology handle that much liquor?

Once again I asked, "Gideon, what's the matter?" I hoped if I could get him talking, then maybe he would slow down with the drinking. Then again, maybe the question would only infuriate him, make him pour another shot.

Since I couldn't take it back, I had to stand there and wait to see what he would do.

Very deliberately, he set down the shot glass and turned toward me. The dark mark left behind by his father's blow seemed to stand out even more in the bright light cast by the luminous ceiling overhead. Then he smiled, but there was no humor in his expression. That smile might as well have been the empty grin of a shark.

"What's the matter?" he repeated, and paused as if considering the answer. His shoulders lifted. "I would say you are the matter, Taryn Oliver."

"I am?" I responded. A chill began to creep its way down my spine. I wanted to back away from him, but that would be far too obvious, wouldn't it?

"Yes, you." He took a step toward me, and I forced myself to stand my ground. "I think I've been very patient."

"P-patient?" I managed, feigning incomprehension. Unfortunately, I thought I had a very good idea of what he was talking about, and the chill that had begun in my spine started to spread throughout my entire body.

Again he moved. This time, there was less than a foot between us. I could smell the alcohol on his breath, see the look of baffled fury in his eyes. And I could feel the war inside him, the need to show who had power here battling with the part of him that had, against all odds, begun to care for me.

I didn't know which side would win. I could hope, but hope wasn't knowing. Every instinct in me was telling me to run, to bolt for the door and get the hell out of there. Problem was, I didn't think that door would open for me.

But I couldn't keep myself from taking a step backward, and I saw the answering flicker in his eyes, as if my small attempt at escape was enough to convince him of something he'd suspected all along. Moving so quickly it was terrifying, he had me backed up against the wall, his hands planted against the metal surface on either side of my head so I was well and truly trapped.

"So you don't want this," he said.

"I didn't say that," I replied. My voice sounded horribly shaky, but there wasn't much I could do about it right then.

"You might as well have. But you realize you don't have much choice, don't you?"

For a long moment, I didn't answer. Nothing I could think of to say seemed as if it would make any difference. In my mind, I heard once again the horrible smacking sound of Lir Shalan's hand striking his son's face. That single blow had to be the reason why Gideon was acting like this now.

Then I took a breath and forced myself to meet his glaring ruby eyes. "No, I don't have much of a choice," I retorted. I didn't stop to think—the words spilled out of me as I added, "After all, your mother wasn't given a choice, either, was she?"

Dead silence. Gideon stared at me for a long moment, and again I caught a flash of guilt, of anger. But not directed at me. At least, I didn't think so.

I didn't dare move. Didn't dare breathe. Had I said exactly the right thing...or exactly the wrong one?

Then he muttered something under his breath, words I couldn't understand because they were in the Reptilian tongue. But I didn't need to know the vocabulary to guess he was cursing, although I had no idea whether those curses were directed at me, at his father, or at himself.

After a span of a few seconds that felt like an eternity, he pushed himself away from me, then picked up the bottle of bourbon. He stared at it, and I wondered if he'd decided to dispense with the shot glass and was going to drink directly from the bottle.

Again he moved so quickly that I didn't even have time to blink. In the next instant, the bottle was smashing against the wall, glass and bourbon flying in every direction. I threw up my hands to shield myself and could feel sharp, tiny pinpricks as some of the shattered glass touched my skin. Right then, I could only be thankful I was wearing one of the bulky dresses Gideon had provided, because most of me was safely covered.

Then he said dully, "You've won."

Won what, I wasn't sure, but in that moment, I

wished I'd never made that comment about his mother. There was something defeated in his expression, and, as much as he'd just frightened me, I didn't want him looking that way.

"Gideon, I—"

"Don't." He paused for a few seconds, then shook his head. "I knew this would never work. He didn't want to believe that. He made it all sound so simple. But now...."

Even though he'd scared me senseless, I found myself wanting to reach out and take his hand, offer him some sort of reassurance. But I didn't quite dare. His behavior had been erratic enough that I didn't want to take the chance.

His eyes met mine. In them, I saw the beginnings of some sort of resolve. About what, I didn't know, because the emotions that had been flaring out from him just a few moments earlier had been banked down, like a roaring fire knocked down into ash.

"I'll take you now," he said.

"Take me?" There it was, that awful quaver in my voice. I really needed to get a handle on that.

"Home," he replied. "Isn't that what you've wanted all along?"

I must be hearing things. After almost three weeks of keeping me trapped here, he was going to ferry me home, just like that?

"Well, yes," I said. "But your father—"

"I'll handle him." His tone was dismissive, but I felt a short, sharp burst of fear before he locked it down. Not that I could blame him for being afraid of his father. I'd seen what Lir Shalan was capable of... and I worried a blow to the face would only be the beginning, once he realized his son had let their prized captive go free. "So where do you want me to take you? To the home of your parents in Sedona?"

I didn't bother to ask how he knew where our house was. They knew a great deal, these Reptilians; they'd been watching my family and my parents' friends since before I was even born.

But I hesitated. Oh, I wanted to go home...but I also knew what would happen once I was there. The whole gang would be called together for a "briefing" at Kara and Lance's house, and I'd have to answer far more questions than I was willing to handle at the moment. I needed just a little breathing space, a chance to absorb everything that had happened to me over the past ten days.

"No," I said at last, willing myself to meet those dark, defeated eyes. "I want to go to my brother Michael's apartment in Flagstaff."

CHAPTER SIX

GETTING AWAY WAS FAR EASIER THAN I'D THOUGHT IT would be. Although the device Gideon used was a short cylinder of dark metal rather than the gleaming opal jewel I'd seen hanging from Raphael's belt, it appeared to do pretty much the same thing in terms of getting people from place to place. As Gideon swiped a finger down one side, glaring yellow light surrounded the two of us, and a few seconds later, we were no longer standing in the kitchen area of his suite, but in the shelter of one of the pine trees that surrounded Michael's apartment complex.

Good thing, too, because appearing in a burst of yellow light was enough to attract attention on its own, let alone when the people stepping out of said yellow light included a man with green skin and a young woman in a long black dress who looked like she might be late for a coven meeting.

I turned toward Gideon. Something in me wanted to urge him to stay here with me, which was crazy. He didn't belong here, would most likely be hauled off to be experimented on as soon as people began to report seeing a strange green-skinned man wandering around their neighborhood.

My words stumbled over themselves. "I don't know what to say—"

His expression was stony. Was he imagining what his father's reaction would be once he found out what his son had done? "Then don't say anything."

A flash of light, and I lifted a hand to shield my eyes. When I lowered it, Gideon was gone.

A sudden tightness filled my chest, and I was pretty sure the stinging in my eyes didn't have all that much to do with the brilliant illumination that had accompanied his departure. Damn. I really had screwed that up, hadn't I?

Probably. Not that I'd wanted to fall in line with Lir Shalan's crazy plans, but at the same time, I couldn't help feeling that there must have been some way for me to show Gideon that my reluctance to become his mate—for lack of a better term—had nothing to do with him and everything to do with not wanting to be his father's pawn.

So much I could have said, or done. If I'd only reached out to him, laid a hand on his arm...something. But I hadn't, and now he was gone, and the wind was cold, biting through the thin fabric of my dress. February was gone and now it was March, and the weather should have been a little milder, but I'd never spent much time in Flagstaff during the winter months and so didn't have much basis for comparison.

Trying to ignore the chill, I gathered a handful of skirt so it would be out of my way, then headed toward the back of the complex where Michael's apartment was located. I prayed he would be home; I didn't know his schedule, but I seemed to recall that he taught morning classes and worked on his dissertation in the afternoons and evenings. From the slant of the light, I guessed it must be late afternoon now. Not that the time of day necessarily indicated he would be home, since he spent a good deal of time on campus even when he wasn't teaching.

With my luck, he'd be gone altogether, getting in some hours on one of Lowell's remote telescopes, which meant he could be miles and miles away. Then I shook my head. No, that wasn't right. You didn't go stargazing at five o'clock in the afternoon.

And if he wasn't home, well, I'd make my way over to the mall and use one of the pay data kiosks there to call the house. The idea of walking around the Flagstaff Mall while wearing this getup wasn't exactly appealing, but better than sitting on the landing outside Michael's apartment and praying that he'd come home before I froze to death.

Going up the stairs in that skirt wasn't much fun. I kept the folds of bulky fabric out of the way as best

I could while I climbed to the second floor, although I did nearly trip once or twice.

When I got to his door, I used my free hand to knock, praying all the while that he would answer. I knew I wouldn't be marooned here in Flagstaff indefinitely if it turned out he wasn't home, but sitting around and waiting for my parents to come fetch me would be uncomfortable and anticlimactic.

I was tired, and I didn't want to think about the look in Gideon's eyes just before he turned away from me and disappeared.

To my relief, the door opened. Not immediately, and Michael was wearing his familiar distracted expression, which meant he'd been buried in something on his computer and hadn't quite snapped back to reality yet.

But then his hazel eyes—so much like mine— widened, and he said, "*Taryn?*"

"Yes, it's me. Can I come in? It's freezing out here."

Looking positively flummoxed—not that I could blame him—he replied, "Um—well, of course."

He backed out of the way so I could head into the apartment. I'd been here once or twice before, and nothing much seemed to have changed. The place was small, occupied by a hand-me-down leather couch that had originally lived in the family room back home, with a cheap glass and metal coffee table in front of that sofa. You could barely see the surface of the table, though, because

Michael's laptop took up most of the space, and a pile of notebooks and some actual books covered the rest.

After shutting the door, he said, "What's going on, Taryn? Mom and Dad said you were—" He stopped there, as if he wasn't quite sure how to say "abducted by aliens" without sounding like an idiot. True, those same aliens had revealed themselves to the world, so talking about such things wouldn't be an automatic ban to advancement for Michael the way it had been for our father. Even so, my brother looked vaguely embarrassed by having to say the words out loud.

"Yes, they took me. But one of them brought me back." I headed over to the sofa and more or less collapsed on it. That confrontation with Gideon had taken more out of me than I'd thought. "Can I have some water, please?"

Brow still puckered in concern, Michael nodded and went over to the small galley-style kitchen. After extracting a bottle of water from the fridge and handing it to me, he said, "They brought you back? Why?"

I really didn't want to go into the whole Gideon thing with Michael. Frankly, I wasn't sure if I understood the situation myself. The truth would have to come out at some point, but it didn't have to be now. "They just got tired of me, I guess."

An eyebrow went up. Right then, Michael looked a lot like our father, although in coloring, he resembled our mother more. "You really think that's the reason?"

Of course it wasn't. "I don't know, Michael," I said, my tone growing waspish. "They didn't exactly explain themselves to me. It was just, 'we're done, where do you want to go?' So I told them."

"You asked them to bring you here? Why not Mom and Dad's?"

At least his question was something I could answer truthfully, because I knew that sometimes Michael felt just as overwhelmed by the combined Oliver/Rinehart/Jones dynamic as I did. "I wasn't ready for the third degree yet."

He nodded. "I can understand that. Well, of course you can crash here—but you're going to have to call them eventually."

"I will. Tomorrow morning. I just need to catch my breath."

His gaze flickered to the dark dress I wore. "Did they give you that?"

"Yes. Apparently, Reptilians have issues with jeans. Who knew?"

My tone was flip, and he frowned again. To my relief, though, he didn't ask any other questions, only said, "Well, I'd give you something to change into, but you'd be swimming in it."

True enough. I took after our mother and was barely average in height, while Michael was tall, like our father. "I know. But could you do me a huge favor and go pick up a few things for me at the mall? Mom and Dad will pay you back."

"Like that matters." He hesitated, then added, "I'm not exactly what you'd call an expert at shopping for women's clothes."

"It's all right," I said, relieved that he hadn't shot me down immediately. "I can make a list."

In answer, he dug in his jeans pocket and pulled out his phone. After having it read his thumbprint to unlock it, he handed the phone to me. "Just dictate your list. It'll be a lot easier than writing it all down."

Which was what I did, asking for a pair of jeans and a shirt, some shoes in a size seven, a pack of underwear, a toothbrush. I figured I could steal some toothpaste from him and borrow his deodorant as well. And I wasn't going to ask him to get me any makeup, since I'd only be crashing overnight and then heading back to Sedona in the morning.

I handed the phone back to him. He looked at the list without comment before sliding the phone back into his pocket, although, judging by the way his brows pulled together, I could tell he was less than thrilled at having to purchase a few of the items I'd included. "Do you want me to go now, or should I wait a little while? I mean, if you don't want to be by yourself—"

"I'll be all right," I said, and hoped that was true. There was always the chance that Lir Shalan would come rampaging back here to collect me. However, I doubted even he would attempt that kind of maneuver in broad daylight in a crowded apartment complex. Full dark was still a few hours off. Plenty of time for Michael to run over to the mall and get back.

"If you're sure—"

"I am."

My brother gave a fatalistic sort of shrug, and got his jacket from the hall coat rack that stood in the corner near the door. "I'll be back as soon as I can," he said, then headed out.

I'd heard him lock the door, but I still went over and tested it, just to be safe. Stupid, I knew, because aliens intent on abduction really weren't deterred by locked doors. Anyway, Gideon knew where he'd dropped me off, but no one else did, and I doubted he was going to reveal that information to his father any time soon.

The shopping trip probably wouldn't take Michael that long anyway, since his apartment complex was just down the street from the mall. I'd asked him why he wanted a place so relatively far from campus, and he'd told me he spent so much time at the university that when he came home, he wanted to feel entirely separate from it so he could decompress.

That explanation made sense to me, and anyway, the location was convenient in a lot of ways; in addition to the mall, there was a shopping center nearby with a Safeway and then another center with a Home Depot and a bunch of other useful places. Having everything clustered together like that meant my brother wouldn't have to go very far to get what he needed.

After peeking out the window to make sure no flying saucers were hovering overhead, just waiting to beam me away, I wandered idly around the apartment, looking but not touching anything. Michael's laptop was closed, and I wouldn't snoop, but his big desktop computer with the thirty-inch screen had been left on. I couldn't make heads or tails of what was on there, though, because the screen was covered in formulas and notations and wireframe models of what could have been a black hole, or maybe a coffee filter. To tell the truth, I wasn't even exactly sure what he was writing his dissertation on. Something insanely technical that he could debate for hours with our father, but made my eyes want to roll back in my head whenever he tried to explain.

There were more notebooks piled on the computer desk. And the middle drawer was partway open, as if Michael had been about to start rummaging in there for a pen or something when I'd knocked at the door.

A flash of color inside that drawer caught my eye, and I sidled closer so I could take a look. Maybe that wasn't a very nice thing to do, but right then, I was just trying to keep myself from brooding about Gideon, about what might be happening to him at that very moment. I hated to think what his father might do to him in retaliation for his act of defiance.

What I'd spotted in the desk drawer turned out to

be a photograph. I even recognized it, because an identical one sat on the mantel in the living room at my parents' house. It was a snapshot Lance had taken with his phone, a picture that Kara had liked so much, she'd gotten duplicates made at the local drugstore and then had given them to everyone.

The photo was from a barbecue last summer at the Rineharts', everyone looking tanned and relaxed and happy after an afternoon of splashing in the creek and enjoying the shade of the big oak trees that sheltered its banks. Callista and I were caught mid-giggle, while Grace stood behind us, annoying the crap out of her younger brother Kevin by tousling his already messy bright blond hair. Their little sister Melissa looked on, grinning.

And off to the side, there was Kelsey, looking bright and windblown and casually gorgeous in her cutoff shorts and tank top while she gave the whole group an indulgent smile. That side of the photo was slightly dog-eared and rumpled, as if it had been handled much more often than the other.

What in the world?

It was a not-so-secret secret in our little extended family that Kelsey had had a crush on Michael for years. He'd ignored her attentions as best he could, and because my brother was one of those rare people whose thoughts I couldn't read, I never could figure out exactly how he felt about her—whether he was embarrassed by being crushed on by the daughter of a family friend like that, or whether he was simply so absorbed by his studies that he couldn't be bothered to waste any mental energy worrying about the situation.

But this photo—

It hadn't been handled that often because Grace was in it; she and Michael didn't get along all that well. And he'd never paid much attention to Callista, except to tease her the same way he'd tease me, like she was just another little sister.

Kelsey, though....

Had he been hiding feelings for her all this time? What would be the point?

Well, the point was that he didn't think he had time for a girlfriend. He'd had a few casual girlfriends in high school, but by the time he got to college, he was pretty focused. If he'd dated anybody during his time at NAU, those relationships clearly weren't serious enough for him to mention them to his family.

The door opened then and I started, turning guiltily toward it, photo still in my hand. Michael came into the apartment, hands full with shopping bags, and then stopped when he saw what I was holding. The frown came back full force.

"Sorry," I said immediately. "Your desk drawer was partly open, and I saw this...."

He didn't reply. In silence, he went over to the drop-leaf table that was placed up against the wall in the dining area and deposited the shopping bags on it. When he turned around, he said, "Look, I know you've been through a lot, but that doesn't give you the right—"

"I know. It doesn't." I slipped the photo back into the desk drawer and then shut it. "But Michael—"

"I don't want to talk about it." He unzipped his jacket and hung it on the coat rack. Without looking at me, he went on, "I got everything you asked for. Just please don't ask me to buy you a bra again, okay?"

"I won't." I approached the table and gathered up the bags. "Thanks for this, Michael. I'll go change now."

"Sure."

Still with that grim set to his mouth, he went over to the sofa, sat down, and opened up his laptop. I decided it was probably better not to say anything else right then. Michael's usual strategy when he was upset about something was to take refuge in his work, and I figured I should probably give him a little cooling-down time.

Taking the bags with me, I headed into the bathroom. At least I could trust my brother to have a reasonably clean bath. He didn't mind a little clutter, but he hated dirt.

He really had gotten me everything I'd asked for. I slipped off my borrowed dress and then pulled on the new jeans, along with the bra and the black long-sleeved T-shirt I found in a different bag. He'd gotten me some black flats, and I put them on as well.

It did feel strange to be wearing regular clothes

after spending nearly three weeks wandering around in those flowy dresses that were just a step up from a nightgown. I finger-combed my unruly hair as best I could, then took a breath and headed back out to the living room.

At least Michael looked up from his laptop when I came in. That meant he was probably still annoyed with me, but not so angry that he would keep typing away without even acknowledging my presence.

"Feel better?" he asked.

"Much," I replied. The couch was the only real place to sit, unless I appropriated the desk chair. I didn't know which was the better choice, so I went and perched at the far end of the sofa.

"You really need to call Mom and Dad, you know."

I knew that. And of course I would...eventually. But the second I got in contact with them, the whole UFO-hunting crew would come down on me, wanting to know every last detail of what had happened on board the Reptilian ship.

I was still trying to figure that out for myself.

So I muttered, "Yeah, I know," then picked up the bottle of water Michael had fetched for me earlier and took a few sips. He was studiously not paying attention to me, his gaze fixed on the screen before him.

A few seconds later, though, he closed the computer and expelled an annoyed-sounding breath through his lips. "Are you going to tell her?"

Playing dumb, I asked, "Am I going to tell who what?"

"You know what I'm talking about."

I played with the cap on the bottle. "You know I wouldn't," I told him. He didn't look all that relieved, however. Since he didn't seem inclined to speak, I went on, "I guess I just don't understand why you thought you had to hide it all this time. You know everyone in the family would be thrilled if you and Kelsey got together."

"Even Grace?" he asked, tone ironic. He'd never gone into any details, of course, but that one date our mothers had kind of forced on him and Grace Rinehart must have been spectacularly disastrous for him to still be put off by it years later.

"I think especially Grace," I replied. She really did just want the best for him. Of course, it was easy to be magnanimous when everything in your own love life was going well.

He was silent for a moment, apparently pondering my reply. Then his shoulders lifted, and he gave a brief glance around the apartment. "I suppose I didn't feel as if I was in a position to start anything. School takes up all my time. Besides, look at this place. I doubt Kelsey would want to be cramped in a crappy one-bedroom apartment. Just her room at her parents' house is almost as big as this."

"And that's the only reason?"

"Jesus, Taryn. Aren't I the one who's supposed to

be asking you questions? Just what the hell did happen up there?"

Damn it. I really wasn't ready to talk about that yet. But I should have known that Michael wouldn't allow me to stick on the topic of him and Kelsey for very long. Would admitting that he felt something for her—even if he had done so very obliquely—be enough for him to bring things out in the open? I didn't know. And even though I couldn't read his mind, I knew my brother well enough to know when I needed to back off.

"Nothing happened," I said in a careless tone that I doubted fooled my brother for an instant. "They were studying me, but not in an invasive way. No anal probes or anything like that."

A pained expression crossed Michael's face at the phrase "anal probe." He really hated that stuff because it was the sort of thing he'd invariably get teased about once people found out that his father was Paul Oliver, the famous ufologist. Everyone seemed to conveniently forget that our father had been an astronomer and double Ph.D. before he was a UFO expert. I supposed no one was laughing very hard now, though, since those aliens had turned out to be all too real.

There probably hadn't been any anal probes at the Reptilians' meetings with the President, though.

"Studying you. How?"

"They wanted me because I'm psychic. That is, a human who's psychic. Callista wasn't worth as much to them because she's mostly Pleiadian and is expected to have unusual powers. But me?" I shrugged. "I'm a freak."

"You're not a freak," he said immediately. We'd had this almost identical exchange numerous times in the past, and he was probably getting fairly tired of it.

"Okay, an anomaly. I can't say a biological sport, exactly, because Mom has her own set of powers, even if they're not identical to mine."

"So they examined you?"

"Um, not really."

That reply only made the puzzled frown my brother wore deepen that much more. "So what *did* they do?"

I didn't know how to reply. I turned the bottle of water I held around and around in my hands, knowing I'd have to tell him something but not sure what that something should be. If I started talking about Gideon, then it would come out soon enough that a fairly weird dynamic had developed between the two of us. It wasn't really the sort of thing I felt comfortable discussing with my brother. Yes, he'd always been there to watch my back, but I knew better than to confide in him when it came to boy stuff.

Boy stuff. There was a joke. I didn't really know how to classify my strange relationship with Gideon, but it was about as similar to the casual relationships I'd had with the few guys I'd dated as the Reptilians' starship was to a tugboat.

So I drank some more water while Michael watched me with an increasingly concerned expression on his face.

"Taryn…if they hurt you, we need to know. If nothing else, we need to get you to a doctor—"

"I don't need to go to the doctor," I broke in. "No one hurt me. No one even really touched me." I figured it was probably best not to mention how Gideon had grabbed me by the arm that one time. "I guess they decided I wasn't worth wasting any more energy on, so they let me go. You know it happens all the time with abduction cases. The aliens get what they want—whatever that is—and then they release the abductees. Why should I be any different?"

"Because they were pretty blatant about it this time, from what Kirsten and Martin had to say about what happened. This wasn't your standard 'abducted from a deserted highway' scenario."

He was right, of course. And, being Michael, he wanted concrete answers. He dealt with facts and numbers and formulas. True, you had to be something of a dreamer to want to spend your life staring up into the night sky, but only up to a point. After that, the hard data needed to kick in.

"Well, they didn't tell me," I said. "So I don't have any answers for you, Michael."

I hated to lie…if I really even was lying. After all, Gideon hadn't articulated his specific reasons for getting rid of me, although it didn't require a rocket scientist to figure out that his father had demanded that he do the unthinkable, and Gideon had almost capitulated before coming to his senses.

A long silence. Michael took his laptop and set it down on the coffee table. Without exactly looking at me, he asked, "Are you hungry?"

A rush of relief went over me. I knew that question meant he didn't intend to pry any further. Most likely, he knew that my parents—and the rest of the group—would put me through the wringer anyway, and so he didn't see the point in bothering me when I was tired and clearly a little shell-shocked.

And maybe he was also thinking that if he didn't push me on this, then I wouldn't push him about Kelsey. Which was correct. I didn't think I could let the matter slide completely, but I had a whole lot of other things to worry about besides my brother's love life, or lack thereof. I certainly wouldn't say anything to Kelsey. Why get her hopes up when I didn't know if my brother would ever get the guts to talk to her honestly?

So I told Michael I was hungry, and he suggested pizza, and I said that sounded like a great idea. After all that time with basically no carbs, I felt as if I could eat two or three pizzas on my own, and possibly a couple of loaves of bread, too.

We both studiously avoided talking about anything except trivial stuff. And that was good, because I'd begun to have the oddest sensation, like a building force somewhere off in the distance, the way you could feel the pressure drop that preceded a thunderstorm like a physical weight on your chest.

I didn't know what it was, but I worried that a very different type of storm was coming.

CHAPTER SEVEN

MY PARENTS CAME AND GOT ME THE NEXT DAY. Michael was the one who called them, actually, because when the moment came, I found I didn't have the nerve to say that I'd been returned the day before. The truth came out while he was on the phone, of course, but I figured my parents would have the entire drive up to Flagstaff to shake off their worry and anger.

Well, some, anyway. When Michael opened the door to their knock, both my mother and father looked uncharacteristically grim-faced. But we weren't the kind of family to have explosive arguments, and so Michael more or less handed me off in a casually civil manner, saying he needed to get back to work but that he'd come down to Sedona on the weekend if he had the time.

That comment didn't exactly mollify them, but

my mother did look slightly less strained, and even managed something of a smile. "We'll see you then," she said, just before she gave him a quick hug.

We walked to the family SUV in silence. After throwing the shopping bag with my meager belongings in the cargo area, I climbed into the back seat. Still, no one said anything until my father was pulling onto the interstate.

Then, in the sort of quiet tones I knew were a sign of how truly angry he was, my father said, "Do you want to explain yourself, Taryn?"

No, I really didn't. And since I could feel the mixture of worry and anger that surrounded him, that he was angry with me precisely because he had been so worried, I did what I could to temper my reply. "I know it's hard for you to understand. But I'd just gone through...something...and being at Michael's place seemed the best way for me to decompress."

"I can understand not wanting to get mobbed right away," my mother put in. "But you could have called to let us know you were all right. Or had Michael call, if you didn't want to talk to anyone else right then."

An entirely logical request. And if our family dynamic had been different, maybe I would have called right away. But.... "So, are you taking me home first, or are we going straight to Kara's house?"

My parents looked at each other. Then my mother gave a rueful little smile as she said, "We're taking you home, and they'll come there rather than having us over at Kara and Lance's place. But naturally, everyone wants to talk to you."

Naturally. Voice tight, I told her, "And that's exactly what I wanted to avoid."

"Taryn, you can't run from this thing," my father said. "We don't want to do anything that makes you uncomfortable. But the more information we have, the better-informed our decisions about what we should do next will be. And so it's better to talk to us —especially to Martin and Raphael—while your experiences are still fresh in your mind."

Under any other circumstances, I would have agreed completely. The thought of facing everyone, though, made me quail inside. I could hide things from Michael. I could probably even hide them from my parents. My mother had her powers, but she'd respected my boundaries and had done a remarkably good job of not prying too much. But Martin and Raphael—and, to a lesser extent, Kirsten and Callista —were their own form of psychic. Telling them as much as I could without revealing anything of what had passed between Gideon and me was going to be difficult.

I knew I didn't have much of a choice. My parents weren't doing this to hurt me, but they needed to know what had happened so they could pass it along to others in their UFO network. Now that the Reptilians had revealed themselves, we needed more than ever to share information.

And that was when I felt it again...that strange, looming pressure. Only this time it seemed to be coming from both my parents, a preoccupation that didn't have anything to do with me.

"What is it?" I asked then. "What happened while I was gone?"

They exchanged another glance.

"We don't know for sure," my mother replied after a long pause. Since she sat with her back to me, I couldn't see much of her expression. But I really didn't need to see her. Usually, she was very good at shielding her emotions and thoughts so they wouldn't intrude on me. Right then, however, I could sense the pulse of her unease, so I knew whatever it was, it couldn't be good.

"We've been getting...reports," my father said. "People going missing."

I sat up straighter, ignoring the tug of the seatbelt against my chest. "Missing? Who?"

"No one here in Sedona," my mother said quickly. "Not that that makes the situation any better. But people have been contacting your father, saying that they know a friend of a friend who's gone, or that a disappearance was reported on the local news before it was hushed up. In almost every state, and overseas as well."

It had to be the Reptilians. I didn't know why, or how, but you didn't start getting mass vanishings of people unless some kind of evil intelligence was at work behind the phenomenon. "Is there a pattern to the disappearances?"

"Yes," my father replied. Right then we reached the roundabout that would slingshot us onto the south-bound State Route 89A and down to Sedona. He waited until he'd finished negotiating the curve before he continued. "They're always taken at night from their homes. No one sees anything. They're just…missing."

"It's more than that, though." My mother was fiddling with the straps of her purse where it sat on her lap, and that bothered me more than I wanted to admit. She was a high-energy person, no doubt about that, but she wasn't given to nervous tics. This whole thing had gotten to her, whatever it was. "All the people taken have been young women. Mostly between twenty and twenty-five, although there are a few who were a few years older than that."

The temperature in the SUV was mild enough, the climate control on vent because of the gentle spring day outside—considerably warmer than the blustery day that had preceded it—but I went cold anyway. Young women, taken by the Reptilians. You didn't need a degree in advanced mathematics to do the calculations for that one.

The question was, why now? Yes, I'd obviously thwarted Lir Shalan's plans in some way, but I was only one person, no matter what my talents might be, while my parents had made it sound as if scores of women—if not more—were involved here.

"And it's not all over the news?" I asked.

"No," my father said, still in that dire tone. "That is, there've been a few times when something made the local news, but you'd never hear about it again, and those stories have been scrubbed from the archives. The people who contacted me said it was as if the abduction had never happened."

"But what about the police?"

"It sounds like the police are stonewalling them," my mother replied. "They say that the women must have left on their own, since there was no sign of a struggle in any of these instances. Never mind that, according to the information we've gathered so far, it doesn't seem as if any of those who've disappeared had a reason to take off like that. Most of them were in college or had jobs they enjoyed. They tended to be high achievers."

A suspicion began to form in my mind. "Attractive?"

"Yes. That is, we don't have photographs for all of them, but the ones we do—yes, they were pretty." She shifted in her seat so she could look back at me. "What are you thinking, Taryn?"

Did I want to tell them? Yes, my parents knew about the Reptilians' penchant for genetic experimentation, that they could create hybrids who looked just like regular human beings. What they didn't know was that the aliens could reproduce with humans the normal way, without the aid of a test tube. Yes, it was more difficult, and the offspring of those pairings could vary wildly in their appearance, but it was possible.

So the Reptilians had come to Earth and had pretended to be the saviors of our astronauts in order to earn some political capital. And what better way to use that capital than to convince the governments of the world that it was in their best interests to look in the other direction when a few of their women went missing?

Another shiver passed over me. Yes, it was all conjecture, but I could somehow feel, in the pit of my stomach, that my guesses were the truth, or at least pretty close to it.

"They're taking the women so they can breed with them," I said bluntly.

The Range Rover shuddered as my father startled, then regained control of himself so we wouldn't go careening off the side of the road. A red light on the instrument panel flashed, indicating that the vehicle would take over if he made another erratic movement. "They're *what?*"

It wasn't that he'd never heard of such a thing before. Abduction reports were full of stories about hybrids, breeding programs. It was just that those stories had always been conjecture. No one had ever been able to offer any real, definitive proof. But he'd heard the truth in my voice. He knew I wasn't making this up.

My mother turned so far around in her seat that I knew her seatbelt wouldn't do a damn bit of good if we did end up having an accident. Her hazel eyes, the same color as mine, were wide, staring. "You sound very certain."

"Well, I'm just guessing," I said. "But, based on what I learned when I was on board the Reptilians' ship, I think it's pretty plausible."

"They didn't—" my mother began, her face white, and I shook my head at once.

"No, they didn't touch me, or hurt me. But...." I trailed off then, wondering how much I should say about Gideon. Then I realized that at least some of the truth would have to come out at some point, simply because I knew everyone would have questions about the green-skinned man who had taken me by the hand and whisked me away from the abandoned alien base. "But I know that the Reptilians can breed directly with humans, instead of just manipulating their DNA in a lab. I know this because that's who the green-skinned man is. He's the son of Lir Shalan, the Reptilian leader, and a human woman who was taken from someplace here in Sedona."

My mother had looked pale before, but now she was positively sheet-white. "But...how? I mean, how is this being allowed to happen?"

I had no answer for that. My father just gripped the steering wheel more tightly and said, "I think that's what we all need to figure out. Unfortunately, because of the near blackout on the news about this, I have to believe that the suppression of information is coming from pretty high up."

In general, when my father started to go down the conspiracy rabbit hole, my mother would make some attempt to find other rational explanations, even though she knew as well as anyone else in our group that all sorts of hidden plots were bubbling beneath the surface at any one time. Now, though, she only shook her head. "But why? Even if the governments of the world are being overly generous in their thanks to the Reptilians for 'saving' our astronauts"—she made air quotes around the word "saving," since we all knew they'd done pretty much the opposite—"I can't understand how they would stand aside and allow hundreds of innocent women to be kidnapped by aliens."

I didn't really want to believe it, either. But I could feel the strong pulse of worry coming from my father, and I knew he was extremely troubled. If I'd wanted to, I probably could have gone into his mind and seen for myself the very reports that had caused so much concern, but no way would I do that. I'd wait to see what everyone else had to say on the subject.

Right then, I realized that, as much as I'd dreaded getting bombarded by questions from so many people, I also looked forward to being surrounded by everyone in our little extended family. Somehow with them around me, I wouldn't feel quite as afraid.

I was given the time to take a long, hot shower and then get myself as ready as I could be. Yes, I'd taken a quick shower at Michael's apartment, but I hadn't washed my hair or done much of anything to get myself prepped. Now at least I was wearing my own clothes, and had put on a bit of makeup, and generally felt a lot more like myself than I had when I'd begun the day.

The whole time I was getting ready, though, I kept thinking about Gideon. I was far more worried than I wanted to admit. Lir Shalan had already proven that he seemed to be capable of just about anything. The question was, how important was his son's life to him? Would the alien leader be able to look past Gideon's betrayal because he didn't have much choice? After all, Gideon was Lir Shalan's only child, as far as I could tell.

I told myself that Gideon would be fine. Lir Shalan wouldn't do anything that would permanently injure his only son.

I just wished I believed that.

But then I had to push thoughts of Gideon away, just in case Callista or Kirsten or Martin might be able to pick up some of my inner turmoil. I didn't want them to know how much it hurt to think of something terrible happening to him. I wanted him to be safe. I wanted….

I didn't know what I wanted. And that was the real problem.

From the front of the house, I heard the murmur

of voices, and I knew that the gang had begun to arrive. I paused in front of the mirror and wished I didn't look so pale. True, I'd been stuck in Lir Shalan's ship for the better part of three weeks without ever seeing the sun, but I guessed that my current pallor couldn't be entirely blamed on my confinement.

Putting on more blush would only look unnatural. I gave my curls one last scrunch, then headed out to face the horde.

They'd all gathered in the living room, which was the only place in the house big enough to accommodate everyone. My parents had brought in chairs from the dining room so there would be enough places to sit. All those chairs were occupied now, by Kirsten and Martin and Callista and Raphael, and then Kara and Lance and Kelsey. I didn't see either Kevin or Grace or their younger sister Melissa, which didn't surprise me too much. Grace would be at work up in Flagstaff, Logan with her, and Kevin probably at work as well, heading up a Jeep tour. Melissa could have been at school, or at work; I didn't really keep track of her schedule, since she was just enough younger that we didn't hang out together too much.

So it wasn't quite as big a group as I'd been expecting, although it was certainly large enough. My parents sat on the couch, and I saw that the accent chair off to its side was empty. The place of honor, apparently.

As I headed for the chair, Callista got up from her seat and came toward me. Before I could react, she was wrapping her arms around me and giving me a fierce hug.

"I was so worried," she said, and I could see tears shining in her eyes. Although I sensed that she was trying to keep it together, huge pulses of guilt kept emanating from her. She'd been blaming herself that I'd gone with the aliens, although that had been my decision. She couldn't have stopped me even if she'd tried.

"It was fine," I told her. "I'm fine."

She pulled away and gave me a long, hard look. "Maybe." And then she paused. A thought coalesced in my mind, a thought that wasn't my own.

But you and I are getting together later and having a drink, and really talking this over.

I knew she'd never been able to do anything like that before. Apparently, she and Raphael had been practicing their mental communications skills, and now she was using them on me.

Since I couldn't really protest, I gave a tiny nod, one she would be able to see but no one else probably could. Looking somewhat relieved, she went and sat back down in her chair, and I settled myself in the accent chair that had been reserved for me.

Before anyone could say anything, I spoke. "I just want to let you all know that I'm okay. The Reptilians didn't hurt me, or perform any kind of tests on me. I know they were observing me, but whatever instruments they were using to do so, they weren't invasive at all."

"Then what was the point?" Lance asked. Trust him to get straight to the heart of the matter.

I couldn't tell them that Lir Shalan had wanted me as a psychic mate for his son. Maybe I could confess that horrible little detail to Callista when it was just the two of us alone, but to say something like that in front of everyone, especially the hard-faced Lance? No, thanks.

"I guess you'd have to ask them that," I replied with a shrug. "My best guess is that they were interested in my psychic abilities and wanted a chance to see them at work firsthand."

"Were you able to get anything from them?" Kara asked.

"No," I said. "I think their brain physiology and chemistry are different enough from a human's that my gift—or whatever you want to call it—doesn't seem to work when they're involved."

My mother frowned. "That's too bad. I'm certainly the last person to advocate tromping around in someone's mind uninvited, but if you'd been able to do that, then maybe we would have been able to understand how they're getting away with these abductions."

"I thought we hadn't definitively proved it was the Reptilians," Kara said, and Lance gave her an ironic look, complete with lifted eyebrow.

"Who else could it be?"

"I'm pretty sure it must be," I said hastily. The last thing I needed was for them to start picking at each other. Their marriage was rock-solid, but they still tended to get a little snipey when they disagreed with one another. Before either one of them could say anything else, I came out with basically the same theory I'd given my parents in the car—that these women were being taken for breeding stock, even though the results couldn't be controlled the way they might if these offspring were being created in a lab.

Kara went pale, and Lance ran a hand through his short-cropped graying hair. Kirsten looked at her husband and said, "Martin, did you know anything about this?"

A shake of the head, while Raphael put in, "It is news to both of us. Of course, we've known for some time that the Reptilians have been experimenting with human genetic material, but we've never heard of them breeding directly with human women. On the surface, it doesn't make a great deal of sense. As Taryn just pointed out, the results of these pairings would vary wildly. They wouldn't be of much use in creating an army in the way that the hybrids were."

Right then, I was glad that Grace and Logan weren't present. I could tell that Raphael hadn't meant any real insult, but he did have a way of talking about the hybrids that was impersonal to the extreme. It was possible he really didn't think of Logan as a hybrid, since he had clearly developed as an individuated person, no matter what his Reptilian creators might have intended. But Grace was touchy about those things. I couldn't really blame her, since her father had been a hybrid and she was now basically hooked up with one as well. However, the situation was complicated enough without her taking offense at an essentially innocent remark Raphael had made.

"Did you see anything, hear anything?" Martin asked then. "Anything that would indicate they were gearing up for something big?"

That was one question I could answer honestly enough. "No. I was given a room to stay in, and I wasn't let out very often. I didn't interact with any of the Reptilians except Lir Shalan—briefly—and Gideon."

"Gideon?" Callista inquired. The glint that appeared in her eyes told me she'd noticed something about the way I'd said the name. Well, I supposed it would all come out sooner or later, but I really wanted to hold off until the two of us could talk in private.

"The human-looking one with the greenish skin," I explained. "He's Lir Shalan's son."

Martin leaned forward in his chair, elbows propped up on his knees. He looked surprised—but not too surprised, as if he'd begun to put two and two together as soon as I'd mentioned the part about Reptilians being able to breed with human women.

"So, you had the most interactions with this Gideon?"

"I—I suppose so. But obviously, he wasn't going to tell me anything about their plans."

"So what did you talk about?" Kirsten asked, tone frankly curious.

"Um...things," I said lamely. "He wanted to know about my psychic abilities. We talked about that a good bit. And he told me a little about his mother, how she'd been here in Sedona for the solstice and then was taken when the remnants of the force Kirsten destroyed fled back to their ship."

"Poor woman," Kara murmured.

I nodded. But I really didn't want to go into too much detail; it wasn't my story to tell, and I didn't want to betray Gideon's confidences. Besides, his mother's tale, tragic as it might have been, didn't have much bearing on what was currently going on.

Well, except how each of the women being abducted might this moment be suffering her exact fate. Would Lir Shalan take his pick of those women so he could start over and try for a son who would be a little more loyal?

A shiver went over me, and I clasped my hands on my knee as I did my best to dispel that terrible thought from my mind. "But I didn't see anything much. Definitely no other human women, so if they were taking them to the ship, then they must have kept them well hidden."

My father spoke then. "So you were able to move

about, even if you spent a good deal of time in your cabin?"

"Yes, a little," I said. "Obviously, I was never allowed to go out alone. Gideon always went with me. But I did get to see some of the ship." I decided it was better not to mention the astral projection, at least not right then. They'd start asking me questions about that instead of focusing on the real issue.

"Can you describe it?"

Of course my father would want to geek out over the Reptilians' ship. I knew he was jealous that he'd never gotten to see Raphael's sleek spaceship, even though Kirsten had kindly spent an afternoon at our house, describing it as best she could so my father would have some sort of record. At the time, I'd been kind of surprised that no one had tried taking a few surreptitious cell phone shots of it when Raphael wasn't looking, but I supposed they'd all had other things to occupy them at the time.

"You've seen their base," I said. "The ship really didn't look all that different. Everything was squared off, and the lighting was dim. The walls and ceilings and floors were all made of metal, a dark kind of alloy. I don't know what it was. There was this one place where Gideon—" As soon as I spoke his name, I flushed, and belatedly realized it was probably better not to confess that he'd taken me to his own suite. I took a breath and tried to backpedal a bit. "That is, there was a sort of observation deck where he took me so I could see Earth."

"Trying to be nice, or just torturing you?" Lance asked in that dry way of his.

"I think he was trying to be helpful," I replied. "That is, he could tell I was homesick, so he took me to a place where at least I could see home, even if I couldn't go there."

"Compassion from a Reptilian?" Raphael said then, with the faintest curl of a sculpted lip. "I find that difficult to believe."

"Half Reptilian," I pointed out. It took a good deal of effort to push the image of Gideon's face from my mind, to attempt to forget the torment and longing in his expression as he wrestled with his father's impossible demands. I couldn't think about that, because if I did, I'd start to wonder what would have happened if I'd let him kiss me then, take me in his arms.

Which was…no. Just no.

"He looks a lot more human than Reptilian," Callista put in. "So maybe emotionally he's more like a human. What do you think, Taryn?"

I thought that I really didn't want to talk about Gideon at all. But if I was too obvious about trying to deflect the conversation, then that would probably invite even more questions. "It's hard to say for sure," I said carefully. "I mean, he was raised by Lir Shalan, so I'd say his outlook on the universe was more like that of a Reptilian."

"Hmm," Callista said. From the way she tilted her head and lifted an eyebrow, I could tell she didn't exactly believe me. To my relief, though, she settled back in her chair and went quiet, which meant she intended to let it alone…for the moment, anyway.

"But what do we do now?" my mother asked. "They returned Taryn to us, but what if they change their minds?"

That exact fear had crossed my mind multiple times the night before as I lay wrapped in a blanket on Michael's sofa. I couldn't help worrying that a blare of sulfuric yellow light would surround me once again, and I'd be whisked back to the *Eclipse*.

It hadn't happened, obviously. But that didn't mean it couldn't.

A brief silence fell.

"She could stay with us," Kara offered. "Grace's room is empty, and the creek will help to provide protection."

"And so will I," Lance said, the glint in his silver-gray eyes making it clear that he'd cheerfully blow a few holes in any Reptilians who might attempt to trespass on his property.

I appreciated the offer, but I didn't want to accept it. My mind and my heart were still too unsettled, and I knew that being in the casual tumult of their crowded household wouldn't help me to heal. Clearing my throat, I said, "That's very kind, but—

"But it's probably best if Taryn goes to stay in the cottage," Martin cut in, sending me a knowing look. He must have sensed my discomfort and stepped in to save me so I wouldn't look ungrateful. "It sheltered Kirsten against a similar threat, and I think it's the safest place for her now."

Of course. The "cottage" had belonged to Michael Lightfoot, one of the original group of UFO hunters my mother had met when she came here to Sedona in pursuit of the agents who had kidnapped my father. Michael was killed during the confrontation with the aliens on that solstice night twenty-five years ago, but he'd left his house to Kara and Kirsten, since he'd had no children of his own. They'd renovated the place and brought it up to date, and it was used as a sort of guest house for visiting friends and relatives.

More importantly, though, the house sat within a hundred yards of Oak Creek. Call it whatever woo-woo you like, but the creek had mystical properties of its own, somehow seemed to carry much of Sedona's power within it. While in the protective field generated by Oak Creek, you were effectively shielded from the Reptilians' surveillance. They couldn't invade your mind while you were there, and neither could they abduct you from your home.

It really was the perfect place for me to stay. I would be safe at the cottage. Safer than at the Rineharts' home, because the cottage sat a good deal closer to the creek than their house did.

My parents knew it really was the most logical solution. Even so, my mother said, "And maybe one of us should stay with her—"

"No," I cut in. I didn't know exactly why, since at first glance, it would have made a lot of sense to have someone there to watch over me. But the creek could do that, and I knew I needed to be alone. "I'll be fine. We all know the aliens can't hurt me when I'm at the cottage."

"But you'll need to leave it sometime—"

"Yes, but I promise I'll only leave to go to work." I paused then, realizing I'd been basically AWOL from my psychic gigs for almost three weeks. Luckily, I'd cut back on my hours at most places so I could concentrate on doing readings at Crystal Vision, which had always been my favorite venue. So I really only needed to make my excuses to one person. "That is, assuming I still have a job. What did you tell Leila?"

"We covered for you," my father said. "We said you'd come down with strep and were highly contagious, and so you needed to stay home until it had cleared up completely. That was the first and best thing we could think of. And we figured we'd come up with another excuse once it became obvious that even the world's worst case of strep throat wouldn't have kept you out of work for that long."

"Thanks," I said, and I meant it. Working at the crystal shop where I gave readings could sometimes be tiring or even depressing, but Leila, the owner, was like the big sister I'd never had, and I hated the thought of letting her down by disappearing off the face of the planet without offering a single word of explanation. "So anyway, we know the Reptilians are all about stealth. They're not going to beam me out of a store in the middle of Uptown Sedona."

"No, but what about when you're driving to and from there?" my mother asked. "There are some awfully dark stretches of road in between."

"I never really work into the evenings," I replied. "The shop closes at six, and the days are getting longer now. I'll be fine."

My parents traded an eloquent glance. "Well...." my mother began.

"I think it'll be okay," my father said.

A long silence. No one else spoke, since this was clearly something that had to be hashed out between my parents and myself. Then at last my mother nodded. "I know the cottage is safe. And I guess I'll just have to pray that being out in daylight and around crowds will be enough of a deterrent."

"It will be fine," I said. But that was just me talking. I didn't have a premonition, or a feeling that nothing bad was going to happen.

Right then, I had to go on blind faith.

CHAPTER EIGHT

I PACKED UP EVERYTHING I THOUGHT I MIGHT NEED FOR a stay of indefinite duration and loaded it into my hand-me-down Honda. My parents insisted on driving over with me, even though it was still broad daylight and I should have been fine. They probably just wanted to be with me for as long as possible, and I couldn't blame them. After all, until earlier that day, they'd been facing the very real fear of never seeing me again.

While I was packing, Kara and Lance had gone back to their place to fetch the keys to the cottage, along with the remote for the garage door. They'd already left again by the time I was ready, for which I was grateful. Of course, I loved Kara and Lance— they were like the aunt and uncle I'd never had, since both my parents were only children—but right then, I wanted to be with my mother and father.

I pulled into the cramped one-car garage at the cottage, and my parents parked their Range Rover on the street. They got out and met me on the front walk.

"Ready?" my mother asked.

"Sure." I didn't know why I was hesitating; I'd been to the cottage many times before, although I'd never stayed there overnight.

Maybe it was simply that it all seemed so irrevocable. Yes, the cottage was a good solution to my current predicament...but was I going to end up having to stay there indefinitely?

I bit back a sigh and pulled the key Kara had given me from my jeans pocket. All of my stuff was still in the car, since I knew I'd have plenty of time to unpack later. Actually, I was looking forward to it, just because the activity would give me something to do.

Inside the house, everything looked neat and clean, groomed as a hotel room. I knew that Kara had someone come in to dust and scrub once a month, more often if someone had actually stayed there. A faint scent of wood smoke lingered in the air, as if it had embedded itself in the paint and the wooden beams overhead.

"Well, everything looks fine," my mother said, glancing around.

"Would you expect anything less of Kara?" my father asked, a laughing glint in his eyes.

"I suppose not."

I set down my purse on a side table and wandered into the kitchen, then opened the refrigerator. It was empty except for a half-consumed flat of bottled water on the lower shelf. Good thing that my mother had loaded up a cooler of food for me before we left the house.

Both my parents followed me into the kitchen. I caught my mother giving the barren refrigerator a sideways glance before I shut the door.

"It's fine," I said. "You gave me more than I can eat in a week, especially since I grab lunch Uptown when I'm working. And the grocery store isn't that far away from here. I doubt the Reptilians are going to zap me out of the Safeway."

"You're right." Something about her shoulders sagged, and suddenly, she looked very tired. "I just hate the idea of leaving you here alone after everything that's happened."

Now that I was actually inside the cottage, I was feeling a little weird about that, too. But I knew the creek had protected Kirsten twenty-five years ago, and it would protect me now. I had to trust in it. Anyway, I'd survived almost three weeks on an alien ship. I should be able to handle being alone in the cottage, especially since my parents were only a five-minute drive away.

"I'll text you right before I go to sleep," I told her. "And I'll text you when I get up, so you'll know everything is okay."

"And you're going back to work tomorrow?" my father asked.

"Yes. I got in touch with Leila before I started packing and let her know that I was feeling well enough to come back to work."

My mother actually appeared relieved by that piece of information. She was probably thinking that the chances of me having any problems with marauding aliens would be greatly reduced when I was in a shop in Uptown surrounded by tons of tourists.

"If you see or hear anything strange, you call us right away," my father said. "I don't care what time of day or night it is. Got it?"

"Aye, aye, captain," I replied, lifting one hand to my brow in a mock-salute.

He looked far from amused, however. "I mean it, Taryn."

"I know you do. But really—I'm going to be okay. I think it'll be good for me to be here. I'm starting to feel better already."

That last bit was possibly a teeny bit of prevarication. True, some part of me had relaxed somewhat, knowing that I was safe from alien incursions here. But the rest of my mind was jangling with too many worries—what might be happening to Gideon, the problem of the disappearing women and what in the world our little UFO group could do to stop it.

But it didn't seem as if any of those troubles showed in my expression, because after giving me a long look, my father nodded slightly. And once he did so, my mother seemed to relax a little, too, although not enough that she was willing to let one particular matter go.

"I still think you should have stayed at the house for dinner at least," she said.

"I know I'm better off here," I told her. "This way, I can relax into being alone. It would have been harder if I'd come back here in the dark."

There didn't seem to be much she could say in reply to that, so she lifted her shoulders and turned toward my father. "Then I guess we'd better go, Paul."

He looked resigned. "I suppose so. Lance said he was getting some new reports, so we might want to head up to their place and see if there's any new information that might be helpful."

That was my parents, always trying to save the world. Or at least, trying to save their little corner of it. I gave them both a hug and saw them out, then shut the door and looked around at my new home.

It was cozy, with its rustic furniture and leather sofa and the Navajo rug on the floor. The fireplace looked inviting, too, although the day had really been too warm to even think about lighting a fire. Still, I might make one that night, if only to give me something to occupy a little time. The house had full internet, so I wouldn't lack for entertainment.

Sunset was still several hours off. I knew what I

needed to do then, while the sun was relatively high in the sky.

The little patio off the back door had been swept recently, although the outdoor furniture there still had its winter coverings on. There was a storage shed around the side of the house where I could put the coverings away if I decided I wanted to sit outside and enjoy the unseasonably mild weather.

But the patio wasn't my current destination. I crossed the flagstone surface and headed down the narrow path which wound through the trees, some of them just beginning to bud. Most of the cottonwoods had a thin film of fresh green along their branches, a sure sign that they'd be in full leaf in a few more weeks.

Through the trees, I heard the sound of water chattering away, rushing over the worn stones of the stream bed. After covering a few more yards, I emerged into the open, then went down almost to the water's edge.

It was rushing and lively, fed from the snow melt up in Flagstaff. I bent down and trailed my fingers in the waters of the creek, letting them flow over my hand. The water was bitterly cold, even on a sunny day such as this, but I didn't mind. That water, and the positive energy behind it, was the greatest ally I had at the moment.

My phone, which I'd shoved in my pocket, buzzed. Sighing, I straightened up and wiped my damp fingers on my pant leg. Really, my parents had only been gone for ten minutes, tops. You'd think they could have lasted just a little while longer before checking in to make sure I hadn't been kidnapped by aliens.

But the message showing on my home screen wasn't from them. It had come from Callista and said, *Coming over for pizza and drinks at six. We need to talk.*

That was so like my friend. She didn't bother to ask, but just steamed ahead as if she knew everything would fall into place neatly around her.

The sound of the water was loud enough that it probably would have interfered with any dictation I attempted. So I typed back, *Cal, you know I don't drink.*

Much, was her prompt reply. *And earlier this afternoon, you looked like someone seriously in need of a drink.*

Well, I couldn't argue with that observation. I'd always been take it or leave it when it came to alcohol, but if someone had stuck a margarita in my hand during the "interrogation" at my parents' house, I would have wanted to name my firstborn after them.

Okay, you win. I'll see you at six. What about Raphael?

He's a big boy. He can take care of himself for one night.

As no doubt he could. I wondered if he would meet up with my parents for a council of war at Lance and Kara's house. If new reports were coming in, that meant more information to dissect and discuss.

And while I knew I would need to pitch in with my own theories and insights soon enough, it did feel good to know that I could stay here tonight and hang out with Callista and pretend everything was going to be fine.

Actually, scratch that. I somehow doubted she was coming over just so we could watch TV and braid each other's hair—if my mane of curls would even cooperate with such an activity.

No, she could tell I'd been holding back. Being Callista, she'd no doubt decided that it was her duty to find out exactly what I'd been omitting from the discussion.

Six o'clock. I looked down at the time stamp on my phone. I had a little more than an hour to figure out what I was going to tell her.

Or, more to the point, what I needed to avoid telling her.

————

She showed up right on time, a bottle of wine in her hand. "I know you don't like red, and white seems wimpy for pizza, so I compromised and got rosé."

"Sounds good to me," I said, moving out of the way so she could go on into the living room and set the bottle down on the coffee table. Since I'd known that was where we'd be eating, too, I'd already laid out place mats and napkins, plates and wine glasses, all available from the well-stocked kitchen. "The pizza should be here soon, too."

"Girl pizza?"

"What else?"

Callista and I both shared an unholy love for Hawaiian-style pizza, a trait our families teased us about unmercifully and which the two of us indulged whenever we could.

"Perfect," she said. Spotting the corkscrew I'd put out on the table, she bent and retrieved it, then got to work on the wine bottle. "So," she continued, as she started twisting the corkscrew in, "you know I want to hear *everything*."

Just what I'd been dreading. I managed to say lightly, "Can it wait until after I've had a few sips?"

The cork came out with a satisfying *pop*. Callista poured a healthy amount into each glass and set down the bottle when she was done. I went over and picked up one of the wine glasses.

"Drink up," she said. "Because I want to hear all the dirt."

"There is no dirt," I protested.

She raised an eyebrow at me and retrieved her own wine glass. "Maybe you've got your parents fooled, but I know you. There was something going on with you and that green-skinned hottie, wasn't there?"

In desperation, I took a swallow of wine, then another. It was light and tart, not sweet at all. I wouldn't say that it exactly gave me courage, but it did allow me to shrug and reply, "You think Gideon is a hottie?"

"For someone with green skin and red eyes, yes. But my opinion isn't what matters here. So tell me all about it."

"There's nothing to tell."

That reply elicited another raised eyebrow. Callista settled herself on the couch and took a couple of swallows of wine as well. "Sit down," she commanded. "You're making me nervous, hovering over there like that."

Since there wasn't much else I could do, I sat.

"You were on that ship for twenty days," she went on. "And you told everyone that you'd spent a lot of time with Gideon. So you must have been doing something when you were with him."

"Just talking," I said. "That's all."

"About what?"

"I told him about growing up psychic, and he told me a little bit about his mother. Not a ton, though—I still don't know her name, or how old Gideon was when she died." At least, I had to assume she was dead. Gideon always talked about her in the past tense.

"I'd want to die, too, rather than have sex with a Reptilian." Callista gave an exaggerated shudder and drank some more wine. "Talk about your fates worse than death. Can you imagine?"

I really couldn't, and I didn't want to think about it too much. "No. I'm sure it must have been awful."

"I don't understand why they'd want to be with human women at all," she continued, even though I would have preferred to have the conversation go in a very different direction. "I mean, it's not as if we find them attractive, so why would they be attracted to us?"

"I don't know," I answered slowly. "I'm not sure it's even really an attraction, actually…more like a desire to dominate."

A shiver went over her, but the doorbell rang before she could say anything. I set down my wine glass and hurried over to the door. The delivery guy from Moon Dog Pizza was out there, so I dug my phone from my pocket and signed off on the bill they'd emailed me. The delivery guy got the confirmation on his phone, saw the size of the tip, then grinned before murmuring a quick thanks and heading back out to his truck.

"I'd planned to cover that," Callista protested.

"You brought the wine," I replied, balancing the pizza box on one hand while I shut the door and locked it with the other. "It's no big deal."

She didn't look that convinced, but she didn't say anything as I brought the pizza over and set it down on the coffee table. I opened the lid and dished a slice each onto our plates.

"Okay," she went on, as if there hadn't been any interruption in our conversation, "I suppose I get the domination thing, but there are other ways to do that without having sex with someone."

"Aren't you kind of fixating on this?"

"No. It's just...weird. And now these women disappearing...." She shivered slightly, although her apparent disgust didn't prevent her from picking up the piece of pizza on her plate and taking a large bite.

I couldn't really argue with her. "One thing I did notice," I began.

Her big blue eyes lighted up with curiosity. "What?"

"Now, I'm not an expert on Reptilians, even though I was on their ship for a while. But I did notice that I didn't see any aliens who looked like they were female."

"Really? How could you even tell?"

"Well, that's the problem. I couldn't tell for sure, and I suppose a biologist would argue that their differences in physiology wouldn't mirror those of us humans, since reptiles are cold-blooded and don't nurse their young. But still...." I stopped there and shook my head. "I still can't help thinking that there really weren't any of their women on board that ship."

"Maybe they're big old raging sexists and don't believe in having female crew members."

Considering what I'd seen so far of the Reptilians —Gideon being an exception—I could accept Callista's explanation as to why I hadn't encountered anyone on the *Eclipse* who appeared to be obviously female. But again I had that feeling of missing something, that there was more to the story than I'd been able to piece together so far.

So I said, "Possibly," and took a bite of pizza.

Callista also had some of her pizza, then washed it down with rosé. To my surprise, I'd discovered that it was actually a fairly decent combination. After she was finished chewing, she said, "Maybe they don't have any. Maybe that's why they're taking our women."

"That doesn't make sense," I replied. "I mean, there have got to be millions of Reptilians out there in the galaxy. The way Raphael talks about them, they seem like a force to be reckoned with, one the Assembly sort of considers a thorn in its side. Or am I misinterpreting things?"

"No, you're right." She deposited another slice of pizza on her plate and sprinkled some extra parmesan cheese on top from one of the packets that had been included with our delivery. "That's basically exactly the way he's made it seem. When I went in front of the Assembly, the Secretary seemed to be doing his best not to antagonize them too much. But…." Her words trailed off, and she took a big bite of Canadian bacon and pineapple, chewed quickly, then said with some excitement, "Clones!"

"What?"

"Maybe they're all clones! The Reptilians, I mean. We all know they're really good at the genetic stuff, so maybe they've been using cloning to keep their race going."

That actually sounded like a good theory, and one I wasn't sure I would have thought of. While Callista sipped at her wine, a triumphant gleam in her eyes, I picked at the problem some more. If the Reptilians were such masters of genetic manipulation, then why were they resorting to the very unpredictable method of natural biological reproduction?

I asked Callista as much, and she shrugged. "I don't know," she said. "God forbid I should ever have the knack of being able to figure out how a Reptilian thinks. It just seemed like the cloning angle would explain a lot of things."

It would. But not all of them. And with me back here on Earth and Gideon up there in orbit somewhere—if the *Eclipse* was even still here in the solar system—I didn't think I'd be getting the answers I needed anytime soon.

"Enough of that," Callista went on. "You're pretty good at angling a conversation the way you want it to, Taryn, but you still haven't given me much of an answer about you and Gideon."

"That's because there *is* no me and Gideon," I protested. "Nothing happened."

"I know. You told me that." Her eyes, the same smoky gray-blue as her father's, glinted with interest and a good deal of speculation. "But did you *want* something to happen?"

Oh, damn, she had me there. Yes, I could hedge and say there had been no attraction, no spark between us, but I really hated to tell such an outright lie to the best friend I had in the world. There had been...something. I'd fought it, hadn't wanted to admit that I liked him very much, despite our differences in background and biology and...well, pretty much everything.

Liked. There was a weak word. In fact, my feelings for Gideon had gone way beyond like, into an attraction I couldn't explain, had wanted to give in to, even though I'd known that would be a terrible idea.

"You did!" she said, setting down her wine glass. "I knew it!"

I wanted to tell her that she didn't know anything, but that would have been both rude and untrue. "I just...." I began, and stopped there. Problem was, I really didn't know what to say. If I admitted to her that I cared for Gideon, then I'd also have to admit the same thing to myself.

Her expression altered, and the triumphant gleam in her eyes faded immediately into worry. She came closer, then leaned over and gave me a quick hug before scooting back over to her side of the couch. "It's okay," she said. "There's nothing wrong with caring for someone, you know."

"Even the half-alien son of an enemy leader?"

"Maybe *especially* because he's the half-alien son of an enemy leader. Give him a little Earth-style lovin', and maybe he'll see the error of his ways."

"Callista!"

"I'm just saying." She took a large swallow of her rosé, and poured some more into her glass. "Seriously, he's half-human, right? So maybe if you could reach out to him—"

"How?" I asked, not bothering to keep the bitterness out of my voice. For all I knew, she could sense what I was feeling anyway. Some of those insights were a little too close to home, unless she'd been able to pick some of that stuff right out of my mind. "He's up there, and I'm down here. What am I supposed to do, stand out in the front yard and put up the bat signal or something?"

"Okay, you have a point. But we should be able to figure out something. I mean, your father *is* a rocket scientist."

"Astronomer," I corrected her. "And astrophysicist."

"Still."

Despite his impressive credentials, I really didn't think my father could do much to help me. Yes, there was the communications center at the Reptilians' abandoned base, but I could only imagine the look on his face if I went to him and asked if he could show me how to use the equipment there so I might reach out to my would-be alien boyfriend.

That would go over really well.

"I don't think we can do anything," I said, and followed Callista's lead by pouring more wine into my glass. Unlike me, since I hardly ever had more than a second glass. But if this wasn't the correct occasion to get mercifully drunk, what was?

She hadn't missed the way I'd topped off my drink. "Taryn, I don't think that's the solution."

"Probably not," I agreed.

Right then, she looked as if she wanted to say something else, but stopped herself. After a pause, she raised her glass and clinked it against mine. "To drowning your sorrows."

I only hoped they would be drowned. I had a feeling that, like a body which hadn't been properly weighted down, they'd inevitably float to the surface to remind me of what I'd lost.

Callista left about an hour after that. My head felt swimmy, but even though I knew I should go to bed and sleep off the half-bottle of rosé I'd just drunk, I felt restless. I didn't want to go to sleep. I wanted….

I wanted answers. Maybe not the ones everyone was looking for, but something to satisfy my own personal curiosity.

My laptop was in its bag in the bedroom, along with all the other luggage I'd brought with me. I retrieved the computer and then took it out to the living room so I could sit down with it on the couch.

Gideon had never mentioned his mother's name, but I refused to believe it could be that difficult to track her down. After all, Sedona was a sleepy little place despite its brisk tourist trade. How many people could have disappeared here over the years?

Also, I knew exactly when she'd been taken. December twenty-first, twenty-five years ago.

I went to the search page and typed in "woman missing, Sedona, Arizona" and the date. Immediately it flipped over to a list of hits, the top one being a piece that had run on the AZCentral website.

Phoenix Woman Missing, the headline said.

And there was her picture.

God, Gideon looked just like her. Or rather, his features were a masculine echo of hers: the full mouth, the somewhat hooded dark eyes, even the wave in her near-black hair. Elizabeth D'Onofrio. An Italian surname. So that odd impression I'd had when I'd first met him, that he wouldn't have looked out of place in a Renaissance painting, hadn't been so far off the mark after all.

Tearing my eyes away from the image, I tried to focus on the text. Elizabeth Angela D'Onofrio, twenty-four, had gone to Sedona with a group of friends for the solstice. But because it had been cold and windy, her two friends had begged off and decided to stay in. Elizabeth had gone out anyway. Her friends had been concerned but not overly so; she was an experienced hiker and had been to Sedona numerous times. She knew the trails. She'd gone out well-equipped, in all-weather gear and carrying several flashlights, and with enough food and water to last her for two days.

And then she'd vanished.

The Forest Service and the local sheriff's department combed the hills and canyons and dry creek beds, but no sign of her was ever found. Her parents, Gideon and Maria, hired private investigators.

Gideon, I thought. *So he's named for her father. I'm surprised Lir Shalan allowed that.*

I pulled in a breath and returned to reading the article. Eventually, the FBI was called in, but they couldn't find anything, either. It was if Elizabeth D'Onofrio had disappeared off the face of the earth.

Which was, as I knew by now, exactly what had happened.

I stared at her photo, which appeared to have been a professional head shot. Had she modeled? She was pretty enough. I supposed if I dug some more, I could find that out, along with anything else I wanted to know.

But I didn't. It seemed disrespectful to be snooping around in her past when I didn't have any idea how much Gideon actually knew about her. At least I'd been able to discover who she was, and what the world thought had happened to her. I didn't want to learn about her hopes and dreams. Had she been seeing someone? Engaged? I supposed if she'd been married, the article would have mentioned that, but it didn't say anything about her relationship status.

"I'm sorry," I told her picture. "I'm sorry for what happened to you. But you would be proud of your son. In the end, he did the right thing." It could have been the alcohol, but I felt tears begin to sting at my eyes, and I had to swallow past a lump in my throat. "And I'm so grateful to him for that. But now...."

I had to stop there for a second. Because now I wasn't sure what I'd meant to say.

A tremor went through me, and Elizabeth D'Onofrio's image blurred as my eyes clouded with tears.

"But now," I murmured, as I closed the laptop, "now I wish he hadn't...because I miss him."

And I buried my face in my hands and wept.

CHAPTER NINE

IT WAS NEVER A GOOD IDEA TO DRINK TOO MUCH WHEN you had to go in to work the next day. It was an even worse one when you weren't used to drinking in the first place, and your job involved peeking into other people's minds. And let's just leave aside altogether my meltdown over Elizabeth D'Onofrio's picture. My eyes had looked puffy and red when I woke up, but after I pressed a cold washcloth against them for a bit, they seemed to go almost back to normal.

Thank God the cottage was well-stocked with coffee and tea. I drank coffee when I really needed an extra jolt, but tea was gentler on my system, so I got out a box of Darjeeling and set the kettle to boil. Even after I'd had a few sips, though, I realized the Darjeeling wasn't quite enough to quiet the headache raging inside my skull.

I made two cups anyway, since I knew coffee

would be too hard on my roiling stomach, and then had toast and cheese, because yogurt didn't sound so good to me right then. There was also some leftover pizza in the refrigerator, but just looking at it was enough to make me feel vaguely queasy. After that, a long hot shower, some ibuprofen, and I was almost ready to face the world.

Luckily, I didn't have to be at work until eleven, which gave me time for the painkillers to kick in, and also allowed my hair a sufficient span in which to dry. Every once in a blue moon I'd blow-dry it straight and use a flat iron on it, but that took hours. It was so much easier to allow it to bounce naturally into its own springy curls.

Although I'd driven over from my parents' house the afternoon before, it still felt strange to slide in behind the wheel and say, "Crystal Vision, please."

The engine started up, and the car backed out of the driveway. From what I could tell, the neighborhood surrounding the cottage was a quiet one, with most of the people who lived there locals. By that hour of the morning, it seemed as if just about everyone was at work, though I did see an older man walking a big golden retriever before the car went around the corner and headed out to the highway.

It did help that I'd come back in the middle of the week. Not as many tourists, although the traffic seemed unusually thick for a Thursday morning. I frowned at the car with Texas plates sitting in front of me at a stoplight, and then wanted to groan. Middle of March. Spring break.

Great. Dealing with alien invasions could really push the mundanities of earthbound life right out of your head.

But there wasn't much I could do about it now, since I'd already promised Leila that I would be in today. With any luck, because the weather was so beautiful, people would be more interested in hiking or going to Slide Rock State Park or participating in any one of the outdoor activities Sedona offered, rather than sitting in a cramped back room at a crystal shop and having their cards read.

I left my car on the lowest level of the parking structure adjacent to the store, making sure that my monthly parking permit was showing on the dash so I wouldn't get a ticket, or worse, towed. My life was complicated enough without having to get my car out of impound.

The familiar scent of sage incense hit me as soon as I walked into the shop. I blinked; I'd been so used to it that I hadn't even noticed the smell anymore, but now, after being away for so long, the intense perfume almost made my eyes water.

Or maybe it was just the effects of my rosé binge from the night before.

"Taryn!" Leila called out. She was off to one side, an elderly, intense-looking woman with a shock of white hair standing next to her. "How're you feeling?"

"Much better," I said. That morning, my reflection in the mirror had been sort of pale, but I figured my pallor only made my father's story about me having strep that much more plausible. I'd gone easy on the blush and used a natural rosy lip stain, just so I wouldn't appear too blooming.

Leila's head tilted slightly, and she gave me a critical look up and down. Although when I wasn't working I tended to be a jeans and T-shirts kind of person, the tourists expected a psychic to look like a psychic. So today I had on a long skirt decorated with sequins and embroidery, metallic ballet flats, and a white scoop-neck top that fit a good deal more snugly than my casual clothes, along with big silver hoop earrings and my favorite turquoise and silver cuff bracelet.

Apparently, I passed muster, because Leila gave a nod, then said, "Your first isn't until eleven-thirty."

"Thanks," I told her, and meant it. That gave me some time to take a few breaths and get myself together, to forget about Gideon and the Reptilians and everything else for a little while. The problems wouldn't go away, of course, but I couldn't allow them to take up too much space in my head, or I'd do a terrible job for today's clients.

The room we psychics used at Crystal Vision was a small space carved out from the storage area at the back of the store. Some places just had a screen to keep the psychic and her client separated from the rest of the shop, but Leila always said that didn't provide enough privacy, and I agreed with her. At least here, though the space was a little cramped, there was a door I could shut and close out the rest of the world.

The air here also smelled of incense, although not as intensely. A table with two chairs sat in the middle of the room, and the walls were draped with sari silks from India. More silk covered the table. In one corner stood an extra chair for those times when a couple wanted to get a reading together.

If I laid out the cards for myself now while I was waiting for my first client, what would I see?

I didn't want to know. The flashes and visions I got from time to time were enough for me. I didn't look down on the people who came to me asking about their futures, but I was content to allow my future to reveal itself to me on its own time.

My deck was one of the things I'd brought with me to the cottage. I dug it out of my purse, then idly shuffled the cards, letting my energy re-imprint itself on them after my long absence. A lot of the time, I didn't really need the cards, could allow the sensations and impressions I got from a client to filter into my mind and tell me what I needed to know, but people found them reassuring. They wanted a psychic who laid out the cards in the prescribed patterns, or looked at their palms. They didn't want someone who seemed to be plucking their fortunes right out of thin air.

My first appointment was, thank God, a nice,

normal woman in her early thirties who wanted to know if her upcoming relocation to San Diego for her job would be a good thing. Her family was all here in Arizona, and so on. But almost from the moment she sat down, I could sense the enthusiasm in her, the desire to try something different. She was experiencing doubts because of her family's wanting her to stay in Phoenix, that was all.

So I laid out the cards and explained that the patterns showed the upcoming change in her world as a very positive thing, and how she needed to listen to her inner voice and trust its guidance. I also hinted that a change in venue would bring about a positive shift in her love life as well. She beamed at that revelation—she was very pretty, with big green eyes and blonde hair, so I didn't think it was stretching things to tell her that her love life was about to see an improvement—and at the end she gave me a twenty-dollar tip above and beyond the usual forty it cost for a half-hour session.

Yes, pretty good pay for someone not yet twenty-two and without a college degree, even with the twenty-percent cut I gave to Leila for using the shop's facilities. Psychic powers didn't have to be a complete burden.

After my sessions, I always went out to the store to take a look around and see who might be lingering there, who might be working up the nerve to visit a psychic for the first time. The shop was fairly crowded, but I didn't notice anyone looking particularly in my direction, so I went over to inspect the sign-up sheet Leila kept behind the counter. If the store was busy, I tended to be busy as well, although my most hectic times were later in the day, after people had stopped for drinks and were feeling a bit more adventurous.

Then I noticed a pair of dark eyes staring at me from across the store. Something about them was familiar, although I couldn't quite—

Oh, my God.

There was a reason why those hooded eyes had seemed so familiar. Only the last time I'd seen them, they'd been a deep ruby color, rather than dark brown. As recognition flooded through me, I realized the rest of him was altered as well. That is, the green skin was gone, replaced by the equivalent of a nice, healthy tan.

Gideon approached me as I stood by the cash register, frozen in place. No one gave him a second glance, but why would they? He looked like a completely normal guy in his mid-twenties.

He stopped a foot or so away from me and said, "We need to talk."

Somehow, I managed to respond normally enough, even though my heart had started pounding away a mile a minute. "I'm working."

"I can see that. But I still need to talk to you."

Helplessly, I looked past him to see Leila sending a curious glance in our direction. Clearing my throat,

I said, somewhat loudly for her benefit, "It's forty dollars for a half-hour session."

Gideon's eyebrows went up for a second, and then he nodded in comprehension. "That sounds reasonable," he said, going along with it. "Are you available now?"

"Yes," I replied, marveling that I could sound so calm. "Come with me, please."

He followed me back to the reading room and shut the door behind us. "Excellent solution," he said, looking around. "Very private."

"Gideon, what you doing here?" I demanded, now that I didn't have to pretend to Leila that he was just another client. "And how can you look like— well, like *that*?"

"Oh, this?" He reached down to his wrist, where he wore what appeared to be a brown leather wristband studded with three silvery buffalo-head nickels. A press of the center nickel, and he became the Gideon I knew, with his greenish skin and ruby eyes. Another press of that same button, and the disguise was back in place. "Protective camouflage. A simple enough illusion, but a necessary one."

"It's—" I had to stop myself there, because I wasn't sure what to think of his altered appearance. Yes, he was, to use Callista's word, a hottie, but I actually thought I preferred him the other way, which seemed to be a clear indication that I was losing my mind. "It's very effective," I finished lamely. "Anyway, you didn't answer my first question."

"What am I doing here? I'd think that would be obvious. I need to talk to you."

"Only talk?"

His mouth tightened. "Perhaps more than that."

"Did your father send you to fetch me back?"

Without looking at me, Gideon pulled out one of the chairs from the table and sat down. "He gave me a chance to redeem myself."

"For letting me go? Since when do you have to redeem yourself for doing the right thing?"

"In his eyes, it was not the right thing at all, but rather weakness."

Since I didn't want to remain standing and talking down at him, I took the other chair and sat down as well. "Well, I think your father has a pretty skewed view of the universe."

Gideon frowned. It was fascinating to watch those same expressions of his play out on a face that was so similar to his own, and yet so different. Amazing what a change of eye and skin color could do to alter someone's appearance. Ignoring my comment, he said, "I had to come see you here because our instruments could not pinpoint exactly where you were staying. Not at your parents' house, or at the home of any of your friends here in Sedona. It wasn't until you were out on the main highway that we were able to pick up your trail again."

So everyone had been right about the way Oak

Creek would shield me from the Reptilians' surveillance devices. Yes, I'd believed the stories—or at least, I thought I had—but belief wasn't the same thing as having someone basically corroborate the thing you'd been trusting in. "I'm staying at a safe place," I said, tone neutral. A part of me was very glad to see him again, but I wasn't so glad that I was about to abandon all caution and tell him where I was currently living.

"Here in Sedona?"

"What does it matter?" I countered. "I'm not coming back with you."

Once again, I saw that tension pull at his jaw, the strong muscles in his neck. "I could take you now," he said, fishing something from his pocket. When he laid it down on the tabletop in front of him, I realized it was the metallic device that activated the teleportation beam which had brought me back to Earth.

"You could," I said evenly, although I felt my heart begin to race, and it took everything in me to keep myself from trying to bolt out of there, out into a public space where I wouldn't be so vulnerable.

So much for me blithely declaring to my parents that the aliens wouldn't have the nerve to zap me right out of the store.

"But I don't think you will," I continued, forcing myself to sound as calm as possible.

Gideon stared at me, face expressionless. "Why not?"

"Well, for one thing, that's not exactly the best

strategy for winning hearts and minds, don't you think? Forcing me to come back with you? That's your father's idea, not yours."

His fingers tightened around the device and I stiffened, sure I was going to be surrounded by acid yellow light at any second and taken right out of the reading room. "Are you saying that I don't want you back?" he asked.

"No," I said. This time I did get up from my chair, but only so I could go around the table and stand next to him. He gazed up at me, eyes narrow. "I think you do…only not like that."

A long pause. He continued to look up into my face, his own expression still impassive, revealing very little. I'd been praying for one of those flickers of emotion, something to tell me what might be going on inside his head, but I couldn't sense anything.

Then, very slowly, he stood as well, and reached for the device and slipped it back into his pocket. I didn't dare let out a sigh of relief, only stood there in silence.

He was so tall. I'd noted his height before, but for some reason, it seemed even more impressive now when he was dressed like any guy you might see walking down the street, in his jeans and sneakers and untucked black T-shirt. His biceps pulled at the sleeves, and for the first time, I could see his fore-arms, see the dusting of dark hair on them, the muscles under the skin.

I wanted those arms around me. Not here, though. We were private enough for the moment, but if someone signed up for the one o'clock hour to have a reading, Leila would be knocking on the door if we lingered for too long.

Something told me I needed to be alone with him, though. Someplace where he could begin to understand why his father's way wasn't the only way.

"I found her," I said softly, and Gideon's unnaturally dark eyes narrowed.

"Found who?"

"Your mother."

Oh, that got him. He stiffened, then crossed his arms as he stared down at me. "How could you have possibly found my mother? She's been dead for nearly fifteen of your years."

Well, that told me something. She'd passed away when Gideon was only ten years old.

As they had the night before, tears stung my eyes. This time, though, I blinked them away. I knew that dissolving into a mess wouldn't help matters at all, could very well make them worse. "I looked her up," I said. "When someone disappears like that, it's all over the news." *Or at least it used to be,* I added mentally. *Someone's doing a pretty good job of covering up that kind of thing right now.* "It might have happened a quarter-century ago, but the records are still there. Her name was Elizabeth Angela D'Onofrio, and she lived in Phoenix. She was twenty-four."

"I knew that," he said stiffly. "Except about Phoenix. She said she wouldn't bother to tell me about where she'd come from, who her family was, because she knew she'd never see them again...and that I'd never see them, either."

The barely masked pain in his voice was too much for me to bear. I didn't stop to think. I only reached out and wrapped my arms around him, then drew him to me.

He resisted for a second, body rigid against mine, as if he was worried that his father would be able to see even this one small moment of weakness. But then a sigh escaped his lips, and he was pressed against me, arms tight around me, his hands tangling in my hair.

It had never felt like this before. Of course, my ex-boyfriends had hugged me, but they hadn't held on to me as if I was the only thing keeping them from drowning.

Maybe for Gideon, I was.

He didn't weep, though. He only stood there for a long time, clinging to me. I didn't say anything, because I knew that wasn't what he needed right then. And he didn't try to kiss me, because I think he knew the time wasn't right for that, either.

Finally, though, he let go of me and stepped back a pace. With a shaking hand, he lifted a curly tendril of hair away from my face, watched as it sprang back into a corkscrew when he let go of it. "Your hair is amazing," he said quietly. "It is so very alive. Just like you."

The tears threatened again, but once more I pushed them back. "You're alive, too, Gideon," I told him. "You can make your own choices."

"I can?" Then he shook his head. "I'm afraid it's not that simple."

"Maybe it can be." I hesitated, then said, "I need you to trust me."

His lids dropped, hooding his eyes, and he wouldn't look at me directly. "Trust is not something that comes easily for me, I'm afraid."

"I know." I reached out and took his hand. His fingers were cold. Nerves, or was his body temperature lower than the average human's? "I'm going to ask a lot of you, Gideon, but it's only because I know you have the strength to do the right thing."

"The right thing?" He frowned then, although he didn't try to pull his hand from mine. A bitter laugh, and he added, "I'm not sure you know me as well as you think you do."

"I know you let me go, that first time." I tightened my fingers around his, hoping that some of my warmth might penetrate his chilled flesh. "And if you were really intent on carrying out your father's orders, you would have already taken me away from this place. You wouldn't be standing here and talking to me."

"I—" His shoulders drooped slightly, and yet I could still sense the tension in his body, the way he seemed like an animal ready to startle at the slightest sound. "I'm not sure I can be what you think I can."

His doubt worried me, but I couldn't let that shake my resolve. He'd spent his whole life trying to live up to Lir Shalan's completely unrealistic expectations for him, of trying to be what he never could, because his heart wasn't cold. Gideon might have done his best to stamp out the gift of humanity that his mother had given him, but no one who was completely lost to compassion would have let me go, risking his father's wrath and so many other complications.

"Will you try, though?" I asked. "I said earlier that I need you to trust me, and I do. I want to show you something."

A ghost of a smile touched his mouth. "That sounds…intriguing."

I had to hope so, but I didn't want to play my hand just yet. What I did know was that we needed to get out of there, and so I had to figure out how best to do that gracefully. The last thing I wanted to do was leave Leila in the lurch while Uptown Sedona was swarming with spring-break tourists.

"Can you wait in here for a minute?" I asked, and Gideon nodded, although he looked slightly confused.

"If you need me to."

I flashed a grateful smile at him and said, "I'll be back in just a minute."

Then I slipped out and went to find Leila, who

had just finished putting away the cash register receipt from her last sale. Good. At least she wasn't occupied with explaining to someone how the magnetic vibrations from quartz crystals worked.

"Hey, Leila," I began, and she looked up from the register, big blue eyes curious.

"Done with your twelve-thirty so soon?"

"I—" Right, she thought Gideon was a client. I should have picked up on that, but his sudden appearance here had really rattled me. "Um, sort of. Something's come up, though. I don't think I can stay for the rest of the afternoon. Is there anyone who can take over my shift?"

"Well, you're in luck, because Shelli called not five minutes ago, asking if there was any way I could get her some extra hours this week. That jerk of an ex of hers conveniently 'forgot' to send her child support again, and she's at her wit's end."

"Oh, wow, I'm so sorry about that," I said, and I meant it. Shelli was about five years older than I, and would have been pretty if she didn't look so tired all the time. Raising a child on your own wasn't easy, and having an unreliable ex just made the situation that much more difficult. "Then please tell her she can take my shift, and all the rest of them for the weekend, if she wants them."

"She'll want them, I'm sure. She said she would be able to get Tina in daycare if she could get a shift, so that part's handled." Leila's expression grew rather sly. "Does this 'business' of yours have anything to do with the young man who took the twelve-thirty appointment?"

"Um…sort of."

She chuckled. "Well, have fun. I don't know where you found him, but I'd be wanting to take the weekend off, too, if I had someone who looked like that to share it with."

Heat flooded my cheeks, but I managed to nod. "Sure. I mean, thanks, Leila. I'm glad you'll still have someone to cover the shift." *And someone who needs the money a lot more than I do,* I thought.

Leila seemed to agree. "Shelli will be thrilled. And relieved. Just give me a call on Monday so we can get your schedule for next week figured out."

I promised that I would, and hurried back to retrieve Gideon from the reading room. He was still standing, but was turning over the cards in the tarot deck I'd left on the table one by one, appearing to study the different faces and figures on the cards.

Normally, it really wasn't a good idea to let someone else handle your tarot deck, because their vibrations could get mixed up with yours, and your readings might be muddy for a while until you could get things sorted out. Right then, however, I didn't bother to say anything, only gathered up the cards and slid them back into their box, then slipped the box into the little velvet pouch I used to hold them. Gideon watched this procedure with open curiosity on his face, but he didn't ask why I took such care in how the cards were stored.

"Good news," I told him as I opened the door and stepped out into the little hallway that separated the reading room from the break area at the back of the shop. "I was able to get the rest of the weekend off, so we have plenty of time."

He shot me a curious look. "Time for what?"

"Lots of things, I hope. But there's something we need to do first."

"What's that?"

"I need to take you to the place where I'm staying."

CHAPTER TEN

It was a gamble, and I knew that. Here I was staying at the cottage so the creek's energies could protect me from the aliens, and yet I planned to take one of them there with me now.

All right, Gideon wasn't exactly an alien. He was...something different. Unique. And I wanted to do everything I could to persuade him that it was far better for him to embrace his human side, to experience all the wonderful things his existence so far had deprived him of.

He did look around from side to side, frankly curious, as I led him from the store and to the parking garage so I could retrieve my car. I had no idea where the Reptilians had dropped him off, so to speak, but clearly, he hadn't had much experience with observing humans in their native habitat.

"They all look so cheerful," he said, as if that observation surprised him.

"Well, they are mostly here on vacation," I pointed out. "They're supposed to be enjoying themselves." I glanced up at him, still somewhat unnerved by the change in his appearance, although I knew it had been necessary. Even in airy-fairy Sedona, someone walking around with greenish skin was bound to attract attention. "And some of them aren't as cheerful as they look."

That was the problem with crowds; people tended to broadcast unintentionally, and I could get bombarded from all sides. I'd had enough practice by that point to tune most of it out, but things still got through occasionally.

Gideon sent me a quizzical look, and I tilted my head very slightly toward a dark-haired couple who'd paused to look in a shop window.

"Those two? They had a huge fight this morning and are trying to decide whether to cut their vacation short. That woman?" I glanced very briefly at a tall, thin woman in her forties who'd stopped to consult something on her phone. "She's afraid she has cancer, is waiting for the test results to come back. She came here to soak up some healing energies."

"It must be difficult for you," he said quietly as we crossed the driveway that led into the parking structure. "Do you try to avoid crowds?"

"Not really. My mother taught me how to deal with it. Sometimes the pressure can be difficult, but

I'd rather feel other people's pain than try to hide from the world."

In silence, he reached out and took my hand. His fingers felt warmer now, possibly because of our walk in the sunlight. The bright light didn't seem to bother him, which seemed to mean that his eyes were more human than Reptilian, despite their color. And I couldn't prevent the thrill that went through me at his touch, but I tried to seem calm as we walked, fingers interlaced, down to the level where I'd left my car.

Gideon didn't seem to have any problem getting in or negotiating the seatbelt, which made me think he must have spent a good amount of time studying our technology and customs. As we left the parking structure, I noticed his gaze was fixed on the people who thronged the sidewalks in Sedona's Uptown district, rather than on the red rocks that had brought them there in the first place.

It was the same way on the drive to the cottage— he looked at the other cars, at the people who stood on the sidewalks, at the businesses we passed. But he didn't seem all that interested in the astonishing natural beauty of the landscape which surrounded the town. Were people and their artifacts really that much more intriguing to him?

We pulled off the main highway and into the quiet neighborhood where the house was located. As we drew closer, I could see his hand wrap around the seatbelt and grip it tightly.

"What is that?" he whispered, face pale under its faux tan.

I didn't have to ask what he meant. "It's the creek," I said. "It's what's been protecting me."

"It's very strong." His jaw clenched, and I saw how the muscles in his neck stood out.

"I know," I said quietly. "But it won't hurt you."

I had to hope that was true.

The car pulled into the garage and shut itself off, and we both got out. Gideon followed me inside the cottage, gazing around with some curiosity.

"So this is what a home looks like?"

"It's what this house looks like," I said. "There's a lot of variation. And no one actually lives here full-time. It's kind of a guest house."

"Because of that?" he asked, looking past me to where the creek lay, although it wasn't visible from where we stood.

"No. We all love the creek. No one lives here full-time because it belongs to Kara Rinehart and Kirsten Jones, and they have their own—much bigger—houses elsewhere in Sedona. They loan this one out for friends—or friends of friends—to use when they come here to visit."

We'd gone through the living room and had stopped in the kitchen. Gideon kept shooting those wary glances in the direction of the creek, and I realized we needed to go ahead and get this over with. Either my hunch would be correct, or this would turn out to be one of the biggest mistakes I'd ever made.

"Come outside with me?" I asked.

A look of something close to terror passed over his features. "Why?"

"Because I think it will help. I need you to trust me, Gideon. Please."

He hesitated, reluctance obvious in every inch of his body. I turned away from the back door and came close to him.

"Do you think I would do anything that would hurt you?"

"No," he said at once, then added, "That is, I haven't seen you exhibit the sort of behavior that would indicate you enjoy seeing others suffer."

Well, that's something, I thought wryly. His dark eyes met mine, and I realized he needed to be himself for this. Wholly himself.

"We're alone," I said softly. "You don't need that." And I pointed at the leather wristband he wore, the one that seemed to be the source of his altered appearance.

"You don't like me like this?"

"I like you as you. I understand the need for the disguise when you're out in public, but—"

His fingers found the center button on the wristband and pushed it. Immediately, the Gideon I knew stood there, his deep ruby eyes locked on mine.

My breath caught. There was something about the contrast between his alien appearance and the ordinary clothes he wore that made him all the more striking.

"Better?" he asked.

"Much better." The words sounded somewhat strangled, but at least I was able to force them out. I laid my hand on the doorknob and turned it. "Let's go down to the creek."

His brows pulled together, but he didn't protest. I wondered what the creek felt like to him. Something inimical that should be avoided? He'd reacted negatively to it at first, although now he seemed more curious than anything else as I led him down the back steps and across the patio. The sun slanted down from above, warm and gentle, although the breeze was fairly cool. It ruffled Gideon's crisp dark hair, and something about the way it waved in the breeze made me wish I had the courage to run my fingers through it.

I didn't, of course. The creek chattered at us through the trees, the sound of the water growing closer and closer. An enormous yellow butterfly fluttered across the path and disappeared into the woods, and I felt rather than saw Gideon's amazement at the sight.

And then there was the creek, slipping over the smooth stones of its bed, the water dancing and flashing in the sunlight. If anything, it seemed even more full than the day before, the warming temperatures melting more of the snow on the San Francisco Peaks in Flagstaff so the water here could run high and fast.

"There it is," I said, quite unnecessarily.

Gideon stopped a few feet from the bank. "It's beautiful."

"Yes."

"I hadn't been expecting that."

Our eyes met for a moment. The fear was receding, replaced by something I didn't quite recognize. Wonder? Awe?

"Why is it so powerful?" he asked.

"I don't know for sure. I mean, we all believe it has something to do with the vortexes, but even the people who are experts in vortex energy don't know for sure why Oak Creek itself has such strength. Maybe because it draws from all of the other vortexes as it passes through town?"

"Possibly," he said. "We've studied the vortexes, but we're not sure we understand them. They are a phenomenon unique to this world, this place."

As he spoke, he was drawing closer and closer to the water. Or maybe it was drawing him toward it. I didn't know, but it was fascinating to watch, almost as if he had no real control over his actions, was being compelled to draw near.

He paused on the bank, head up into the sunlight. It glinted off his near-black hair, and made his skin seem even more greenish in hue. Or maybe that was only a reflection from all the cottonwoods and sycamores and oaks with their brand-new leaves.

Then he was bending down, pulling at the laces on his tennis shoes. He kicked one off, then the other, before removing his socks and stuffing them inside.

"Gideon," I said, "what are you doing?"

But I thought I knew.

He stepped out into the swirling water and I couldn't help wincing, because I knew just how cold it was. A tremor went through him, followed by another. He bent down and dipped one hand into the water, letting it flow between his fingers.

I stood on the bank, knowing that I shouldn't speak, or interfere. I needed to let him do this.

He lifted his hand from the water and looked at the droplets glittering on his fingers. And then he turned and looked at me, and I saw tears gleaming in his eyes, diamond-bright as the creek water on his hand.

"Taryn," he said. His voice was a broken whisper, one I could barely hear above the rushing water.

"I'm here." I wanted to wade out to him, but I forced myself to stay where I was. Unlike Gideon, I had no need to make my peace with Sedona. It was my home. It was a part of me.

"The things I've done…." he began, then shook his head.

It couldn't possibly be that bad, I thought, but then, did I really know for sure? He'd had a life before we met, a life more or less ruled over by Lir Shalan. The Reptilian leader wasn't exactly a shining paragon of moral rectitude.

"You can change that," I said.

"Can I?"

I held out my hand. "Let me show you."

We sat on the couch in the living room. Gideon had dried his feet off and replaced his shoes and socks, but he still looked shaken.

There had been some bottled iced tea in the care package my mother sent over with me, and so I'd poured two glasses for Gideon and myself. He picked up his glass and drank, although I could tell by the expression on his face that he wasn't overly thrilled by the taste.

"Do you want to tell me?" I asked softly.

"No," he said. "Because then you will think the worst of me. But I must be prepared for that."

"It's all right," I told him. "I won't. I promise."

"Better not to promise things before you know the truth," he said, his tone a warning.

I tilted my head at him. "Just tell me."

"We were—we are—taking your women."

"I know that," I said calmly.

The ruby eyes widened before he did his best to cover his shock. "You know?"

"My parents told me. Remember, they're part of a large network of people who share anything that seems out of the ordinary. So when the stories started up, the news ran through the grapevine pretty quickly."

He settled back against the sofa cushions, clearly attempting to figure out what to say next. "Is it common knowledge?"

"No. As far as we can tell, the media and the government are doing all they can to suppress the information." I shifted on the couch, then tucked one leg under the other so I could face him directly. "Is there anything you want to tell me about that?"

"It is part of the agreement."

"What agreement?"

"The agreement we made with the governments of your world." He drank some more of his iced tea. This time, he barely grimaced. "We offered some of our technology, but in exchange, we asked for a number of your women."

"But...why?" Even as I asked the question, I had to wonder how close to the truth Callista's hypothesis about clones would turn out to be.

He didn't answer right away. The iced tea glass went around and around in his hands as he turned it while staring down into the pale brown liquid inside. At last, he said, "Because our race is failing."

"Failing? Failing how?"

With a sigh, he reached over and set down the glass, then turned back toward me. "It is a long story."

"I have time."

An improbable smile touched his mouth. "I suppose you do." He stopped then, looking up at the beamed ceiling and over at the fireplace before his gaze returned to me. "Will anyone be stopping by to check on you?" he asked. "I'd rather not face your family right away, if that can be avoided."

"It's fine," I told him. "They all think I'm at work. I texted my mother to let her know I was okay, and I need to do that again around the time they'd be expecting me to be home, but that's hours from now."

He nodded and seemed to relax slightly. Then he said, picking up the earlier thread of our conversation, "For generations, my race has used cloning to keep its bloodlines pure."

Ha, I thought. *Callista's going to be thrilled she was right.*

"And for generations, everything was fine," Gideon went on. "But then something went wrong. We were unable to clone our females."

Part of me wanted to interrupt him, to point out that it wasn't entirely accurate for him to keep saying "we" and "our" when he was half human. But I had a feeling he wouldn't appreciate that sort of observation, so I remained silent.

"Why would you need them, if you were reproducing by cloning anyway?" I asked, genuinely curious.

Gideon's shoulders lifted, but I didn't believe the negligence of that shrug, not for a second. "Sometimes, genetic anomalies would occur. When that happened, the bloodline in question would be terminated and a new one begun. Naturally, we needed to combine male and female genetic material for that to occur, for us to create new life."

I didn't think there was anything natural about it at all, but I only nodded.

"And so when a bloodline was corrupted, without the necessary female biological material to create a replacement, we could do nothing except close it down, and we would have no one to replace those who were lost. That was when the first hybridization attempts were made, with races from subject worlds. But those experiments were all failures."

"You did well with your hybrids here," I pointed out. More than well, if Logan was an example of the Reptilians' genetic experiments. He looked completely human. Well, the epitome of human, anyway—handsome, strong, intelligent.

"Yes, because of the human genetic material we used. It is extremely malleable and adaptable, more so than anything else we've found in the galaxy. But those hybrids were designed to be indistinguishable from humans. They did very little to help with our own particular problem of vanishing bloodlines."

"And so you decided to leave the laboratory out of the equation and reproduce the old-fashioned way." I tried to make the comment in as neutral a way as possible, but I knew I wasn't very successful. The image of Elizabeth D'Onofrio haunted me. She'd looked so beautiful and bright, and she'd been taken and used by a monster.

Gideon didn't quite wince, but I could see the

way his shoulders stiffened. "Yes. With varying success, as I told you before."

Something was bothering me, but I didn't know if I had the courage to ask. But I recalled how he'd looked, standing there in the creek, grief and remorse as clear on his face as the bright sunshine above us. He was being honest with me now, so I needed to be brave and not shy away from the hard questions.

"I don't understand, though," I began, and paused as I tried to figure out the best way to ask the question. He tilted his head, waiting for me to go on. "If you were reproducing with cloning, why the"—I hesitated, then forced myself to go on — "why the sex? You'd think your people would just take what they needed from human women to create little test tube babies."

"You misunderstand," Gideon said, apparently not offended at all. "We reproduced by cloning to ensure the purity of our race. That did not mean we —I mean they—did not engage in sexual activity purely for pleasure's sake."

His sage-green skin took on the slightly deeper hue I'd come to recognize as his form of flushing, and I knew I'd hit a nerve. Well, I'd gotten the distinct impression earlier that he was just as inexperienced as I, so I figured the embarrassment was natural enough.

"And when you ran out of your own women...."

He looked away. "Yes. We—they—that is, they do find human women sexually appealing."

Well, there it was, stated far more baldly than I'd expected. I couldn't say I was surprised, not after some of the things Kirsten had said, not after the stories I'd found circulating on the internet, stories I was sure my parents would have rather I'd not known about.

And the one persistent rumor, rigorously debunked on more than one occasion and yet which refused to die, that sex with a Reptilian could be a transcendent experience.

Personally, I'd just as soon never find out.

With a half-Reptilian, however....

To break the awkward silence that fell after that particular revelation, I let out a not very convincing chuckle and said, "Should I be flattered on behalf of human women everywhere?"

He didn't smile. "That depends on whether you would find those attentions appealing."

"God, no," slipped from my lips before I could stop myself. A flash of disappointment came and went in Gideon's eyes, and I immediately reached out and put a hand on his knee, saying, "But I definitely don't think of you as one of them."

"But I am."

"Half," I said firmly. "The other half is just as human as I am."

No response. He watched me for a moment, and then his gaze flicked down to where my hand was resting on his knee.

Maybe I should have pulled it back. After all, we

were sitting very close. But I realized then that I didn't want to. I wanted—

I wanted what I knew he was going to do then.

He leaned forward, his face scant inches from mine. Finally, there was a pulse from him—of need, of worry…of self-loathing. Everything in him wanted this, but he thought he wasn't worthy.

Well, I'd have to correct that notion right away. I lifted my hand from his knee so I could cup his face in my fingers. I brought him close, and in the next instant, our lips touched.

Heat moving all through me, raging down into the pit of my stomach and out along every limb. The world shimmered around me. A kiss wasn't supposed to do *that* to you, was it?

In this case, it did.

Our mouths opened, and I tasted him, clean and light, like the mineral-laden water we'd drunk on board his father's ship. His arms were around me, and then he was pushing me down against the sofa cushions, his weight on top of me, his hands tangling in my hair.

I wrapped my legs around him, pulling him close, even though I knew that was crazy, that I shouldn't be pushing things along so fast. But, oh, God, feeling his body pressed against mine was divine, and I never wanted it to end, wanted the whole world to be the two of us together like this, everything else forgotten.

But it couldn't be forgotten. I needed to take some

control of myself, because dimly past the heat and the blood that seemed to pulse in every square inch of my body, I realized Gideon was in possession of information that needed to be shared with everyone in the group.

So I broke the kiss, but gently, pulling my mouth from his as I reached up to run a hand through his heavy, wavy hair. "Gideon—"

At once, he looked stricken, and raised himself from me as he practically propelled himself upward from the couch. "I should not have done that."

"Why?" I asked candidly as I sat up and got everything more or less back in place. "I wanted you to. In fact, I started it."

He stopped where he was and stared down at me. "You wanted that?"

"Of course, I did," I replied, then got up from the sofa as well so I could go over and take his hand in mine. "I realized I needed to stop fighting it. Unless —" I paused then, not wanting to say the words but knowing I must. "Unless this was all a trick, and you're still planning to take me back to your father."

"No!" The word burst from him with such force that I knew he could only be telling the truth. "I would never do that. I—I don't know for sure what to do next, but I would never betray you to him."

His words rang with truth. I could feel it radiating from every syllable. Relieved, I tightened my fingers on his. "So…does that mean you're throwing your lot in with us humans?"

"I—" He stopped there, clearly warring within himself. "I suppose I must. I can't support what he's doing. Not any longer. Besides...." His mouth twisted, and he stopped there, eyes dark with memory.

"Besides...?"

"I can't forget what my mother told me as she was dying. 'Always remember,' she said."

"Remember what?"

He gave me a sad smile. "'Remember that you're half human, too.' I can't make a decision without betraying some part of my heritage, and yet I know what Lir Shalan is doing is wrong."

The very fact that he'd used the alien leader's full name rather than saying "my father" told me a great deal. I waited in silence, since I worried that interrupting him would only serve to shake his resolve.

Then Gideon lifted first one of my hands, and then the other, laying a gentle kiss on each one.

"Tell me what I should do next."

CHAPTER ELEVEN

I TEXTED MY PARENTS AND SAID THAT I HAD SOMETHING important I needed to discuss with them, and would it be okay if I came over?

My mother replied almost immediately. *What's the matter? Aren't you at work?*

I left early, I texted back. *Are you busy?*

No. I had a client earlier, but he's gone back to his hotel. And your father is working on his book, but he can take a break.

I'll be over in fifteen, I typed, then closed the messenger window.

My father was always working on a book. I honestly didn't know how much those books actually earned him, since I'd always had the impression that a large chunk of the family's income came from residuals from his television show *Paranormality,* even though it had been canceled years earlier, as well as the speaking engagements where he made appearances at UFO conventions around the country. Well, that, and from my mother's private clients, many of whom flew out from L.A. to see her, since the majority of them were entertainment types. Apparently, word had gotten out about her abilities, and she had a steady stream of well-heeled people coming to Sedona to have her do readings for them.

Anyway, I'd long since stopped worrying about whether I was interrupting my father while he was writing, because otherwise I would never have gotten to talk to him. I also had a feeling he wouldn't mind this particular interruption.

"We can go right over," I told Gideon, who'd been hovering nearby while I conducted my text exchange with my mother.

He didn't look exactly overcome with excitement at the prospect of going to my parents' house. "Are you sure this is necessary?"

"They need to hear it from you, Gideon." I could have been impatient with his reluctance, but I thought I knew where it was coming from. Meeting someone's parents for the first time was hard enough without also being the son of an alien enemy leader.

"I know. And it needs to be stopped, but...." He paused then, searching my face. "You understand what we're facing here, don't you? The people who entered into these agreements with Lir Shalan are very powerful. They think the lives of a few women are a small price to pay compared with the technology we can give them. They will not be happy that someone is trying to stop them."

"True," I said, trying to sound unconcerned, even though a shiver of anxiety went through me at the thought of having to somehow take on a global conspiracy. "Then again, they've never gone up against the Sedona UFO hunters."

Gideon activated his disguise again, just because we had to drive through a good chunk of town to get to my parents' house. The windows of my car were tinted, but not so much that they could hide the unusual hue of his skin. Anyway, we'd also have to park in the driveway and come in through the front door, which meant any neighbors out walking their dogs or watering the potted plants on their porches would be able to get a look at him before we went inside. Better safe than sorry.

Besides, I thought it might be a good idea to ease my parents into this. Seeing a green-skinned man on their front doorstep might give even them pause.

Traffic was heavier than usual because of all the spring-breakers. I tried not to curse as we missed yet another light. Gideon looked over at me and said, "This is a highly inefficient form of travel."

"No kidding," I replied. "But we still don't have our flying cars, so we have to put up with traffic."

"You don't have your flying cars...yet," he said, rather cryptically.

Or maybe his comment wasn't so cryptic. I could see why some politicians in Washington and elsewhere might think it was a fair trade to hand off a few women in exchange for flying cars and nonpolluting renewable energy and....

My fingers tightened on the steering wheel, even though the car was in self-driving mode and I didn't need to be involved at all. Somehow, I doubted the Reptilians would be quite that altruistic with their "gifts." More like they'd be all too happy to give us a bunch of new and improved weapons, and they could swoop in and steal away even more unwilling breeding stock while we were busy picking up the pieces. Nothing powerful enough to make us a threat to the aliens, but bad enough that there might not be a lot of civilization left by the time they were done.

No, it wouldn't come to that. My mother had stopped the Reptilians on the first go-'round, and Kirsten had finished the job a few years later. True, she hadn't completely gotten rid of them, but the aliens had left Sedona alone for the past twenty-five years.

Problem was, when they'd returned, they'd returned with a vengeance. And they weren't working in the shadows anymore, but were out in the world, pretending to be saviors when in fact they were the exact opposite.

The car finally eased itself around the traffic circles near Tlaquepaque Village, and I let out a relieved breath. Just a little farther, and then I'd be off the highway and into the hilly neighborhood where I'd grown up.

"You're worried," Gideon said.

"Not exactly worried," I replied. "Anxious, I guess. I was just thinking about what the Reptilians have been doing, and I'm getting myself all worked up. But I know we need to be calm and methodical about this."

"I'm glad that you're getting worked up. It shows you care. I enjoy your passion."

I could think of something else I'd rather be passionate about. Just recalling the way Gideon had kissed me was enough to send that flooding warmth all through my body again. I'd have to push those feelings out of my mind for now, though. It was never a good idea to show up in front of your parents when you were all hot and bothered...especially when one of them happened to be a psychic.

The car pulled into the driveway and shut itself off. We both got out, Gideon gazing around at his surroundings as he did so. I had to wonder what he thought of the neighborhood; it was a lot more upscale than the area where the cottage was located, with bigger lots, each property carefully situated to make maximum use of the spectacular red rock views all around.

"This way," I said, guiding him along the walkway that led into an enclosed entrance. It was cooler in there. A gardenia bloomed in a pot next to the front door, its fragrance seeming to fill the sheltered spot.

I almost knocked, then realized that was foolish. This was my home; I still lived here, even though I'd already begun to feel detached from the house, as if my future belonged somewhere else. And though it was broad daylight and technically we should have been safe, I realized it probably would have been safer for my parents to come to the cottage, rather than Gideon and me coming here.

Well, there wasn't anything I could do about it now. I dug in my purse for a key and let us into the foyer. As I shut the door behind us, I called out, "I'm here!"

"In the kitchen," my mother called back.

That could be a good thing. There was something intrinsically relaxed about having a conversation in a kitchen, rather than facing one another in the far more formal space of the living room.

"This way," I told Gideon.

He followed me toward the back of the house where the kitchen was located. As we went, I could see him glancing around with a good deal of interest. The house was almost twice the size of the cottage, and more elegantly furnished. "Tuscan villa" was how my mother always described the decorating style, and I supposed that fit. There were a few Southwest pieces here and there, mainly Navajo pottery and the rug in the dining room, but she hadn't gone full-bore with those kinds of accents the way Kara tended to. But maybe he wasn't comparing the house to the cottage at all, but instead to his surroundings back on the *Eclipse.* Had he ever lived anywhere else, or was the Reptilian ship his only home?

The kitchen at my parents' house was large and had always felt friendly to me, with its warm maple cabinets and the big window in the breakfast nook, the one that gave an amazing view of Cathedral Rock. My mother stood in front of the refrigerator, the freezer compartment open in front of her as she stared into it. I recognized that pose all too well; it meant she had absolutely no idea what to make for dinner and was hoping inspiration would strike.

Experience had taught me that at least two times out of three, we'd end up going out to eat or ordering in when she resorted to hoping for divine inspiration in her meal planning. At the sound of our footsteps, she shut the freezer door and turned toward us, surprise flaring in her eyes when she caught sight of Gideon.

"Well, hello," she said, as her gaze flicked toward me in question.

"Sorry," I told her. "I guess I should have told you I was bringing company. Mom, this is Gideon." Her eyes widened as she recognized the name, and in the next second she frowned, as if attempting to reconcile the normal-looking young man in front of her with my stories about Lir Shalan's half-human son. "Gideon, this is my mother, Persephone Oliver."

"Hello, Ms. Oliver," Gideon said, and she waved a hand, although a frown still pulled at her arched brows.

"Persephone is fine. It's very nice to meet you, Gideon." The glance she sent me next was clearly speculative, but she only said, "Let me go get Paul. I told him to come meet me in the kitchen, but it looks like he probably got sucked right back into that book he's working on. Taryn, why don't you see if Gideon would like some iced tea, or some water?"

"Water," he said immediately as she headed out to pry my father away from his computer. "Thank you."

I flashed a grin at him—obviously he wasn't going to warm up to iced tea any time soon—and went to get the filter pitcher from the refrigerator, then filled a glass for both of us. "Ice?" I asked.

"Excuse me?"

"Would you like ice in it?"

"Isn't it already cold?"

"Well, yes, but we add ice so our drinks don't come up to room temperature too fast."

He frowned. "Why aren't your drinking vessels made of materials that would prevent that from happening?"

Good question. I supposed such things must exist, but most of us still just drank out of glass. "Tradition, I guess."

He shook his head. "Well, I think I will be all right without the ice."

With a smile, I brought his glass over to him. As he took it from me, his fingers touched mine for a second, just long enough to send that warm, shivery heat all through my body again.

At that inopportune moment, my parents reappeared in the kitchen. I pulled my hand away from Gideon's, hoping they hadn't seen. Not that I was embarrassed by how I knew I felt for him, but because they were about to hear some very unsettling things, and discovering that the half-alien man and I shared some kind of connection probably wouldn't make them jump for joy.

"Paul, this is Gideon," my mother said, and my father reached out to shake his hand. Obviously, he hadn't made the connection yet, was still lost in his own thoughts the way he usually was when interrupted during a writing session.

Gideon extended his hand as well. "It is very good to meet you, Mr. Oliver."

"Paul," my father corrected automatically, his tone somewhat vague. It always did take him a little while to reconnect with reality.

I had a feeling he was about to reconnect with reality in a very big way in about a minute.

"So what's this about?" my mother asked then,

glancing from Gideon to me. The frown had returned, but it was clear enough that she wanted me to explain things in my own time.

"It's—" I paused then. What was the best way to broach the subject? I looked over at Gideon, who wore a look of resignation. He seemed to have already guessed what I wanted him to do. But, as they said, a picture was worth a thousand words.

"It's because I possess information you will probably want to hear," he said. His fingers moved to the band of leather he wore in his wrist and pressed down on the metal disk in the center.

My parents had both seen and experienced enough crazy things in their lives that they didn't jump, or gasp. Eyes widened, yes, and my mother pressed her lips together, as if she was trying to hold in an exclamation.

"So you're the one who took our daughter," my father said then. All absentmindedness was gone, and the way his friendly hazel eyes narrowed seemed to indicate he was none too thrilled to have Gideon in his house, even if I'd brought him there.

"I went of my own volition," I protested. "And he brought me back, so can we just forget about that for now? We have more important things to talk about."

"More important things than kidnapping my daughter?" he asked. My mother laid a hand on his arm, as if to tell him to take it down a notch, but he ignored her, instead kept his gaze fixed on Gideon.

"Perhaps. I wanted to tell you of the women who are being kidnapped."

Something in my father's body language altered. It wasn't exactly that the fight had gone out of him. Rather, it seemed that he had found something else to focus on.

"What do you know about that?" My mother's pretty features suddenly seemed quite grim.

"A good deal, if not everything." Gideon hesitated for a moment, then gave the slightest lift of his shoulders, as if he'd realized he couldn't hold back what he needed to say. "You see, I was privy to most of Lir Shalan's plans and designs, since I am his son."

Of course they both knew that already, even though Gideon didn't realize I'd told them. He probably thought he was sharing a huge revelation. What he thought of their lack of reaction, I couldn't tell, because his expression was still calm, almost bland.

My father said, "That does explain a few things."

"Such as my appearance?"

"Yes. We'd been wondering about that. Both Martin and Raphael swore that they'd never seen anyone who looked like you before."

"No, they wouldn't have."

I decided it was time for me to break in. "His appearance really isn't what's important here. What's important is that the reason we haven't really heard anything about these kidnappings, why they haven't been all over the news, is that governments worldwide actually are suppressing those reports. Lir

Shalan has promised to hand over some of the Reptilians' technology if people keep their mouths shut about the women being taken."

"I see," my father said heavily. "That...complicates things."

"But why?" my mother asked, and Gideon and I looked at each other.

He was the first to speak. "Perhaps we should sit down. This may require some explanation."

"Of course." She headed over to the table in the nook and pulled out a chair, and after a brief hesitation, my father followed her.

Both Gideon and I picked up our water glasses and went to sit down in the two unoccupied chairs. For just a second or two, I thought about how familiar those surroundings were to me, and yet how they were made strange by having Gideon sitting there, his greenish skin a stark contrast to the black T-shirt he wore.

Then he launched into basically the same explanation he'd given me about the Reptilians relying on cloning to reproduce, and how they'd found themselves boxed into a corner when that method of ensuring the survival of their species began to fail them. He didn't go into any great detail, but he did explain how his mother had been taken from Sedona.

During that part of the narrative, I watched my parents' changing expressions. My father had shifted into analytical mode, brows raising or scrunching together as he took in each piece of Gideon's story and thought it over. As for my mother, well, I could tell she was shaken by Elizabeth D'Onofrio's fate, her pale face and the strained look in her eyes telling me how much she worried for the women who were being taken for that same purpose even now.

"How many?" she asked, once Gideon had paused and picked up his glass of water.

He didn't pretend to misunderstand her. After he'd swallowed a mouthful of water, he replied, "A little over a thousand so far."

"A thousand," she murmured. Right then, I could feel the worry and sorrow pulsing from her as she thought of the shared fate of those women, taken by a hostile race for a single terrible purpose.

"From where?" my father asked. I could tell he was wondering if only a few nations had submitted to the aliens' terrible request, or whether this was a worldwide conspiracy.

"Everywhere," Gideon said simply, and both my parents winced.

"We have to stop it," I said.

"How?" Gideon asked.

He wasn't being mean, or being obtuse on purpose. I could tell he genuinely wanted to know.

The problem was, I had no idea. My parents and their little group of UFO hunters had accomplished some amazing things over the years, but they weren't exactly equipped to take on a problem of this magnitude.

My father's jaw hardened. Right then, I got a

glimpse of the man who'd evaded pursuit by Men in Black and traded potshots with hybrid soldiers. He wasn't afraid of this challenge.

"First thing," he said, "is to get the word out. I'll pass along everything you've told me to Lance, and he'll make sure it gets through the network. And then we can start digging into the stories of the women who've disappeared, find as many common-alities as we can, and try to spread word as to how women in the target demographic can protect themselves."

"Were the ones taken women who lived alone?" I asked.

"I don't think Lance said one way or another," my mother replied. "So we'll have to look into that. It would be an easy precaution to take—just make sure you never sleep alone."

"Thus encouraging tons more college hook-ups and one-night stands," I said dryly, although actually, better to go to bed with someone you just met in a bar than to get beamed up to be a Reptilian's sex slave.

My mother slanted a look at me. "That's not what I was suggesting. I was thinking more about getting a friend to stay over or something along those lines."

"It really wouldn't change the situation all that much," Gideon said. His tone wasn't quite defeated, but he didn't look terribly enthusiastic, either. "If my people have decided on a particular target, then they can take her right out of her bed, even if someone else is in the same room, or sleeping next to her."

Mouth dry, I asked, "Seriously?"

"Seriously. In the past, they would have preferred to avoid such maneuvers, since they were riskier, but now, with your governments covering up for them, they don't need to be quite as discreet."

A silence fell. My father drummed his fingers on the tabletop, clearly sorting through what Gideon had just told us and attempting to see if he could find any kind of a loophole, something that would make it so those women's fates weren't already predetermined. I looked across the table at my mother, saw how the fine little laugh lines around her eyes appeared to deepen with worry. She'd never been the type to sit by when there was an injustice that needed to be righted, but at the moment, I could tell she didn't know what she could possibly do to fix this problem.

"They use a version of these," Gideon said as he laid the transporter device on the tabletop. His words fell cool and clear into the silence, although again I sensed those waves of shame coming from him, as if he still thought this was all his fault. Maybe in his culture, the sins of the father were just as much the sins of the son, since they were all clones.

My father's eyes lit up with curiosity, and he made a movement toward the silvery cylinder, then stopped himself. "Do you mind if I pick it up?" he asked.

"Go ahead," Gideon replied. "It's keyed to my biometrics, so there's no chance of you setting it off."

Lying there in my father's hand, the device did look pretty harmless. But I'd seen how Gideon had used it to transport me back to Earth, so I knew it could do exactly the opposite, bringing unsuspecting —and most likely terrified—women up to the Reptilians' ship.

My mother spoke then. "Is there any way of, I don't know, blocking it? Creating a sort of field that would disrupt its effects?"

A flicker of surprise went through Gideon's deep red eyes, as if he hadn't ever considered that question before. "I don't know for sure. That is, I've never heard of such a thing, but I suppose it's theoretically possible."

"Of course, Persephone," my father said, his face lighting up at the prospect. He put his free hand on top of hers where it rested on the tabletop and gave it a squeeze. "If we could analyze the beam, discover the energy waves it's using, then generating a counter-energy that would block it is entirely possible."

"You could do that?" I asked. That is, I knew my father was brilliant, with degrees in astronomy and in astrophysics, but still, it sounded as if what he was proposing would need an engineer to implement the hack once the physics had been figured out.

"By myself? No. That's not my background. But we can put the call out, get some particle physicists and a couple of engineers to come and analyze it. I know Jeff Makowski knows some people at Caltech. They'd kill to get their hands on something like this."

And when that call went out, my father wouldn't have to hide the origins of the device. He might have spent years being mocked by the scientific community for believing in UFOs, but no one could laugh at him now. The images of Lir Shalan and his delegation greeting the President had been carried around the world, and now nothing would ever be the same.

"Do you mind if they take it, Gideon?" I asked gently, because I realized that in his scientific zeal to start taking the device apart, so to speak, my father hadn't actually asked permission to start reverse-engineering the thing. Also, with it disassembled, Gideon would have no way of getting back to the ship.

Then again, maybe that was a good thing.

"No, it's fine," he replied. "When the time comes, I can unlock it so they're able to analyze the beam without my handling it. Besides, if the device is out of my possession, then Lir Shalan cannot use it to contact me. You see, they are used both for transportation and for communication."

Those words made me go cold. I'd almost forgotten, in everything which had happened that afternoon, how Lir Shalan had sent his son down here to fetch me back.

Voice tight with worry, I asked, "How long before he gets suspicious?"

"I'm not completely certain. But he's probably already wondering why I haven't returned."

"He sent you here to get Taryn?" my mother said, looking even paler.

"Yes. He was not happy to learn that I had let her go. She's quite a prize, you see—a human with strong psychic powers. Her genetic material would have made a significant contribution."

Gideon's reply made her wince and look over at my father, whose jaw had set even more firmly. It was clear that if any aliens showed up to take me back to the ship, they'd be doing so over my father's dead body.

That wouldn't happen, though. The creek would protect us during the dangerous nighttime hours, and during the day, we'd just have to make sure to be around plenty of other people.

A thought occurred to me. "If I'm that important, why hasn't Lir Shalan just beamed me up anyway without waiting for you to bring me back?"

"It's very difficult to get a lock on an individual here in Sedona," Gideon replied. Both my parents visibly relaxed, and I let out a relieved breath as well. "Yes, the protection is strongest by the creek, but the effects of Oak Creek and the various vortexes are also distributed through the area. They create a lot of interference. It's one thing to come down here with a device and take someone directly, but attempting to do it from up on the ship would be nearly impossible."

"So someone would have to come down here to get her," my father said.

"Yes. And Lir Shalan wouldn't risk that. The chances of discovery would be much higher."

My mother's head tilted to one side, as if she was trying to determine whether we'd covered every angle. "Couldn't he or one of his people disguise himself the way you did with that wristband you're wearing?"

"No. The field it generates is a subtle one—it can alter my skin and eye color, but it doesn't have the power to effect such a radical change."

"And even if he can't beam Taryn right out of here," my father said, "what's to stop Lir Shalan from sending a team down to the cottage to take her back in the middle of the night?"

"The creek is stopping him," Gideon replied. "Taryn will tell you that I felt its effects as well, but because I'm half human, I was able to work past that to understand its healing energies. But those energies are actively hostile to a full-blood Reptilian. It's like trying to walk into—" He broke off then, frowning slightly as he attempted to describe what it did really feel like.

"Like walking into an F5 tornado," I said. "Or trying to push your way through a tsunami. The energy is just too strong. I doubt it was coincidence that their base was located way out in Secret Canyon, far enough away from Oak Creek to be safe."

"So you're safe here, then," my mother said, relief

clear in her face. I could tell from the way she pulsed with worry that she'd been imagining Lir Shalan and his minions swooping down tonight as soon as my head hit the pillow.

"Safer than anywhere else," I told her, which was true enough.

However, that wasn't quite the same as being completely safe.

CHAPTER TWELVE

My parents wanted us to stay for dinner, but I didn't think that was a very good idea. Yes, I was heartened by how kind they were being to Gideon, and it made me hopeful for the future—whatever that future turned out to be. However, I knew I wanted to be back at the cottage long before night fell, and since it seemed as if Gideon was going to be staying there with me for the duration, I realized that I'd need to get him a few supplies.

So I thanked them but said we needed to go to the outlet mall in Oak Creek to get Gideon a few changes of clothes. He looked surprised by that comment but didn't argue. And my father said he was going to be in touch with Lance and then Jeff Makowski, his hacker friend, and we'd see what we could do to circumvent the alien gizmo.

Right before we left, though, Gideon went out

into the courtyard with my father so he could show him how to disengage the biometric locking mechanism and use the device's backup lock instead. He needed to do that outside, away from us, just in case something went wrong.

My mother looked as if she wanted to protest, since risking my father's safety wasn't something she appreciated. But then she saw the light in his eyes and kept quiet, knowing that he was willing to take the risk in the pursuit of more knowledge.

After they'd gone outside, though, she turned toward me, a question clear in her face. "So," she said, "do you want to tell me about you and Gideon?"

"There isn't much to tell," I replied, although I could feel the blood rise to my cheeks.

"Really? I would have guessed otherwise, from the way he was looking at you."

I couldn't deny that. From time to time during the conversation, probably when he thought they weren't paying attention, Gideon had glanced over at me, his gaze catching mine. I'd always looked away quickly, worried that my parents might notice. My father, obviously excited to play with a new toy, didn't seem to have detected any undercurrents between Gideon and me. But my mother must have been observing us with a much clearer eye.

"Does it bother you?" I asked.

The worry line between her brows deepened. "Of course, it bothers me," she said, then held up a hand as I began to protest. "Not for the reasons you might think, though. I'm not going to hold his father against him. It seems pretty clear to me that Gideon's had a change of heart. And lord knows we have enough aliens and hybrids and so on in this little extended family of ours that it would be hypocritical of me to judge him solely on that. But Taryn...." She trailed off, as if she wasn't quite sure what she'd meant to say, or at the very least had thought better of it.

"You're afraid he's going to hurt me?"

"Not intentionally. But he must have even less experience than you do, sweetie. This could just be an...infatuation."

She was right, of course. I didn't want to admit it to myself, but Gideon had literally never been around a human girl until he met me. He could have latched on to me simply because there was no one else.

Even as the thought swirled through my mind, I knew it was wrong. Gideon and I had only spent a few weeks together, and we'd only kissed once, but that was all I needed to convince me of the way his soul fit into mine.

I expected that most people wouldn't understand. That was all right, though. The two of us understood, and that was enough.

In the meantime, though, I needed to set my mother's mind at ease.

"I know it's not like it was with Callista and

Raphael," I said. "That's the way they're made—to be able to recognize their soul mate when they see them. There isn't that kind of connection between Gideon and me. But *something* is there, and I need to find out what it means."

"I hope you can," she replied. Her gaze shifted toward the ceiling, although I knew she wasn't looking at the overhead light fixtures, but much farther away, to a place where the Reptilian ship circled the Earth in stealthy silence. "I hope they give you the time for that."

Gideon was mostly silent during the drive from my parents' house to the outlet mall. He stared out the window, looking at the red rock formations as they passed by. When we drove slowly past Courthouse Butte, though, a tremor went through him.

"That is where it happened, isn't it?" he asked in an undertone.

"Yes, it's where Kirsten Jones defeated the forces from your base."

"One woman." The words came out flat, but I could still feel the disbelief in him, as if he was trying to figure out how that possibly could have happened.

"One woman channeling the power of Sedona," I corrected him. "Also, she had a little help." From Martin, the man who loved her, and Michael Light-foot, who'd given his life to ensure that she would succeed. I wouldn't mention his name, though. Gideon and I had already talked about Michael Lightfoot, and bringing up the subject again would make it seem as if I was reproaching him for that brave man's death. As if Gideon had anything to do with it. He hadn't even been born yet.

The shopping center wasn't too crowded. My parents said it had almost folded completely a few years before I was born, but some hard work had brought it back from the brink. Now it was a mixture of several national chains' outlet stores, along with shops and restaurants that were locally owned. There certainly wasn't time to drag Gideon all the way to the real mall in Cottonwood to go shopping, but I figured we could get enough here to manage for a few days.

He was wearing Levi's and a T-shirt with a Hanes label inside. God only knows where the Reptilians had dug those up, but clearly, they'd done their homework. Good thing, though, because that made it easy to scrounge up a few more pieces in the same sizes without him having to try anything on.

I wasn't about to ask to inspect the label on his underwear. He was roughly the same size as my brother, and since I'd gotten stuck doing the laundry more often than not during high school, I knew that meant Gideon was probably a size medium.

By the time we got to checkout, I had a nice stack of several pairs of jeans, some more T-shirts, a couple of button-down shirts just in case, and a duffle coat

I'd found on the clearance rack. He eyed the pile in the shopping cart with some surprise.

"Do you really think I'm going to need all that?" he asked as the woman at the checkout started to scan everything.

"Do you know how long you're going to be here?" I returned, and he shook his head.

"No, I suppose I don't."

"Then let's make sure you have enough clean underwear."

He couldn't help grinning at that comment, although he looked troubled as the clerk told me the total and I passed my debit card over the scanner.

"This is costing you a lot—"

I was a little surprised that he understood the concept of money at all. The Reptilians hadn't seemed like the type to need it. Maybe his mother had told him about it, or maybe he'd learned something of the way our economy worked from watching our films or television shows. "It's fine. Mostly, I let my work money pile up because I live at home and don't have much to spend it on."

My reply didn't seem to comfort him very much, although he didn't offer any further protest. I handed the bags to him and said, "Some shoes, and then we can head back."

"Shoes?" He stared down at the canvas high-tops he was wearing. "Aren't these sufficient?"

"For hanging out in Uptown, sure. But what if something comes up where we need to head out into the wilderness, maybe go back to the base? You need something you can hike in."

Actually, I didn't know how necessary any of that would be, either. But better to be prepared. In a pinch, he might have been able to borrow something from my father, I supposed. We were here now, though, and I didn't see the point in delaying.

Gideon dutifully followed me into the shoe store, and once again we lucked out by finding something that would work—and which fit—in the clearance area.

"They do seem sturdier," he said, taking a few experimental steps in the size-eleven hiking boots I'd found for him.

"They are. That's the whole point. So we'll get these wrapped up and head out of here."

The transaction was handled quickly, and less than five minutes later, we were out the door and headed north on 179. There was some traffic, but not as much as I'd feared. Even so, I couldn't help sending a few wary glances westward, where the sun was beginning to dip toward the horizon.

"It will be fine," Gideon said, apparently noticing the worried looks I'd sent out the driver-side window. "It will not be full dark for another forty minutes."

I sent him a startled glance. "How can you know that?"

"I just do."

Well, I wasn't going to worry about how he'd

apparently analyzed the almanac for this part of the world. It was enough that we'd have sufficient time to get home before dark fell.

Home. Was the cottage my home now? It didn't feel that way, but until we figured out how to send the Reptilians packing, the little house that had once been Michael Lightfoot's was my only sure refuge.

We pulled into the garage just as the sun sank behind the hills to the west. Gideon gathered up his shopping bags and followed me inside. As we went in, I realized we probably should have risked a trip to the grocery store. Yes, my mother had sent food over, but it was all easy-to-fix prepackaged stuff intended for one person. She hadn't really planned on me having a house guest.

Well, neither had I. We'd just have to make the best of it, which probably meant ordering take-out. Luckily, there were a number of places that would deliver to this area. Moon Dog Pizza, of course, but also Thai Gardens and that new Mediterranean restaurant, the one whose name I could never remember. Anyway, we wouldn't starve.

The hard part was realizing that I would be alone with Gideon here. My mother hadn't exactly given me her blessing, but neither had she told me to stay away from him. Not that I necessarily would have done so, even if she'd been that explicit about her wishes. I still lived at home, but I was an adult and my mother and father treated me like one. I paid a modest amount for rent, was expected to contribute to the monthly food budget, even though my parents definitely didn't need the money.

That was the big difference between Callista and me, I supposed. Her parents more or less gave her anything she wanted, while I was expected to work for what I had. That was the way both my parents had been raised, and they'd raised me and Michael that way as well. I couldn't even blame Kirsten for coddling Callista the way she had. I supposed I would have been overprotective, too, if my mother had walked out on me when I was only three years old. And Martin hadn't even been born on this planet. He'd probably followed Kirsten's lead when it came to parenting, since he didn't have much of a frame of reference.

Gideon stopped in the center of the living room, shopping bags in hand, and gave me a questioning look. Diffidence fairly pulsed from him.

And I got it. He didn't know the cottage, didn't know where he was supposed to put his things. And as much as that kiss had ignited something between us, I wasn't quite ready to blithely show him into the master bedroom where I was staying.

"Over here," I said, going down the short hall where both bedrooms were located. I opened the first door on the left, the one to the guest room. It was small, with only a full-sized bed and a single high-boy. Not much else would have fit in there. "And the bathroom is just next door."

If he was surprised to see that I'd shown him to a

different bedroom than the one I was occupying, his manner didn't indicate that. Actually, I thought I could sense some relief, as if he'd been worried I would try to move things along more quickly.

I wasn't that forward. Whatever was going to happen between us, I wanted it to happen on its own time, and not because I'd decided to rush things.

"Well, I'll let you settle in," I said then. "Come find me in the kitchen when you're done."

Gideon only nodded, and I hurried out. Standing next to him in that small bedroom had begun to feel too overwhelming, or maybe it was just that I worried he'd catch me glancing at the bed and get the wrong impression. Anyway, I breathed a little easier when I got to the kitchen. I fetched a couple of glasses from the cupboard and poured some water into each of them. Gideon hadn't mentioned that he was thirsty, but I knew I was after all that shopping.

A few minutes later, he came into the kitchen. Since we were alone here and weren't expecting any company, he'd deactivated his disguise. By then, it really was dark; I'd flicked on the overhead lights, as well as several in the living room. He watched me carefully, eyes gleaming with dark ruby glints in the bright fluorescent light.

"Water?" I asked.

He went and retrieved the second glass from the counter. "Thank you."

"All I have here is some frozen stuff, so I thought we'd order in," I went on hurriedly, rifling through the stack of menus that Kara always kept in one of the kitchen drawers. "What would you like? Pizza, or there's a Mediterranean place that's pretty good, or—"

"Taryn."

His voice was quiet, but something in it made me look up and meet his gaze. "What?"

"I know very little of your food, except the things my mother programmed into our food synthesizers, so choose whatever you would like best. And—" He hesitated, clearly debating something with himself. After a long pause, he went on, "I know it is… awkward…being here like this. We will have to make the best of it."

"'Make the best of it'?" I repeated. "Is that what you think?"

"I'm not sure what to think. You seem different now from when we were together earlier today. Did your mother say something to you?"

Every line of his body was tense, poised for rejection. I knew then that he thought I had changed my mind about him, that I viewed our kiss earlier that afternoon as a mistake.

Well, I couldn't have him thinking that was true.

I set down my own glass and went to him, lacing my fingers through his so I could pull him close and kiss him again. After a brief, startled hesitation, his mouth opened to me, and we were tasting one another, my heart beginning to race at the exquisite sensation of his lips pressed against mine. His fingers tightened on mine, strengthening the connection between us.

After a few moments, we pulled apart, although we still held one another's hands. I wondered if he could hear how hard my heart was beating. Did his beat the same? I didn't even know if it was more human or Reptilian.

"Yes, my mother said something," I told him, my voice somewhat breathless. "She said she could tell you'd had a change of heart. I think she trusts you."

His fingers tightened on mine. "That is something, to have her tell you such a thing after what she has experienced in her past." For a few seconds, he was quiet, watching my face. I tried not to blink or look away, although it was difficult. Being subjected to such scrutiny was not something I was used to. "And you, Taryn? Do you trust me?"

"I wouldn't have let you kiss me if I didn't."

And then his arms were around me, and he was pulling me close. Our mouths met once more, and I let myself be lost in him, in the strength of his body and the taste of his lips. This was dangerous, I knew. If he kept kissing me like this, I was going to forget all about being careful.

I'd never been able to really understand letting passion overwhelm you to the point where you abandoned rational thought and allowed your emotions to take over completely. Because I was that crazy Oliver girl with the supposed psychic powers, I wasn't exactly someone who'd ever had a long string of boyfriends. There had been one or two, guys I thought I'd connected with but then realized were not compatible at all. Maybe I should have realized the first time I kissed those guys that it wouldn't work. There had never been fireworks.

Not like now. Just the way Gideon let go of one of my hands and trailed his fingers up my arm was enough to send a new set of thrills arcing and sparking through my body. The world was spinning around me, and I liked it. I liked being out of control. I'd spent so much of my life keeping everything locked down in order to preserve my sanity, and now I wanted to open myself to him and let fate decide what would happen next.

And yet...with everything that was going on, could I justify being that self-indulgent?

This time, he was the one to pull away from me, as if he'd detected a sudden shift in my expression or my body language. His fingers untangled themselves from mine. "Taryn?"

I didn't want him to think I was rejecting him. This had nothing to do with what I felt about him— or at least, what I thought I felt about him, since I hadn't had time yet to really sit down and sort through my emotions. This was everything to do with knowing that women were in distress, and my government was apparently complicit in their suffering, and I didn't know what the hell any of us could do about it.

"It's—" I'd been about to say that it was all right,

but it wasn't. Instead, I reached out and took one of his hands and held it, staring down at the faint greenish hue of his skin in contrast to my own ivory-pale fingers. His flesh was cool against mine, but not unpleasantly so. "It's just that I feel so helpless right now."

He pulled me against him, not to kiss me, but to hold me close, to wrap his arms around me. Was that something instinctive, or had his mother hugged him, showed him something of what human closeness was supposed to mean?

"You're not helpless," he said, his voice a low, comforting murmur against my hair. "I saw the fire in your eyes when you faced me down back at the ship. A helpless woman would not have been able to muster that kind of defiance."

Had it been defiance? To me, it had felt more like desperation. After all, he'd literally had me backed up against a wall. And that was where the Reptilians probably thought they had all of us now—backs to a wall, no real choice but to go along and pray that their horrible harvest wouldn't touch any of us personally.

"What do you think I should do?"

"What you're doing already," he said. He did release me from the hug then, but gently, and he still remained standing very close. "What all of you are doing. Trying to find a solution. You're not willing to stand by and let this happen. That's the important thing, isn't it?"

I reached up to push some of his heavy, wavy hair back from his forehead, then ran my hand down his face to cup his cheek. His eyes closed briefly, as if in pleasure, but then they opened again, focused on me, on the expression I wore.

"No," I said sadly. "The important thing is actually *finding* a solution, not trying to find one."

He went silent then. I think he knew he couldn't really argue with that statement.

CHAPTER THIRTEEN

ALTHOUGH WE WERE BOTH SUBDUED AFTER THAT, WE also realized we needed to eat something. Gideon again told me I should choose, since he wasn't familiar enough with our food to guess one way or another.

So I ordered from the Mediterranean place, mostly because shawarma and rice pilaf and roasted vegetables sounded good. While we waited for the food to arrive, Gideon helped me set the table, interested in the ritual of it, his fine, sensitive hands running over the edges of the plates as he set them down on the tabletop. They were beautiful, local handmade stoneware glazed in dark red and a warm teal color, and I'd always sort of secretly coveted them, hoping that one day I could have something similar in my own house.

There was wine in the little countertop rack in the

kitchen, but I didn't bring it out. I wasn't the sort of person who thought a meal was incomplete without a glass of wine to go along with it. Also, Gideon and I were already having a difficult enough time maintaining even a semblance of self-control. I knew where all this was eventually going to end up...but I also knew that I wanted to be with him when the time was right, and not because we'd both had too much to drink with dinner and had lost our last vestiges of self-control.

I did put out the wine goblets, though, just because they were lovely Mexican blown glass, their edges a deep ruby shade not too far off from the color of Gideon's eyes. There was a pitcher that matched, and I filled it with ice water. That way, the table looked more festive, and maybe he wouldn't notice that we weren't drinking anything stronger than water.

But then, why would he notice? He hadn't been raised here on Earth, and most likely didn't know that much more about its customs than what his mother had taught him before she died. Somehow, I doubted she'd told him anything about the way many people liked to have wine with dinner. Why would she? When she passed away, he'd been far too young to know or care about such things.

I'd just set down the water pitcher when the doorbell rang. At once Gideon touched his wristband, activating his disguise. I flashed a grateful smile at him as I went to open the door, and he came up behind me so he could take the bags of take-out from the delivery man, leaving my hands free to wave my debit card over the reader he carried.

Once the transaction was handled, the delivery guy wished us a good evening and headed out. Even as I shut the door, I turned to catch Gideon sniffing appreciatively at the bags.

"What is this? It smells delicious."

"It is," I said. "It's beef shawarma and rice and vegetables. Oh, and some pita bread. I think you'll like it." I hesitated, a sudden thought hitting me. "Can you digest grains? I mean, you've never had any—"

"My digestive system is human," he replied. "It will be fine."

I couldn't help smiling in relief. "Well, let's get this dished up, and then you'll be able to find out for certain."

Serving bowls were already waiting for the food, so all I had to do was transfer everything from its plastic containers, then shove them back into the bag and hurry them off to the kitchen. That was something my mother had always done. We might have eaten take-out a good deal of the time—although not nearly as often as Callista's family—but it was always served up in nice dinnerware.

Gideon and I sat down. I hadn't been quite bold enough to light the candles in the centerpiece on the table, so the dining room was illuminated by the small wrought-iron chandelier overhead. Everything looked and smelled wonderful, but you couldn't exactly call it romantic.

Which was fine. There was enough unresolved sexual tension between Gideon and me that I didn't see the need to make it any worse. Besides, I really didn't know if he would have responded to those sorts of cues the way a regular man might. He wouldn't have the cultural context, and I honestly didn't know how much research he'd done into twenty-first-century American customs. Some, because otherwise he wouldn't have been able to get along as well as he had, but many of the nuances had to be lost on him.

Since he looked unsure as to how to begin, I went ahead and dished rice and vegetables onto his plate, followed by a good-sized helping of shawarma. While I was busy with that, he poured water for the two of us. I gave myself a more modest portion of food, although I had a feeling I'd probably go for seconds. It wasn't until the savory aroma reached my nose that I realized how hungry I really was. Things had been so chaotic that I hadn't even eaten lunch.

We both dug in. I saw Gideon's eyes widen as he took his first few bites, and relaxed slightly. It looked like I'd make the right choice, because he was eating with such appetite that I began to wonder if I'd ordered enough food.

After a moment or two, however, he began to slow down a little. "Sorry," he said, flashing me an apologetic smile. "It's been many hours since I last ate."

"It's fine," I told him. "I skipped a meal, too. It's been kind of a crazy day."

He stopped then, fork lowering to his plate, although he didn't scoop up any more food. "Has it? I'm afraid I don't have much context for what would have been a normal day for you. Would you rather it had gone differently?"

"Oh, no," I said at once. I'd been startled to see him come walking into the shop—especially with his appearance altered—but once I'd gotten past the shock, I was happy to see him. More than merely happy. Relieved. I'd asked him to return me to my home, true. However, I'd begun to realize very early on that, while I was glad to be safely back on Earth, I wasn't nearly as glad to be away from him as I'd thought I would be. My talk with Callista had opened my eyes to that particular truth. But because Gideon was still watching me with concern written on his face, I hurried to add, "I wouldn't change a single thing about it."

His eyes lit up. They were now back to their normal reddish color, since he had no need of a disguise around me. "Neither would I." He paused then, shifting in his chair so he could look past me, in the direction of the creek. "I still don't know exactly what to do next, but I know that wherever my path leads, it won't be back there." A flicker of his eyes upward, as if to indicate the *Eclipse,* silently circling the Earth, undetected by any human instruments.

"No, your place is here with us now," I said, my tone fairly emphatic, although inside I couldn't keep myself from wondering if Lir Shalan himself intended to descend upon us in search of his wayward son. The creek was protecting us now, but we couldn't stay in the cottage forever. The alien leader wouldn't even have to come here himself; if he had the power to force our government to look the other way as his people helped themselves to the women they thought they needed, then he probably also had the power to send human agents after us, or at least request that they be sent.

I shivered, my fingers tight on the fork I held.

"He frightens you." It wasn't a question.

"Doesn't he frighten you?"

A shrug. Gideon's hand was resting against the stem of his water goblet, although he made no move to pick it up and drink. "Sometimes. Although before I couldn't fear him too much, because I knew I was too valuable to him. His efforts to produce more children with my mother were unsuccessful, but he had the thing he wanted—a son to take his name, to carry on his line. He knew I was irreplaceable, or at least he thought I was. Now, though…." Those words drifted into the silence that surrounded us; I'd forgotten to put on any music to accompany our dinner. Not that I would have had the foggiest idea what Gideon might have liked to hear.

"Now?" I prompted.

Another lift of the shoulders. He drank some of his water before replying, "Now he has access to human women. He can write me off as a failed experiment, and start over."

I stared at Gideon, aghast. "Do you really think he would do that?"

"Of course. From his point of view, it would be the logical thing for him to do. It is possible that he might attempt to convince me that I have made a foolish decision in rebelling against him. It is also very possible that he has already decided I am not worth the effort."

How could he speak so calmly of these things? Once Gideon had delivered that particular speech, he went back to eating shawarma as if we hadn't been discussing anything more important than the weather.

A question had been niggling at the back of my mind for a while, ever since I'd learned who Gideon's mother actually was. The time hadn't been right for me to ask it, and maybe it still wasn't right now. But I had to know.

"Are...are Reptilians capable of experiencing love?"

Gideon shrugged and finished chewing a mouthful of rice. "How do you define love?"

Well, there was a question. I certainly didn't think I was up to the task of quantifying love, particularly because it could wear so many different faces.

However, everything Gideon had told me so far made it seem as all his father's actions had been dictated by a driving need for power, or control, or even plain old survival.

"I think that particular task is beyond me," I began, speaking slowly as I tried to sort through my thoughts. "Generally, though, there's an element of selflessness involved, or at the very least a desire not to see harm come to the person you care about. But you're talking about your father as if he's capable of tossing you aside like a used candy wrapper or something."

"Are there not fathers here on your world who don't particularly love their children, who abuse them or neglect them?"

"Okay, yes, but—"

"So even though men like that exist, would you ever ask if the human race is incapable of love?"

"Of course not," I said, somewhat offended.

"Well, then." Gideon picked up his water glass and drained half its contents before setting it back down on the table.

"That's not the same thing, and you know it," I added, feeling the need to defend all humanity.

"Maybe it isn't." He shifted on his chair so he could face me a little better. "To clarify, no, the Reptilian race isn't known for outward shows of emotion. That doesn't mean they have no feelings."

I was probably pushing into an area Gideon would prefer to avoid, but I desperately wanted to know more about his mother, about what her life had been like after Lir Shalan claimed her. Maybe that was only because I wanted to believe that it hadn't all been misery. How else could she have been so loving toward her half-alien son? Gideon hadn't said much about her, but I was able to read something into those areas he'd left blank. Also, I couldn't understand how he could be so unexpectedly gentle and insightful if he hadn't learned such things from Elizabeth D'Onofrio.

"Did he love your mother?"

Silence. Since I was watching him closely, I could see a muscle twitch in his cheek, see the hard lines of his throat as he tensed, then forced down a swallow of water.

"Why do you want to know that? What does it matter?"

"It matters because it must have mattered to you."

Another long pause. His fingers tapped against the base of his water glass, and I noticed that he wouldn't look at me. Not directly, anyway. I was able to catch a sidelong flicker of those deep-set garnet eyes before he returned to playing with his glass.

At last, he let out a breath. "I don't know about 'love.' That is a strong word. I think he had some affection for her."

Not the answer I wanted to hear, but I supposed it could have been worse. "How so?"

"If he'd been truly indifferent, he would have had

no reason to interact with her at all, except those times when he was trying to conceive another child. But he would come to our quarters and spend time with us, and ask her how I was faring."

"So he allowed her to raise you?"

"I lived with her, yes." This time, Gideon did meet my gaze fully. He looked dry-eyed and sober enough, but the tension I'd seen earlier was still obvious in the way he sat almost too straight in his chair, in the carefully controlled timbre of his voice. "He had many concerns which claimed his attention, you understand. I was tutored by his science officer, Sal Galen—who is now is second-in-command—and Lir Shalan also spent an hour or so with me each day, so he could ask me about my lessons and assure himself I was making adequate progress. As for my mother...."

"Did he ever see her, other than the times he came to check on you?"

"Occasionally. It was a treat to be invited to his quarters, because he had one of those observation windows there. I looked forward to those visits, since they gave me a chance to look out at the stars, or at whichever new planet we were orbiting. Usually, my mother would bring me, and the two of them would talk."

"About?"

A faint smile touched Gideon's lips. "I don't really recall. I think I was so busy looking out the window, or playing with some of the gadgets he had lying around, that I didn't pay much attention. I usually had a good deal of restless energy stored up after being kept in our suite for so much of the time."

Considering I'd spent a good chunk of time myself locked up on a Reptilian ship, I could sympathize, and I wasn't a young boy, someone who should have been able to go outside and run and play to work out his wiggles. I nodded, and he went on,

"But I remember them sitting down and talking quietly. And once—" He stopped then, and I gave him an inquiring look. "Once I remember her sitting fairly close to him. I think she was upset, although I don't know about what. Then Lir Shalan pointed at me, and she smiled at him. And he put an arm around her and held her close for some time."

Offering comfort, I supposed, although the Reptilian leader seemed about the least comforting person I could think of. Had he shown her even that small measure of affection because he'd truly felt it, or only because he'd analyzed the situation and determined that she would best react to a show of compassion, whether feigned or not?

Based on what I'd seen from Lir Shalan so far, I was inclined to lean toward the latter option. I didn't say that to Gideon, though. If it felt better for him to think that his father had cared for Elizabeth, even a little, then I wasn't going to speak up and try to change his mind. What point would that serve? Gideon had already decided to side with his human half...or at least gave every indication of doing so.

"That sounds...nice," I said, then wanted to wince at the banal words. But I really didn't know how else to comment without sounding skeptical.

"More surprising than anything else, I think. It was the only time I'd ever seen him do anything like that."

"But he did do it. That must have meant something."

Another of those half-smiles. I didn't know Gideon well enough to understand for sure what that expression meant, whether he was attempting to smile for my sake, or whether he couldn't muster the enthusiasm for anything more than that meager gesture. "Possibly. She was already ill then, although she did her best to keep her condition from me. I remember how she would be sick in the mornings for weeks, and then she would disappear for a few days and be brought back to our suite, thin and white and with very little energy."

"Gideon—" My voice broke on the syllables of his name.

He shook his head, that slight motion telling me that he needed to go on. "At the time, I wasn't sure exactly what was wrong with her. It was only later that I realized she was with child and then would lose it, over and over again."

I hated to ask. I shouldn't ask. But somehow, the

question came out in the barest whisper anyway. "How many times?"

"Eight, I think. And after the last one...." Gideon's gaze was fixed somewhere off in the distance, as if he couldn't bear to see the pity in my eyes. "Well, at least Lir Shalan allowed me the opportunity to say goodbye to her."

We both were quiet after that. I knew somehow he didn't want to hear any useless words of condolence from me. She was long dead, and nothing I said now could change that fact. My appetite had fled, but he finished what was on his plate, clearly not wanting to be wasteful.

Afterward, he helped me take the dirty plates out to the kitchen. I could tell he wanted to change the mood of the evening, because he watched with some fascination as I rinsed them off and put them in the dishwasher.

"That seems rather inefficient," he remarked. "To use so much water."

"What do *you* do?" I asked, slightly irritated on behalf of Earth's technology. After all, it was a very new dishwasher, with the latest water-saving design. Kara and Kirsten were nothing if not environmentally conscious.

"Put our used plates and utensils in the recycler. They're broken down into their component atoms and then reconstituted when we have need of them again."

Slick, but as advanced as I generally tended to think my planet was, I knew we hadn't quite reached that level of technology. Rather than trying to defend planet Earth, I instead held one of the plates in my hand and turned it over, watching the way the over-head lights brought out a subtle iridescence in the glaze before I bent and put the plate in the dishwasher. "Well, I could never do that. Someone made these by hand. They deserve to be taken care of and used over and over again so they know they're loved."

Gideon didn't reply at first. One of the serving bowls was still sitting on the counter; he picked it up and ran a finger over the gleaming surface, seeming to trace the slight irregularities in its contours. Then he set it down again and turned toward me. "Yes, I think I can appreciate the idea of showing love for something so beautiful."

Our eyes met. Even though my hands were wet from holding them under the faucet, he reached out and took them, pulling me toward him. In the next instant, he was kissing me, mouth insistent on mine. Not that I minded. I wanted this, wanted to taste him again, press my body to his and feel the strength in his arms as they wrapped around me. Once again, that delicious, insidious heat worked its way through me, telling me that this was all right, that I should be with him completely. Who had I been saving myself for, if not for him?

But somehow I managed to pull away, although

my breaths came far too fast and I could feel the way my hands shook. "Gideon, I—"

"What's the matter?" His expression became all concern, his eyes scanning my face to see what he'd done wrong.

"Nothing's the matter. It's only…." I had to let the words fade away, because I truly wasn't sure if I would be able to adequately communicate my concerns to him. "It's just that this feels so very important to me. I don't want to rush it. Does that made any sense at all?"

At first, I was fairly certain it didn't, because his brows pulled together and the puzzled light in his eyes didn't go away. But then he nodded. "Yes, it does. I understand that whatever it is we share, it's something that should be savored. I just wanted to make sure you didn't think I was trying to pressure you because of—well, because of what happened up there." His gaze flicked upward and back to me.

So he was worried that I thought he was still trying to carry out his father's wishes? "Oh, no, I wasn't thinking that at all," I said quickly, and some of the tension went out of his body. "It's more that I'm having a hard time putting on the brakes myself, so to speak. I want to be with you, Gideon. But at the same time, something is telling me that it would be better to wait, if only for a little bit longer."

Those last words seemed to cheer him, because an actual smile touched his mouth this time. "I can wait for as long as you need me to, Taryn."

I took his hand then. Not to pull him close to me again, but to hold and feel its very human shape, feel the strength and comfort in even that small touch. It was good.

And for right then, it would have to be enough.

We finished the clean-up—what there was of it—and headed to the living room. I'd never been that much of a TV-watcher, preferring to read, but watching television seemed to be the safest thing to do right then, since it was way too early to even think about going to sleep. And I figured that whatever we did settle on to watch, it would be educational for Gideon, and might help to take his mind off the dark memories our dinner conversation had awakened.

Luckily, I was able to locate a somewhat silly but entertaining space opera, complete with improbable light-speed and laser guns and everything else. Gideon watched with his brows drawn together in concentration, although I saw him shake his head from time to time when the action got completely hyperbolic.

"Can you stop this for a moment?" he asked me partway through the proceedings.

"Sure," I said, then picked up the remote and hit "pause." "What is it?"

"People who watch this don't believe any of it, do they? The science is completely fabricated."

"Of course not. It's just for entertainment." I set the remote in my lap and gave him a closer look. Wisely, he'd sat down in the accent chair to the left of the couch. I think it would have been too much for either of us to handle if we'd been sitting next to each other on the sofa. "I would have thought your people would study our movies and television to gain a better insight into how we think."

"We do, somewhat." His gaze shifted to the screen where a fighter ship was frozen, flashy magenta bolts of energy firing from its guns. "But I must confess that I've never seen anything like this."

"Not even in real life?" I asked, teasing him just a little. "You mean real outer space isn't like that?"

"No," he said, his expression quite serious. "The worlds of the Assembly are peaceful, for the most part. In fact, what conflicts do exist—" He stopped there, looking slightly shamefaced.

"Let me guess. It's the Reptilians who stir up most of the trouble?"

"They would never admit to that, but an impartial analysis would suggest that they tend to be the instigators more often than not. Of course, they'll always claim that they were the wronged parties, but…." He gave a shrug, although I noticed how he looked away from me, as if even that small admission had been too much of a betrayal. "Anyway, I will try to look at this as pure entertainment."

"Good idea," I said, unpausing the show so it could continue to play.

However, when I stole a glance at him later, his expression had turned brooding, and I noticed that his gaze was not fixed on the television screen, but on the window. The curtains had been drawn, so there was really nothing to see.

And yet he still kept watch, as if he worried that someone—or something—might be coming for us at any moment.

CHAPTER FOURTEEN

SLEEP APPARENTLY DID NOT WANT TO BE MY FRIEND THAT night. I tossed and turned, moving from one position to another as I tried to find the one that would magically send me off to slumber-land. That wasn't like me, as I usually had no problem falling asleep. Actually, as my mother liked to point out, getting up in the morning was my problem, not getting to sleep.

At last, I lay on my back, eyes wide open, as I stared at the ceiling. Was it simply knowing that Gideon was right across the hall that had me so wakeful? He'd been quiet and subdued after we finished watching the show, and had been quick enough in the bathroom before slipping into the guest bedroom. A quiet "good night," and then he was gone, the door shut behind him.

Shut, but not locked. I knew I could get up and go in there, and....

No way. Not after all that talk about how important it was to wait. In that moment, I was having a hard time determining exactly why my forbearance was so important. I could still feel his lips against mine, his arms around me. I wanted more than that. I wanted all of him.

That was a huge step to take, though. Going to bed with Gideon wasn't exactly the same as sleeping with one of my high school boyfriends. There was no one else like him in the world—in the galaxy, I supposed. He'd turned his back on Lir Shalan, but I had to be sure of him. No, wait…I was sure.

Or was I?

Damn it.

His unease had bothered me, too. That could have been the simple paranoia of anyone who'd had the misfortune to be raised by the alien leader, but I wasn't sure. Gideon had almost acted if he expected something terrible to go wrong, even though we should have been perfectly safe here.

Well, I could always do a little reconnaissance to be sure. No, I wasn't going to put on my robe and slippers and go wandering around in the middle of the night…but I thought my astral self always could. That seemed safe enough.

I began the breathing exercises, putting away the stress and tumult of the day so I could focus only on the necessary separation of my consciousness from my body, could find the stillness to send my spirit out and away from this room.

Yes, there was that strange little *pop*, and then I was drifting upward, staring down at myself as I lay there in bed. I did look very peaceful, eyes shut and curly hair spread over the pillow in its usual mess.

And then I thought of Gideon, lying asleep—at least I hoped he was asleep—in the bed across the hallway.

No, I told myself. *You will not. Because that's just creepy.*

With something like the ghost of a sigh, I moved further upward, going through the lumber and composite shingles of the roof so I could emerge into the night air. It must have been fairly cold by then, despite how mild the day had been, but I couldn't feel the wind, could only sense it because I saw the branches of the trees moving, young leaves fluttering in the moonlight.

I could also sense the creek. It seemed to call to me, and I moved in that direction, drawn by the glitter of the fast-moving water between its banks. Once there, though, I couldn't feel anything else, only the low-level thrumming energy that always seemed like a deep bass note plucked once and allowed to keep on vibrating forever. The creek was safe, just as it always had been, and its pulsing power drifted over the cottage and to the houses on either side. They were all close enough to the creek to share in its blessings as well.

Reassured that all was well here, I began to move back toward the cottage, sailing serenely over the treetops, moving higher and higher. I'd done this several times before, drinking in the beauty of Sedona at night, reveling in the majesty of the red rock bluffs by moonlight. Their colors might have been subdued by the darkness, but when the moon was bright enough, it brought all their edges into sharp relief.

And then suddenly I wasn't sailing, but was being drawn forward, past the cottage, over the blur of lights that was the highway, out toward the north and east.

Toward Secret Canyon, and the aliens' base.

I resisted, tugging backward, but I might as well have been a swimmer caught in a riptide for all the good that did. Gasping, I fought, my astral body writhing against the unseen force. Somehow, I knew that if it managed to pull me all the way to the base, I would never be able to escape.

And Lir Shalan's voice in my head, amused. *Did you think I didn't know about this little trick of yours? I allowed it on board my ship because I wanted to see what you would do with the knowledge you acquired. As it turned out, that wasn't very much at all.*

Let me go, I gritted. At the same time, I couldn't help but be grateful that my astral self was dressed exactly the same as I'd been when I went to sleep, in leggings and a baggy T-shirt. I didn't have to worry about wriggling around in midair in a filmy nightie or something,

Oh, I think not, Lir Shalan replied. *I'd rather see if you're able to free yourself.*

Another few seconds of struggling seemed to indicate that I couldn't. An astral self couldn't exactly become out of breath, but for some reason, I was beginning to feel winded. *How can you do this?*

I am, as your people like to say, a man of many talents. These talents are very rare, and this is why I command. Surely you must know something of this, as my predecessor had similar powers. Or did Kirsten Jones not speak of it? I can see why she might have been ashamed.

Yes, because the former alien commander had basically attempted to mind-rape her. I wasn't about to tell Lir Shalan that, though. *I guess it never came up,* I said, still trying to pull away. To no avail; now I knew what it must feel like for a flood victim to be swept up in a river's current, realizing in despair that it would be impossible to break free and make their way to the safety of the shore.

Ah. A pause, and then he said, tone silky, *There is no reason for you to fight. I don't intend to harm you.*

Oh, really? I shot back. *Then what do you intend?*

I wished I hadn't asked the question. Because then my mind was flooded with—well, not exactly images, but impressions. Sensations. Lir Shalan taking me because his son had turned out to be worse than useless. I, on the other hand, could be useful. My psychic powers could be joined with Lir Shalan's, creating a child who would be worthy to be his heir.

The denial burst from my throat in a tearing scream, one that had no words, only a single long, drawn-out cry of negation. And that scream seemed to shake me loose from his mental grasp, propelling me back toward the cottage as if I'd been shot from a cannon. In less time than it took to blink, I was slammed back into my body. My eyes flew open, and I pulled in a deep, hitching breath, my pulse thundering along every vein.

Had I screamed aloud? If I had, surely Gideon would have come rushing in here to see what was the matter. But the house was still and quiet around me, the only sound the faint whispery scratch of the willow tree outside as its branches trailed against the window, blowing with the night wind.

With shaking hands, I pushed back the blankets and duvet cover, and swung my legs over the edge of the bed. They felt just as shaky as my hands, but I forced myself to get up and make my way out to the kitchen. I'd left the under-cabinet lights on, just in case Gideon had wanted to wander out here and get himself a midnight snack or something. Now I was glad of their warm glow, glad that I hadn't been forced to walk into utter darkness.

I went to the cupboard and got out a glass, then poured myself some water. For a second, I considered the wine in the pantry, but just as quickly, I put that thought away. The last thing I needed right then was to weaken my thoughts with alcohol. Yes, I was shaken—and shaking—but I needed a clear head.

"Taryn?"

I whirled, heart pounding all over again, but it was only Gideon, standing in the doorway to the kitchen, his expression puzzled.

"What's the matter?"

"I—" I drank some of my water, hoping that would help to settle me down, remind me that I was now here in the cottage, far away from Lir Shalan's reach. But it really didn't help that Gideon was standing there in only his underwear and a T-shirt. His legs were long and strong and more muscular than I'd imagined they would be. "I had a bad dream," I said quickly.

His brows drew together. "Are you sure it isn't more than that? I can see your hands trembling from here."

Damn it. Part of me had already resolved not to say anything about what had happened, but I knew that was no solution. Gideon had already broken from his father, true. This information wouldn't change anything, except possibly to harden his resolve.

I recalled what Lir Shalan had said about Kirsten Jones, about how she probably hadn't said told anyone about the previous base commander's threats because she'd been ashamed. Well, that same sort of humiliation preyed on me now. I didn't want to tell Gideon what his father had said because I hated to admit that he even dared to think of me in such a way.

But if I kept quiet, Lir Shalan would win.

"It was more than a dream," I said then, after taking a fortifying swallow of water. "I can do something called astral travel. It involves projecting my consciousness from my physical body so I can move around by spirit only. I did it on your ship many times."

Gideon's eyes widened with shock. "You did? How often? When?"

"I can't remember exactly how many times. Probably at least ten or twelve, I think. And it was at various times…mostly when I'd been left alone for a while and was bored out of my mind."

He shook his head. "I am sorry about that."

"It's all right. I survived. But…." I let the words trail off as I warred with myself. Should I tell him that I'd witnessed that dreadful scene between him and his father? I doubted Gideon would be happy to know that I'd seen him in what he probably considered to be a moment of terrible weakness. On the other hand, if I was going to be honest with him about the dreadful encounter I'd just had with his father, then I should be honest with him about everything.

"I saw you," I went on after a long moment. I made sure to keep my voice soft, as if that would make what I was about to say any less difficult for him to hear. "That time when your father confronted you. I saw him hit you."

A wince, but Gideon didn't say anything. He only

stood there, mouth tight and eyes wary, as I continued,

"He was giving you grief about not trying to sleep with me, wasn't he?"

That question shocked him out of silence. "Taryn!"

"Well, he was, wasn't he?"

"Yes." That single syllable was so weighted with pain and anger that I almost hoped he wouldn't go on. But he did, telling me, "Let's just say he didn't appreciate my reticence. He'd certainly had no such scruples when my mother came into his possession."

"And that's why you were so angry." I paused, then added, "And why you knew you couldn't keep me there, not when you recalled everything your mother had gone through."

"Yes."

He looked so stiff and angry and yet sad that I wanted to go to him and wrap my arms around him. But that was far too dangerous, with him standing there in just a pair of dark briefs and a T-shirt.

I pulled in a breath, knowing that what I was about to tell him was far worse than the ground we'd already covered. "So I went down to the creek to look around—"

"In your astral body."

"Right. I drifted around for a bit, then came back toward the house. But as I came close, something grabbed me and began to pull me away. It was incredibly strong, and no matter what I did, I couldn't seem to break loose from it. It began to pull me toward the abandoned base."

"It was my father." The sentence was uttered so flatly, so utterly without surprise, that I stumbled for a second before replying,

"Yes, it was. He was in my head somehow, talking to me." I paused, then asked, "Do all Reptilians have that kind of talent?"

"No. That is, they can manage some forms of nonverbal communication, but what my father did—exerting his will in such a way that it acted on yours —there are very few with that sort of skill. It is part of the reason why he is the leader here. He can control those under him with his mind."

A shiver went over me, and I had to keep myself from snapping that maybe it would have been a good idea if he'd warned me about some of his father's hidden talents. "Do you have it?"

Gideon shook his head. "No, I did not inherit that gift. I suppose part of the reason he wanted me to—to be with you was he hoped I carried that particular gene dormant within me, and it would combine with your own considerable psychic gifts to create an unusually gifted child."

"About that—" I stopped then, knowing I had to go on with my story and really wishing there was any way to avoid it. "Lir Shalan was attempting to draw me to him so he could take me for himself. He said you'd proved yourself to be useless, and he'd decided it would be better for me to have his child."

Red fury glared from Gideon's eyes, and I had to force myself to remain where I stood and not back away from him. "He said that to you?"

"Yes." I didn't bother to sugarcoat it. That really was what Lir Shalan had said, more or less, and his son had a right to know.

Green-skinned hands knotted into fists, but Gideon didn't move. I saw how his chest rose and fell, the way he was trying desperately to contain his anger. I waited for him to regain some control, knowing that he had to fight this battle himself.

After a long moment, he said, "But you got away."

"I think it was his gloating that worked against him. He made me so angry and frightened that I was able to summon the strength to break free of him and come back here. I fell back into my body, and that was the end of it."

Gideon didn't say anything at first, only went to the window and separated two of the blinds' slats so he could take a look outside. What he expected to see, I wasn't sure. Hordes of advancing Reptilian soldiers?

But no, they couldn't come here because of the creek. Then again, it hadn't done such a good job of protecting me when I was in my astral body. Maybe it could only keep me safe when I was in my physical form.

Either way, I didn't plan to go astral walking again anytime soon.

Then Gideon turned away from the window and took a long look at my face. Something in his expression softened, and he came to me at once, his arms going around me before I could protest or attempt to pull away.

Not that I really felt like doing either of those things. After what I'd just been through, I couldn't think of anything better than having Gideon hold me, of feeling safe in his embrace, even if that safety might not be quite as assured as I had hoped it was.

"You're all right," he said, breath warm against my hair. "You're here with me. I won't let him hurt you."

I buried my face in his chest and breathed in the warm scent of his T-shirt. Or was that halfway familiar fragrance only the subtle and very welcome smell of his skin? I didn't know, and right then, I didn't care. I just wanted him to hold me like this forever.

But even as I reveled in his closeness, the worry came over me again.

Could he really keep me safe? Would I be safe anywhere?

Eventually, we both went back to bed. As much as I would have liked him to crawl into the queen-size bed in my room and stay there with me, I knew I couldn't give in to that urge. After that encounter with Lir Shalan, sex was probably the last thing on my mind, but who knew how I'd feel when I woke up in the morning? Better to avoid temptation altogether.

I did sleep at last, though, and didn't open my eyes until almost eight o'clock the next morning. Faint sounds drifted in through my partway-open door, and I realized Gideon must have been in the bathroom across the hall, taking a shower.

My mental state was still unsettled enough that I only allowed myself a brief image of what he might look like in that shower before I pulled my robe off the hook on the back of my bedroom door and then tied it around myself. I didn't exactly have a headache, but my head was throbbing faintly. I needed some tea.

Getting the hot water going and rummaging through the collection of tea boxes in the pantry helped me to feel a little more normal. As I waited for the water to boil, I went to the window and twisted the wand for the blinds so I could get a look outside.

Warm light slanted across the backyard, and a small, delicate breeze was playing with the leaves on the trees. There was absolutely nothing out there that looked threatening in any way, and yet I still couldn't keep a shiver from passing through my body. The sun was shining, and it looked like a beautiful day, but I was scared spitless to go outside the cottage.

You don't have to, I told myself. *You can just stay here all day and....*

And what? I knew the longer Gideon and I were in each other's laps, so to speak, the harder it would be to resist him. At that point, I wasn't even sure why I was bothering. Yes, Lir Shalan had wanted me for his son, and I hadn't wanted to do anything that would make him happy, so delaying any intimacy with Gideon had seemed like the best thing to do.

But now it appeared that Lir Shalan had decided he wanted to take me for himself, in which case it seemed a better idea to thwart him by being with his son.

That's still playing into his hands, I scolded myself. The water began to boil, so I went over and shut off the gas, then poured some hot water into the mug I'd set out on the countertop. *Whatever you do, you need to do it for you, and for Gideon.*

I couldn't really argue with that. I also couldn't argue with the realization that every time he held me, every time he kissed me, I wanted him more and more. It wasn't as if I'd been holding on to my virginity because it was some precious thing. I was only still stuck with it because I'd never had the right person cross my path.

Now I was sharing a house with him. What the hell was I waiting for?

From out in the dining room, I heard a faint *bing!* and realized it was my phone, lying where I'd left it on the side table the night before. I hurried out to retrieve it, and saw that I'd had a text from my mother.

I just wanted to check in and make sure everything was going okay with you two. Do you need anything? Your father would like to stop by later if you're going to be around. He and Lance had a convo last night, and he wants to update you on some things. I'd come, too, but I have a client flying in later this morning.

Did we need anything? The food situation wasn't great, especially when it came to dinner, but we didn't have to leave the house to get take-out. I supposed I could have asked for some basics to throw together a meal, but the truth was, my mother had never really showed me how to cook, since she wasn't exactly an expert in the kitchen herself. It was probably better to stick with take-out meals. At least that way, I wouldn't have to worry about poisoning Gideon.

So I texted back, *No, I think we're okay. What's going on in the outside world?*

No reply at first. I didn't think much of it, because my mother tended to send a text and then get distracted by something else. While I was waiting for her to get back to me, I took the phone and headed into the kitchen, figuring my tea should be about ready. I'd just lifted the mug to my lips when my phone binged again.

Too much to go into in a text. Your father wants to know if he and Lance can come over around 10.

That sounded ominous, although it was probably better for them to come here. I didn't really feel like subjecting Gideon to the carefully organized chaos of Lance and Kara's house, which was usually where any important conversations concerning our group or UFOs took place. And even though the words had been framed as a request, I got the feeling this was more of a command performance.

Sure, I texted back. *We can be ready by then.*

I'll let him know. XOXO, Mom.

She always signed off like that. I'd tried to tell her that no one really did that in texts anymore, but she'd just laughed at me and said she was too old and set in her ways to change. Which was actually kind of silly, since she was only in her mid-fifties.

Gideon came into the kitchen then, wearing one of his new pairs of jeans and a dark blue T-shirt. This one seemed a little tight on him, but I didn't mind, since it showed off the nicely defined contours of his biceps.

I caught myself staring and said quickly, "Um, my father and Lance Rinehart are coming over later this morning. I guess they have some things they want to talk to us about."

"All right."

He didn't seem particularly fazed by that information, so I asked, "What do you think they want?"

"Well, I assume they have new information. I doubt it'll be anything pleasant, though."

Thank you, Susie Sunshine, I thought. But then I realized he was probably right. With everything that was going on, the chances of the news being unpleasant were pretty high. Figuring we'd find out soon enough, I said, "Tea or coffee?"

"Wasn't that tea we were drinking yesterday?"

"Yes, the iced version. People generally drink it hot in the morning, though."

Apparently the hot variety didn't appeal to him any more than the iced kind, though, because he replied, "I'll try coffee, I think. I've heard a great deal about it."

"Don't believe the hype," I said, and he frowned.

"Do you think I won't like it?"

"I don't know. You don't seem to like tea that much, and coffee has a much stronger taste. But you're down here on Earth, so you might as well try new things."

Our eyes met as I made that remark, and a little shiver went down my spine. Oh, I'd like to try all sorts of new things with him, and if the need that had awakened in his expression was any indication, he was certainly open to new experiences as well.

My cheeks flushing furiously, I went to the pantry and got out the bag of French roast I found there. At least I did know how to make coffee, even if I didn't drink it all that often. It was something I could do for my father when he was buried in a book, trying to meet a deadline.

As I busied myself with getting the coffeemaker going, I said, my tone probably too casual, "Did you ever have your food synthesizer make Earth-style breakfasts? Eggs, toast, that kind of thing?"

"Bread, no. It did not do well with complex carbo-hydrates. I did have eggs." His eyes closed briefly, as if he was recalling a pleasant memory. "And bacon."

It seemed his taste buds were human enough. But there hadn't been any bacon in the care package my mother had sent over with me. Oh, well. Maybe I'd send a text later and see if my father could stop on the way over and get us an emergency supply.

"No bacon, unfortunately. But I'll make some eggs and toast. Maybe the toast will be a treat, since you haven't had much bread in your life."

He didn't seem too disappointed by that prospect. "That sounds very good."

So I got busy with putting a simple breakfast together, and when it was done, we sat down and ate it at the dining room table. Gideon appeared to enjoy everything, even the coffee. I didn't have too much time to savor my meal, though, because the hour was inching toward nine o'clock, and that meant I didn't have a lot of time to shower and get myself together before my father and Lance showed up. Since Gideon was already dressed, I told him he could watch some TV if he wanted while I was getting ready.

"Of course," he told me, and took his freshened-up cup of coffee with him into the living room.

I hurried off to take my shower, glad that it seemed as if it was going to be another mild day, which meant my hair shouldn't take interminably long to dry. Even so, I went as quickly as I could, rushing through the shower and the toothbrushing and all the other things I had to do to get ready. Since it was just my father and Lance, I didn't worry about primping, but just scrunched some product into my wet hair to keep it from frizzing, then put on some colored lip balm and a single coat of mascara.

When I headed back out to the living room, it was five minutes until ten. Not too shabby. Gideon paused the television and turned toward me. He must have been watching how I worked the controls the night before. "You look very well."

I smiled, but thought the compliment was a little misplaced. I hadn't done that much to get ready, and only had on some jeans, a tank top, and one of my denim shirts on over that. But I still thanked him, then said, "We might as well turn that off. They're going to be here any minute."

Gideon obediently picked up the remote and shut down the TV. Not a moment too soon, because in almost the next instant, the doorbell sounded. My heart started to beat a little faster, which I thought was kind of silly. I'd known Lance all my life.

True, I thought, as I opened the door, *but Gideon hasn't.*

My father and Lance came inside, and Lance stopped in the little entryway, his gaze fixed on Gideon.

"So," he said, "this is the alien."

CHAPTER FIFTEEN

"HALF-ALIEN, LANCE," MY FATHER SAID, HIS TONE MILD enough, but there was an undercurrent of steel to it nonetheless. Not that he and Lance didn't see eye to eye on a lot of things, but my mother had probably filled him in on the situation with Gideon and me, and my father wasn't about to let anyone diss his only daughter's boyfriend.

Or whatever Gideon was to me.

He got up from the couch. His expression was nearly impossible to read, but I could feel a pulse of irritation come from him before it was quickly clamped down. "I am Lir Gideon."

"Gideon, this is Lance Rinehart," I put in, even though that was stating the obvious. "He's an old friend of the family."

"Emphasis on the 'old,'" Lance said. He didn't crack a smile. When he got like that, I always had the hardest time trying to figure out whether he was joking or not. But then, he'd had military training in remote viewing, which also meant that he'd learned some insanely rigorous mental controls. He was another person I couldn't read, his thoughts clamped down so tightly that nothing ever slipped out.

"Um, I thought we could sit at the dining room table," I said. "There really isn't enough space in the living room."

"That's fine, Taryn," my father replied. He didn't say anything else, but his expression appeared somewhat relieved.

We all went into the dining room, although I didn't sit down immediately. Instead, I told everyone that I'd bring some glasses and water. That was about all I had to offer when it came to entertaining, but I figured it would suffice. My father and Lance weren't exactly here on a social call.

I fetched the pitcher and four glasses, then sat down opposite Gideon. Lance and my father had already taken their respective positions at the head and foot of the table.

"So," I said, after everyone had some water and I'd set the pitcher down on the tabletop, "what have you found out?"

"Nothing good," my father said grimly. "We got the network on alert and received reports of about eighty fresh disappearances overnight, most of them here in the U.S., but a few in Central America and also in Australia. The word had gone out to tell people to take precautions, but of course we can't reach everyone."

"And there are way too many people who don't believe anything is going on at all," Lance commented with a twist of his mouth. His silver-gray eyes had always looked cold to me, but now they appeared positively glacial. "They all think because something isn't on the news or on the internet, then it can't actually be happening." He shifted in his seat and pinned Gideon with that icy stare. "So, how many of our women *do* your people plan to abduct? Your ship's going to get full pretty quickly at this rate."

If I'd had Lance glaring at me like that, I doubted I would have been quite so composed. But Gideon only lifted his shoulders and said, "As I am not privy to Lir Shalan's plans, I can't say for sure. The *Eclipse* —that is their ship—is large enough to hold thousands. There is also the possibility that they are only holding the women in orbit here until another ship can come to take them away. Again, I can only speculate, because I was not included in any of these plans."

Lance's eyes narrowed. He hadn't missed the way Gideon had referred to the Reptilians as "they" rather than "us." Whether he truly believed that Gideon had switched sides was a whole other story.

"In slightly better news," my father said, "we were able to get a small team from Caltech to come out here and take a look at Gideon's transporter/comm device. They arrived late last night. Jeff definitely came through for us on that one."

Jeff Makowski, a computer hacker that my father had known for longer than I'd been alive. For someone who was, by all accounts, pretty damn anti-social, he did seem to be connected to a lot of people.

"Did Jeff come with them?" I asked. I sort of wanted to see the legend in person. He'd come to Sedona just a few months ago, to help hack into one of the alien's handheld computers, but he hadn't hung around long enough for me to meet him.

"No," my father replied. He didn't say anything else, but he didn't really need to. I'd caught flashes from him before on the subject of Jeff Makowski, so I knew that Jeff had had some sort of crush on Kirsten back in the day, and hadn't been too thrilled when she'd gotten together with Martin instead. And apparently that old wound hadn't healed very well, because Jeff had quarreled with Kirsten when he was here in December, and departed in yet another huff.

It was understandable, but I was still a little disappointed.

"I got them set up in a maker space off Coffee Pot Drive," Lance said.

"'Maker space'?" Gideon repeated, obviously confused.

"A shop with equipment like 3D printers and CNC machines, that sort of thing," my father explained. "People pay a monthly fee so they can come in and use the equipment to fabricate things they need."

Gideon nodded in comprehension, and Lance continued, "The maker space has a good deal of the equipment the group from Caltech might need, and we'll bring in anything else if necessary. I pointed out to Paul that it would have made more sense to take the device to them in California, but he wouldn't hear of it."

"I didn't think it was a good idea to send it out of Sedona." My father's gaze flicked toward Gideon and back over to me. "It's irreplaceable. Better that we have it someplace where we can keep an eye on it."

"Thank you for that," Gideon said. "I would have been...uncomfortable...knowing it was so far away."

My father didn't quite smile, but I saw a corner of his mouth twitch, as if that was his way of saying "I told you so" to Lance. "Not a problem," he said. "About all we can do now is wait, though, and hope it won't take too long for them to figure out how to reverse-engineer the device."

He sounded hopeful, but even the brain trust from Caltech that was on the case couldn't guarantee results in anything close to a timely fashion. And in the meantime, women would continue to disappear while the world's leaders sat back and considered their loss a fair bargain in exchange for Reptilian tech. If it was even the people at the very top who were calling the shots. I couldn't speak for every country around the world, but in the United States, it seemed that half the time, the left hand didn't know what the right was doing.

"Perhaps I could go help," Gideon said. "I'm not a scientist or an engineer, but I am more familiar with the technology than your scientists would be."

"Not a good idea." Lance's tone was flat, and he sent a not-quite-derisive look in Gideon's direction, clearly taking in the green skin and dark red eyes. "We'd have a hell of a time explaining you away."

"They wouldn't have to know." Although Gideon appeared calm enough, I heard an edge to his voice and knew that he wasn't overly thrilled with Lance Rinehart. "I can easily walk among you." His finger swiped over the metal stud on his leather bracelet, and at once he looked like a perfectly normal human, skin tanned and healthy-looking, eyes dark brown.

Lance didn't exactly let out a whistle, but he leaned back in his chair and nodded. "Nice trick. It could come in handy. But even if your appearance didn't give you away, there's too much risk that they'd figure out you're a little too familiar with the Reptilian tech to be a plain old human being. Better for you to stay out of their orbit. If something comes up that gets them really stuck, I'll pass it along."

"If that's what you wish."

"It is."

"Isn't there anything else we can do?" I asked, feeling almost as helpless as I had the night before, when I'd been caught in Lir Shalan's mental version of a tractor beam. "What those scientists are doing is great, but it could take days, or weeks."

"I know, Taryn," my father said. "The problem is, even if we could get every single person in all our UFO networks to work together, we don't have any real power. Yes, we've finally been proven not to be utter crackpots, but none of us hold public office. A few are in the military, but I guarantee that the rank and file—and probably everyone except those at the very top—don't have any more idea of what's going on than the regular person on the street."

"And when someone tries to get the word out, it gets pulled almost as soon as it goes up," Lance added. "A lot of our people have their own internet channels, so they figured that would be the best way to spread the word. But they'll no sooner post a video than it's nuked. Some of them have had their channels shut down altogether and had their accounts yanked. The people keeping a lid on this are too powerful...and there are a lot of them."

I slumped in my chair. Across the table, Gideon watched me with worried brown eyes. They didn't seem quite as unfamiliar now, probably because I knew their shape even if the color was different. Besides, that had been the color of his mother's eyes. From the way he shifted his weight, I had the impression that he wished we didn't have the table separating us, so he might reach out and take me in his arms, give me what comfort he could.

Or maybe he was just wishing that my father and Lance weren't there.

"Taryn, I know how you feel," my father said. "But you have to be patient." He glanced over at Gideon. "I know you said you weren't included in your father's—"

"Lir Shalan's," Gideon corrected him. He sounded calm enough, but there was something in his tone that made it clear he wouldn't be contradicted.

"Lir Shalan's plans," my father went on. "But can you make any kind of educated guess as to how many women would be adequate for his purposes? Are we talking several thousand here? Ten thousand? More?"

Gideon didn't answer right away. His fingers rested at the base of the water glass before him, but he made no move to pick it up. "Their race is very depleted. It's something they've managed to hide from the Assembly for some time, but their numbers are nothing close to what they once were. Because of that, and because this is such a hit-or-miss way of reproducing, I would guess that they would need far more than a few thousand. A hundred thousand?" I gasped, and he sent me a sympathetic look before continuing. "Perhaps a million?"

"That's impossible," Lance said, but the worried flicker in his eyes seemed to indicate he wasn't completely certain, despite his denial.

"Is it? There are how many people here on Earth?"

"A little less than eight billion," my father replied, since Lance didn't seem inclined to answer.

"What is a million, measured against that number? A few drops of water in an ocean."

"These are *people*," I argued. "Not drops of water. They have friends, family who will miss them. Lir Shalan can't possibly think he can take that many without *someone* noticing."

"People are noticing, and yet nothing has changed," Gideon said. His tone seemed cool enough, but I could see the compassion in his eyes, feel it radiating out from him. He wanted to comfort me. The problem was that he had nothing comforting to say. "I doubt there's much we can do—except hopefully come up with a way to create a device that will block their conveyors."

I didn't reply, because it seemed as if every protest I could devise was immediately shot down. All right, there were people in charge who were doing their very best to carry out the Reptilians' agenda. But still, there were far more of us than there were of them. If enough people rose up, something would have to change.

Then I realized I was contemplating an all-out revolution, which I knew was completely crazy. Even if it was somehow possible to get any kind of momentum going for that sort of uprising, I had no doubt that it would be quashed quickly enough. And that would mean even more people hurt. No, I feared that Gideon was right. We needed to cut the Reptilians off at the knees rather than march in the streets and demand justice.

Still, I found myself praying that when this was all over, the people who'd brokered this unholy deal would get what was coming to them.

———

Since we didn't have much more ground to cover, Lance and my father left soon after that. I'd decided not to mention what had happened the night before with Lir Shalan. It would only make my father worry that much more, and there wasn't anything he could do to help. I did contemplate whether I should say something to my mother, just because she'd had some luck in getting rid of the aliens years before. Unfortunately, even though she'd been the one to accomplish that seemingly impossible task, she still couldn't say how she'd managed it. According to her, the power had been fueled by her rage at my father's death, and had blasted out of her without her really knowing how.

Yes, my father had technically died at that base. Luckily for all of us, he hadn't stayed that way for very long, thanks to Raphael's intervention.

I looked out the front window as Lance's Jeep reversed out of the driveway, then turned back toward Gideon, who stood a few feet away. He must have touched the wristband he wore while I wasn't looking, since now he looked like his normal self.

"Well, that was depressing," I said.

At once, he came to me and folded me into his arms. I leaned against his chest, glad for the pillow of muscle, the comforting sound of his heartbeat. "I know, and I'm sorry. But I did not see the point in uttering platitudes. Your father and Lance—and everyone else—need to know what we're up against."

"You're right, I know." I took in a breath and let it out again, the sound too soft to be a sigh.

He passed a hand over my hair, then said, "Why don't we walk down to the creek? It looks like a beautiful day outside, and I know that being by the creek comforts you."

That did sound like a good idea. I could go outside, get some sun, try to shake the cobwebs loose from the corners of my brain. I tilted my head so I could smile up at him. "How do you know me so well?"

"Because you make it so easy." He squeezed my hand, then let go of me so we could head out through the kitchen and down the back steps, then on through the backyard and onto the path that led down to the creek.

Yes, it was a beautiful day. A few lazy clouds moved overhead in a sky so deeply blue it looked as if we were standing inside a hollowed-out Hope diamond. The breeze was fresh, but not too cold, nothing that my denim shirt couldn't handle. And the bright new green of the leaves on the trees comforted me, letting me know that spring would always come again, no matter what else might be going on in the world...or the galaxy.

We came down to the creek, which was chattering away as usual, sunlight dancing on the water as it passed over a small collection of projecting stones just slightly upstream. A few yards away from the spot where the path ended was a large, flat rock. I headed over there so I could sit down, and Gideon followed, his footsteps crunching on last year's dead leaves.

For a few moments, neither of us said anything. I wanted to sit there and breathe in the fresh air, let the soothing currents of the creek work their magic on me. From far overhead I heard the cry of a hawk, which immediately silenced the frenzied little chirps of a bunch of finches clustered in the next tree over.

As I sat there, though, I realized the creek wasn't helping as much as I'd thought it would. Yes, it did feel good to be outside and away from the rather cramped quarters in the cottage. Kara and Kirsten had done their best to make the place cozy and inviting, but they couldn't change the fact that the little house was barely more than a thousand square feet, which felt tiny to me compared to the home where I'd grown up. However, I'd been expecting a little something beyond just getting some fresh air. The tones of the creek, which usually calmed and comforted me, sounded more accusatory than anything else. It seemed as if it was speaking to me in a language that I should have understood but which continued to elude me.

This time, the sigh I let out was clearly audible.

At once, Gideon reached out and took my hand in his. "What's wrong?"

"I don't know." I paused then, trying to gather courage from the sensation of his strong fingers wrapped around mine. "I thought this would help—being by the creek, that is—but all I can do is sit here and think that I must be missing something."

"What do you mean?"

I didn't answer immediately. My gaze was fixed on the water, the way it reflected the sunlight and moved both over and around the stones on the stream bed. I stared so hard that the scene became blurred, the flashes of light morphing into glittering spheres, rather like the otherworldly orbs I'd seen floating in the more desolate areas outside Sedona proper.

But those shapes didn't coalesce into anything resembling a rational pattern. They shattered and burst apart, flying outward like a supernova. I blinked, and Gideon said,

"Taryn?"

"I'm all right." I blinked again and shifted on the rock so I was facing toward him, rather than in the direction of the creek. "It's just that I keep feeling as if the creek's trying to tell me something, and I'm too stupid to understand."

"You are not stupid." He raised my hand and kissed it gently. Warm shivers rippled all through me, like sunlight on water. "You are intelligent and brave and beautiful."

At another time, I probably would have protested that compliment. I really wasn't used to men saying nice things to me. Right then, though, it was good to have the reassurance. "Really?"

"Really." He turned my hand over so the palm faced upward, and traced my life line with one finger. Had his mother told him about palm reading, about how we humans attached a lot of significance to those lines and squiggles on our palms? I supposed it was possible, since it sounded as if she'd been like many of the New Age types who came to Sedona looking for enlightenment. Sometime soon I'd have to look at his palm and see if it carried those same telltales. "Taryn, you can't take the weight of the whole world on your shoulders. Many people are working on this problem. Its solution doesn't rest solely on you."

I knew that intellectually, of course. I didn't have the skills to reverse-engineer his "conveyor" device, and I wasn't someone who could go into the wilds of the internet and quietly get the word out to as many people as possible. Maybe I'd been born with some special talents, but they didn't seem to be doing me much good at the moment.

Gideon stood up then, pulling me with him. Just as well, because that rock got cold after a while, even if you happened to be sitting on it in jeans rather than in shorts. His eyes searched mine, looking for what, I wasn't sure. In the hope that his words might have reassured me, if even just a little bit?

But then he bent and kissed me, his lips warm and welcome. I melted into his embrace, wanting to lose myself in the feel of his arms, the taste of his mouth. And as heat flared all through me, I knew exactly what I wanted most.

"Make love to me, Gideon," I whispered.

He pulled away slightly, eyes widening with surprise as he gave a quick glance around us. "Here?"

I couldn't help chuckling. "No, it's probably better if we go inside. But," I went on, my expression sobering, "I want to. I want to be with you."

Apparently, he needed no further reassurance, because his hand closed around mine and we hurried up the path back to the house. Once we were in the kitchen, I'd barely closed the door and locked it behind us before Gideon's arms were around me again, only this time lifting me clean off the floor.

I let out an excited little laugh and allowed him to carry me from the kitchen, through the dining room, and on into the short hallway where the bedrooms were located. He hesitated in the hall for a second, a flare of uncertainty touching my mind, and I said, "My bed's bigger."

He answered with a quick flash of a grin, and then went into my room, where he lowered me gently onto the bed. In the next instant, he was on top of me, his weight pushing me down into the mattress as his mouth found mine again. The fire in my blood roared at the sensation of his body pressed against almost every inch of mine, even though we were still both fully clothed.

Well, I thought I should do something about that.

I grasped two handfuls of his T-shirt and pulled it up and over his head, then had to keep myself from gasping out loud. The clothes he wore had always hinted at his shape but didn't tell me all that much. Now I could really see the defined muscles of his arms and chest and stomach, perfect as if he spent hours at the gym every day—except I knew he didn't. Was that what having some Reptilian DNA thrown into the mix could do for you?

His fingers found the snaps on my shirt, so I didn't have time to speculate further, could only suck in a brief shocked breath as his hands touched the bare flesh of my stomach. Now his skin felt very warm, or maybe that was my own flush. Either way, I reveled in the sensation of his hands moving upward, the strength in his touch.

And then he paused when he reached my bra. For a second, I worried that he would stop altogether, that he still wasn't sure how much I wanted this. But then his hands moved to the front clasp and unhooked it, and I realized he'd only hesitated because he wasn't sure where to unlatch the bra.

His fingers closed around my breasts, and I made a sound halfway between a gasp and a moan. I'd wanted him to touch me like this, but I really hadn't known what to expect, wasn't sure if he would be hesitant, or unsure.

I certainly didn't sense any uncertainty about him now. His breathing quickened, and he moved from my mouth to my neck, kissing his way down so his lips could fasten on a nipple, suckling, even as the fingers of his free hand found the button of my jeans and popped it loose.

Then he slipped under my panties, sliding into me. Ah, God. Shimmering, pulsing heat, concentrating at the very center of my being, all awakened by Gideon's touch. This time I moaned loudly, unable to keep silent as his fingers stroked me, slipped deeper. I'd gone this far before, but it had never felt this way with Noah, my last boyfriend. Not even close. I clung to Gideon, knowing the climax was going to hit me very soon.

Which it did, rippling through me as the world spun in a mad dance and my body clenched around his long, strong fingers. He kissed my neck gently, cradling me as the last of the shudders rippled through my body.

"That was…all right?"

"More than all right," I replied, my voice breathy, hoarse. "It was incredible."

"Good."

I could hear the relief in his voice, could feel it rippling out from him. He'd been afraid that he would disappoint me somehow. Later, I'd have to ask him how he'd known to touch me exactly that way, but for now I only wanted to return the favor.

His flesh was warm and smooth beneath my lips as I kissed my way down his body, drinking in the beauty of his sculpted chest and stomach. I could hear the breath escape him as I undid the buttons on his jeans and pulled them down, but he didn't try to stop me.

The bulge in his underwear was larger than I'd expected, and I pulled in a nervous little breath, even though I had no intention of turning back now. Before I could lose my nerve, I grasped the waistband of his briefs and eased them down over him, then flung them over the side of the bed, where they landed on top of his jeans.

Damn. In the back of my mind, I'd worried that maybe this one part of him somehow wouldn't be human, but now I knew I needn't have worried. Even so, he was very big, so big that I had a hard time wrapping my fingers around him all the way.

As soon as my hand closed on his shaft, he groaned, a shudder moving through his body as I began to work him up and down. Not too hard or too fast, because I wanted this to end with the two of us fully together...even if his size worried me a little.

"Taryn...."

My name was barely more than a sigh on his lips. The sound of it made a rush of need course through me, and I knew I wasn't going to delay the inevitable for too long. I did want to taste him, though, even though I felt a thrill of nervousness at the same time. I'd never done this before, and I wanted to make sure it was right for him.

After taking a breath, I brought him into my mouth. He groaned again, his body shuddering at the feel of my lips wrapped around him. His skin was like silk against my tongue, the texture finer than I could have imagined. I wanted to keep going, but I could feel another of those shudders run through his body and I had a feeling that I needed to stop there.

So I lifted my mouth from him. He sighed, but then he was moving, shifting so I was buried beneath him, his lips against mine as he caressed my breasts again. There was something almost reverent in his touch, as if he couldn't quite believe he was here like this with me in his arms.

He pushed against me, so hard, so ready, but then he paused. "Are you sure, Taryn?"

"Yes," I said, gazing up into the beautiful wine-colored depths of his eyes, garnet and ruby and rich, rich carnelian. "I've never been more certain of anything in my life."

A moment that seemed suspended in time as he stared down at me, our naked bodies touching but not joined. And then he drew in a breath, and pushed into me with one quick thrust, as if he under-stood it was better to do it that way rather than ease in.

The pain came and went so quickly, I hardly had time to register that I'd experienced it at all. He began to thrust in and out, but not too hard, instead in a gentle rocking rhythm that took him deeper and deeper into me. I wrapped my legs around him, pulling him in even closer, savoring every move-ment, every pulse.

His breathing began to speed up, and I knew it wouldn't be long for him. I hadn't really expected to climax this first time, but it still felt good, felt more right than anything else I'd ever done.

And then he convulsed, driving into me with one last thrust, a groan of sheer animal ecstasy tearing itself from his throat. I clung to him, holding him close while the orgasm thundered its way through his body. He continued to gasp while we lay there for a long moment, neither of us wishing to break the contact.

At last, though, he pulled away, shifting his posi-tion so we could hold one another until our breathing quieted. I knew in a moment I would need to get up, go to the bathroom so I could clean up the inevitable aftermath, but right then I wasn't sure I'd be able to move.

His hand moved over the tangled mass of my hair, his touch so tender it almost made me want to weep. "How beautiful you are."

"So are you," I whispered, snuggling close to him. "Perfect in every way."

"Even though I'm half alien?"

"Because you're half alien," I replied. "Because otherwise, you wouldn't be you."

He didn't reply at first. His arms tightened around me, and he pushed a lock of hair aside so he could place the softest, most feathery kiss in the world on my temple. "I love you, Taryn Oliver."

My heart stopped, shuddered, then remembered to keep on beating. "I love you, too. I think I began to even when I was still on the *Eclipse*, only…."

"Only?"

"Only I didn't want to admit it to myself. It was what your—what Lir Shalan wanted, and I couldn't give in to that."

"Ah." The syllable was hardly more than a sigh, a drift of warm breath against my hair. "He did not want us to be in love, Taryn. He wanted us to have sex. Love can make people unruly, uncooperative."

I supposed I could see that. Two people in love were far more likely to do whatever was necessary to protect one another, and Lir Shalan couldn't have liked that idea very much. "So the two of us falling in love was probably the last thing he wanted?"

"I believe so."

"Good," I said, desire stirring in me as I moved closer to him. My hand drifted lower, feeling how he was almost ready again. "Then make love to me again, Gideon."

CHAPTER SIXTEEN

EVEN THOUGH IT WAS ONLY MID-AFTERNOON, WE DOZED a little in one another's arms afterward, then finally got up and took a quick shower together, the two of us laughing as we tried to negotiate the cramped space. The shower stall had definitely not been designed for more than one person to occupy it at a time, but we struggled along as best we could, neither of us wanting to be separated after sharing such intimacy.

Once we were dressed, we headed out to the kitchen. Lunch was long overdue, but the meager assortment of items in the refrigerator didn't appear terribly appealing.

"Let's go out," Gideon suggested, and I shot him a surprised look.

"Do you really think that's safe?"

"I know it is," he replied, closing the refrigerator

door and taking me by both hands. "It's broad daylight. Lir Shalan won't attempt anything, even with the two of us away from the protection of the creek. And I think it would do us both good to get out for a while."

"Afraid I'll drag you back into bed?" I teased, and an amused glint entered his eyes.

"Afraid? Hardly. But I do think it would be a good idea to get something nourishing to eat before we attempt a third round."

I could only laugh and shake my head at that remark. But his words had given me an idea. I realized there was someplace where we could go to have wonderful food and still be protected by Oak Creek.

"Sounds like a plan. I know exactly where to go." He raised an eyebrow, and I went on, "A place called Hideaway House. We can sit on the deck and be only a few yards away from the creek."

"The perfect solution."

So we finished getting tidied up, then went and got in the car. This time, instead of taking my usual position behind the steering wheel, I got in the back seat. Looking a little puzzled, Gideon followed, then nodded to himself after he settled down next to me. After I'd told the car where we were going, I leaned against the seat back, my hand resting in Gideon's as we were driven out onto the highway.

The drive over to the restaurant would take about ten minutes, so I figured that gave me enough time to ask the question that had been burning in my mind ever since we'd made love. It wasn't the sort of thing I really wanted to discuss in a restaurant, but you didn't get much more private than the back seat of a car.

"So…how did you know exactly what to do?" I asked. "I mean, you've never been with anyone else, have you?"

"No," he said. I'd been expecting that reply, but I still relaxed slightly once he'd told me so emphatically. Maybe it was silly to think that way, but because he'd been my first, I wanted to be his first, too. He went on, "Where would I have had the opportunity? You were the only human woman I'd ever met, except for my mother. No, Lir Shalan wanted to make sure I knew what to do when the time came, and so he provided me with some of your world's erotic films. They did make…interesting viewing."

If I'd been drinking something, I probably would have choked. As it was, my words still sounded a little strangled. "Your father supplied you with *porn?*"

"Well, can you think of a better way to learn about human sexuality, if one has no access to the real thing?"

He had a point. That is, I knew that the vast majority of pornographic materials didn't exactly provide a realistic view of human sexual relations, but I supposed you could learn the basics from them, even if the real thing was very different in terms of nuance and emotional connection.

"Not really," I admitted. "Better that than on the street, I suppose."

Gideon shifted slightly so he was almost facing me. "This bothers you?"

"No." Was that the truth, though? He'd only watched those things for informational purposes. It wasn't as if we'd been dating and he'd been secretly getting his rocks off on internet porn. "I get it. And... I suppose I'm glad. Being with you was amazing."

He leaned over and kissed me, lips warm against my cheek. A slow-burning fire roused in my belly, and I moved so we were really facing one another, mouths meeting, tongues touching. I started to wonder if we'd end up having sex there right in the back seat of the car, but then he pulled away.

"We had better stop," he said. "Or I'm not sure I will be responsible for my actions."

"You say that like it's a bad thing."

A quick glance downward at the noticeable bulge in his jeans, and he shook his head. "It's probably not a very good idea to walk into an eating establishment looking like this."

I couldn't help chuckling. "True. Well, we've got a few minutes until we get there. Just think about something very unsexy so you'll be socially acceptable."

He shook his head and looked out the window. "The best thing is for me to watch something other than you, because when I see you, I can't help thinking about all the things I want to do to you."

Well, damn. A delicious shiver went over me, and I said, "Not helping. You're getting me all hot and bothered, too."

"At least on you it doesn't show."

True. I moved slightly so we weren't sitting quite so close to one another, and he did the same. The rest of the drive passed in silence, which was probably just as well. Gideon and I didn't seem to be too successful at sticking with safe topics of conversation and would only keep getting each other in trouble.

When we pulled into the parking lot, it was only half full. Not that surprising, since it was almost three-thirty by then, in the no-man's-land between lunch and dinner. We didn't have any problem getting one of the more desirable seats out on the deck, where the murmur of the creek drifted up to us from many feet below.

"It's beautiful," Gideon said, gazing past me to the vista of red rocks off to the east.

"I thought you'd like it."

It did make me feel better to know we were so close to the creek, that it would protect us here just as it had back at the cottage. Yes, everyone said that Lir Shalan and his people wouldn't make a move during the daylight hours, and they were probably right. The Reptilians had always worked in stealth, in darkness. But now that they were out in the open, were looked on as the people who'd saved the Mars

mission astronauts, who knew what kind of maneuvers they might pull? They were certainly bold
enough to be stealing women at an alarming rate.

"I think I would like a glass of wine," Gideon
announced as he looked at the menu.

"Really?" I said, amused. "What brought
that on?"

"It's just that I've never tried it. Bourbon, yes, but
people often drink wine with their meals, don't
they?"

"Oh, yes," I replied. "Some of them more than
they should, probably."

"You don't drink?"

"It's not that I don't drink," I told him, trying not
to sound defensive. "It's more that I need to keep
things sort of locked down, so to speak, so I'm not
constantly being inundated by other people's
thoughts. One glass of wine isn't too much trouble,
but anything more than that, and my control begins
to slip."

"Ah." He was quiet for a moment, seeming to
consider what I'd just said. "But one glass is all
right?"

"Usually, yes."

"Then have a glass with me now. Shouldn't we be
celebrating?"

I supposed we should. He loved me, and I loved
him. That knowledge wouldn't fix the problem with
the Reptilians, but it did do a lot to improve my
overall outlook on life.

The waitress came by and asked if we'd like anything to drink. I quickly glanced over the wine selections, then told her I'd like a glass of pinot grigio. Gideon ordered a malbec. After the waitress had left, I tilted an amused eyebrow at him and asked, "Why malbec?"

"I liked the sound of the word."

I couldn't help chuckling. Of all the reasons I'd heard for choosing a drink, that was a new one to me.

Then I heard a familiar voice say, "Taryn?"

I turned in my seat and saw the hostess leading Callista and Raphael out onto the deck. What in the world? That is, I knew that the two of them went out to eat almost every day, since Callista's culinary skills were even more nonexistent than mine, but I didn't really want to calculate the odds of us running into one another out of all of Sedona's numerous restaurants.

Her gaze fastened on Gideon, and she raised an eyebrow. He'd activated his disguise, of course, and so looked just as human as anyone else you might meet on the street, but I could tell that she'd realized who he was. Raphael's gaze sharpened as well, and I guessed that the two of them had just shared one of their rapid nonvocal conversations.

"How about we join you?" she asked then. "Do you mind?"

"Um—"

"Of course you may join us," Gideon said politely. Even though this was the first time he'd encountered the couple here in Sedona, he'd seen both of them when Callista was called in front of the Assembly to make her statement about the accidental death of a Reptilian soldier at her hands. So he knew exactly who he was inviting to sit down with us.

Since Gideon and I had taken the seats closest to the railing when we first sat down, it was easy enough for Raphael and Callista to sit in the vacant chairs next to us. The hostess looked a little puzzled, but only said that the waitress would be back to get their drink orders as well.

"So," Callista said, once we were all alone, "what brings you out this fine day?"

"The same thing that brings you here," I replied. "An overwhelming urge to avoid cooking."

She laughed. "Okay, true. We went to a gallery earlier—they had a new installation, and wine and cheese and all that stuff—and we sort of forgot about lunch. But we decided that wouldn't be enough to hold us until dinner, and we were driving by here, so...." A quick darting look at me, then at Gideon, as if she'd just guessed why we'd ventured out in search of food at such an odd hour. Her lips curved into a half-smile, and I knew she'd probably be calling me later to get all the details... not that I planned to kiss and tell. "Call it serendipity."

I wasn't sure I'd call it that, but I didn't say anything, only nodded. Then the waitress returned so she could get Callista's and Raphael's orders. They requested wine as well, and the waitress disappeared once again so she could get all our drinks at once.

Since we were the only ones out on the deck, I figured it was safe enough to discuss topics I wouldn't have broached if anyone else had been around. "So, a gallery installation?" I asked. "With everything that's going on?"

Callista's lips thinned, but then she gave a philosophical shrug. "What do you think we should have been doing instead? My parents told me that Lance has a team working on Gideon's device"—she inclined her head in his direction, and he nodded —"and everyone's trying to get the word out as best they can. I guess I just don't think there's much else to be done."

Privately, I had to admit she was right. Again I had that sensation of missing something, however, as if voices were murmuring just out of earshot, saying things I should have been able to understand.

I couldn't reply to her remark right then, as the waitress came back with our drinks and asked what we wanted to order. None of us had really looked at the menu, but I more or less had it memorized anyway, and so ordered my favorite caprese sandwich, thus giving the other three time to peruse the offerings and make a quick decision. After we were left alone again, I looked across the table at Raphael, who met my gaze frankly, dark eyes knowing. He probably knew exactly what I was going to ask.

"Why can't we petition the Assembly and have

them step in? What the Reptilians are doing has to be against the Assembly's non-interference policies."

Raphael's fingers wrapped around the stem of his wine glass, but he didn't take a drink. "The Assembly doesn't have jurisdiction here because Earth is not a member world."

I shot a questioning glance at Callista, and she only shrugged, as if deferring to his greater knowledge of the subject. "But the Reptilians are members," I argued. "Shouldn't that be enough to warrant some kind of intervention?"

Next to me, Gideon shifted in his chair. Unlike Raphael, he did raise his glass and help himself to a sip. A flicker of his eyes, and then he nodded, apparently confirming something for himself. "Another reason why they cannot intervene is that the Reptilians' actions are sanctioned by your government, or at least by elements within it. The situation may be horrible, and it may be ugly, but it does not meet their requirements for stepping in."

Raphael nodded. "Gideon is right. Your people elect their representatives to speak for them. If those representatives do something terrible, well, that is between them and those who elected them. The Assembly simply does not have the jurisdiction to go against the will of the people."

"I'm not sure it's all our representatives," I said, speaking slowly as I mulled over the situation, trying to put together a pattern from the little I did know. "In fact, I have a feeling that most of them don't know anything about what's going on. There've always been elements inside the government who work independently and without much—if any —oversight."

"Oh, God, not that whole 'shadow government' thing again," Callista said sourly. For the first time, she sipped at her wine, as if she needed its taste to cleanse her palate of all the conspiracy-theory nonsense. "You sound like my dad."

"Or mine," I said, refusing to get angry. For someone who was mostly alien, and who'd been surrounded by the reality of UFOs for her entire life, Callista could be kind of hard-headed sometimes. Or maybe it was just that she didn't want to have to stop and think about the implications of what the existence of a shadow government might mean. "They both talk about it a lot. But they do that because it's true. Just because something is far-fetched doesn't mean it's not accurate."

"And it is all true," Gideon added. Callista's eyebrows lifted, and Raphael settled back in his seat, a frankly curious expression on his handsome features. "I know this because my fa—because Lir Shalan has had dealings with them."

"For how long?" I asked. The way he'd said it, this sounded like a long-standing relationship, not something that had only occurred in the aftermath of the Mars astronauts' supposed "rescue."

"For as long as I can remember. There are many things that go on without being detected—or at least, not detected by the general public. The Reptilians were driven away from Sedona, but they did not leave this system."

"Well, obviously," Callista remarked. "That Mars base looked pretty well established."

"There was that base, true," Gideon said. "And also one on the dark side of your moon, which made meetings here on Earth easier to manage."

I wanted to ask more, since the possible existence of an alien base on the moon's dark side was something that had been hotly debated in UFO circles for years. But the waitress appeared with our food then, and conversation had to be put on hold until after she'd left again.

Gideon ignored his plate of roasted chicken, however, and went on, "The rescue of the Mars astronauts merely gave Lir Shalan the opportunity he needed to bring things more out in the open. What he needed next—the women who've been disappearing —was something that couldn't be accomplished merely by means of the same back channels he'd been using for years. That would require more people to be brought into the conspiracy."

"And they went along with such a despicable plan, just like that?" Callista asked. Her own Roma-style pizza sat neglected in front of her as she stared across the table at him, challenge clear in her gaze.

"I wouldn't say it was 'just like that,'" Gideon replied calmly. "But once they were convinced of the value of the technology the Reptilians would be providing, their doubts were pushed aside. It's easier to overlook the lives of a few thousand when millions—or even billions—more are in the balance."

Time to ask the question that had been in the forefront of my mind ever since I'd learned of the Reptilians' plan. "Just what kind of tech were they promised, anyway?"

"Clean, renewable energy," he said. "And beyond that, the principles behind our superluminal drives. There were many who thought it a fair exchange."

Yes, I supposed they would. We'd made a lot of advances in the last few decades, using the sun and the wind and the power of water to generate a larger percentage of the world's energy. But we hadn't given up entirely on fossil fuels, and all those other means of producing energy had their own drawbacks. So I didn't doubt for a second that some of the people making decisions behind the scenes would have sold out their own mothers for access to an easy source of endless energy with none of the pitfalls of more conventional sources. Adding some kind of faster-than-light space travel to that was just putting the cherry on the cake.

"Damn," Callista said. She took a large swallow of wine, followed by another. I had a feeling she needed it to steady her nerves after Gideon's revelation.

"Damn, indeed." Gideon picked up his fork and sampled some of the roasted squash on his plate. It seemed to meet his approval, because he nodded and speared another piece.

"So that is the problem, Taryn," Raphael said. "This is not the Assembly's fight, even though any of its representatives would be the first to agree that what is happening here on Earth is a terrible tragedy. But I fear it is your—that is, our—tragedy."

"So it's up to us to stop them." I stared down at the sandwich on my plate, my appetite fleeing. Nevertheless, I made myself pick it up. If nothing else, I needed to find some way to replace some of the energy I'd used up earlier in my exertions with Gideon.

I couldn't really read Raphael, not the way I could most people, but you didn't need to be a psychic to see the compassion on his perfect features. And I did appreciate that "our," even if he'd had to correct himself as he was speaking. He'd chosen Callista, and he'd chosen to live here on Earth. That meant he was as bound up in its troubles as the rest of us, although the two of them did have an option that most of the rest of us didn't. If things got bad enough, they could just...leave.

They wouldn't do such a thing, though. At least, I was fairly certain they wouldn't. And I certainly didn't have that option. Even if I did, I wouldn't choose to exercise it. This was my home. I'd fight for it, no matter what it took.

Down below, the creek rustled, water flowing swiftly over the smooth-worn stones of its bed. The conversation around me seemed to fade as the sound of the rushing water filled my head, echoing with power, moving over and around me. It was such a tangible thing that I could almost feel it brushing against my skin, could almost see the energy flashing and swirling along its surface, like a million fireflies holding their own very special kind of dance.

Through the rippling echoes of the water, I thought I vaguely heard Gideon's voice. "Taryn. *Taryn!*"

I blinked, and saw all three of my companions staring at me with various degrees of consternation in their expressions. "What?"

Gideon's eyes were narrow with concern. "Is everything all right?"

"Why wouldn't it be?"

"You went all zone-y," Callista said. "Like you were having a vision or something. Your eyes are still sort of glassy. What was it?"

"I don't—I don't know," I replied, reaching for my wine glass so I could take a bracing swallow, or at least as bracing as pinot grigio ever was. "I heard… something. But it's all fading now."

"It wasn't…it wasn't *him*, was it?" Gideon asked, his voice pitched low. But Raphael caught the question anyway.

"Who?"

"Lir Shalan," I said wearily. "We had sort of a run-in last night. But I'm fine. Anyway, it wasn't him. He couldn't do anything to reach me, not this close to the creek." The creek. There it was again, that murmur in the background. I knew it had reached out to me, but again, I wasn't smart or psychic enough to understand what it was trying to say.

"A *sort* of run-in?" Callista demanded. "Do your parents know about that?"

"No, and I'm not telling them. It was a stupid mistake. It won't happen again."

She and Raphael exchanged a look. Again I got the impression that they were communicating without speaking aloud, but my psychic powers apparently weren't the sort that was able to pick up their frequency unless they deliberately opened the channel, the way Callista had that one time.

"Taryn escaped unscathed," Gideon said, and I wanted to hug him for coming to my defense. "She saw no need to worry her parents unnecessarily, not when they have so many other matters to occupy their minds."

"Hmm." That was all Callista said. Her bright blue eyes were full of speculation, though, as if she was trying to decide if there was something more to my reticence beyond a simple desire to avoid freaking out my parents any more than they already were.

There wasn't, really. And that encounter had been a valuable one. It had told me I wasn't safe anywhere, that I had to be on my guard at all times. Not that I expected any trouble here; as I'd told Raphael earlier, we were too close to the creek for Lir

Shalan to try anything, even if he was bold enough to have his minions make an attempt to snatch me during daylight hours, in a very public place.

But I wasn't sure if I would ever feel safe on my own again.

CHAPTER SEVENTEEN

THE REST OF OUR MEAL WAS FAIRLY SUBDUED, AND afterward we said our goodbyes and departed in our respective vehicles, Callista and Raphael making a far better show in his sporty red BMW convertible than I did in my older Honda. Gideon didn't seem to notice the disparity, though, only got in the back seat and waited for me to join him.

"Do you want to tell me what happened in there?" he asked quietly as the car pulled out of the parking lot and headed toward home.

"Nothing happened," I said.

His raised eyebrow was eloquent, and I let out a little sigh.

"I don't know what it was. Like the creek was talking to me, but once again, I couldn't understand what it was trying to say. And it was as if I could see the power in it, like bright sparkles of light dancing all along its surface. Not like sunlight, though. Something stronger, but at the same time diffuse." I pulled at one of the curls hanging over my shoulder, watching as it went nearly straight under the tension, then bounced back as soon as I released it. "That probably doesn't make any sense."

"Not completely, but I'll admit I don't know all that much about this creek of yours."

"It's not my creek."

"I'm not so sure about that. It seems to have some sort of connection with you, even if you haven't figured out yet how best to work with its energies."

That was a tactful way of describing the situation. Since I wasn't sure how to respond, I only reached over and took Gideon's hand, held on to it like a lifeline as the car maneuvered through the thick West Sedona traffic and then eventually pulled off into the sleepy neighborhood where the cottage was located.

Everything looked the same, although I had to admit to myself that I didn't know why I thought it would have changed. We got out of the car and went inside, neither of us speaking. It wasn't until I'd dropped my purse on the dining room table and began to head into the kitchen in search of water that Gideon said,

"Have you asked your mother for help?"

Puzzled, I turned back toward him. He stood just inside the front door, arms crossed, his brows pulled together in an abstracted frown.

"My mother?"

"Or Kirsten Jones."

"Why?"

"They drove out the Reptilians before, didn't they?"

"Well, yes, but…." We'd been over this ground already. My mother hadn't really known what she was doing, had acted out of instinct. Or, more to the point, something seemed to be acting through her. As for Kirsten, she had the aliens right in front of her, itching for a fight. It was easier to take on your foe when you knew where to find them. All right, I knew more or less where Lir Shalan and the rest of his cohorts were located, but since I didn't have a space- ship, heading into orbit and confronting them was going to be a little difficult. "This is entirely different. For one thing, they're no longer occupying a base here."

"That you know of."

His remark, offered so casually, made the hair on the back of my neck stand up. Could Lir Shalan have slipped back into the base out in Secret Canyon without anyone knowing? That would make our encounter the night before all the more telling. He'd been able to intercept me because he wasn't on his ship at all, but lurking nearby.

I shivered, and at once Gideon was there next to me, pulling me close, holding me against him so I could breathe in the warm scent of his skin, drink in his nearness.

"I'm sorry," he said. "I didn't mean to frighten

you. But we must accept that as a very real possibility. Now that he knows he has the backing of your government, or at least certain elements in it, he can afford to be bolder."

"Why, though?" I asked. "That is, why would he feel the need to be here at all? The base has been defunct for longer than I've been alive. It certainly isn't going to offer the sorts of comforts or resources he's used to on the *Eclipse*. Unless he's got engineers working in there to get the labs up and running so they can make more hybrid soldiers, I just don't see the point."

Gideon pulled away slightly so he could gaze down into my face. I saw tenderness in his eyes, but also genuine worry, a clawing fear that he wouldn't be able to protect me from his father. His hand cupped my cheek, and he said, his voice barely a whisper, "I think there's a very real point. I think you know exactly why he's here."

I swallowed then, and couldn't come up with anything to say.

———

At sunset, I walked down to the creek. Gideon tried to stop me, saying he didn't think it was a good idea for me to be going anywhere alone. He was probably right. But I couldn't get rid of that nagging sensation at the back of my brain, the one telling me there was something horribly important that I'd overlooked.

I somehow knew I needed to be by myself. Gideon's presence was a comfort, but sometimes just having another person around was enough to keep me from being able to concentrate fully. And if Lir Shalan was strong enough to overcome the energy of the creek and still swoop down and grab me, then I knew I truly wasn't safe, no matter where I was or who I was with.

The mildness of the day was slipping away as the sun set, but I was still comfortable enough in my shirtsleeves. A breeze ruffled my hair, playing with it and sending it to dance around my shoulders. I should have been calm, surrounded by the warm, slanting light of early evening, and yet every muscle in my body was tense, every nerve ending pinging with brittle energy.

I really didn't want to know if I'd come out here alone as a sort of challenge to Lir Shalan. The underbrush rustled to my right, and I came to a stop on the path, heart beating wildly—only to let out a relieved breath a moment later when a rabbit bounced out from under some sumac, paused right in front of me, and then took off again, bolting into the thick stand of cottonwoods to my left.

The rest of my short journey passed without incident, although I had to keep telling myself not to have a panic attack at every shadow of a bird that moved overhead, every rustle of the leaves on the trees. I wasn't alone out here at all; the wildlife of Sedona seemed to be keeping watch over me.

When I came to the bank of the creek, I stopped, then bent down and unlaced my shoes, pulled off my socks, and rolled up the legs of my jeans. Walking into the water seemed to have helped Gideon, and so I thought it was time for me to try.

The current that flowed over my bare feet as I ventured out into the creek was so cold that it made me want to gasp, but I gritted my teeth and ignored the discomfort.

"All right," I said aloud. "Tell me what you want."

Nothing, of course. Only the sound of rushing water and the wind rustling in the trees.

Except....

The tingling began in my toes. At first, I thought it was only my extremities going numb from the icy water, but then I looked down and saw a flare of light under the creek's surface, winding around my feet, then flowing up my legs, shimmering and a yellow so pale, it was almost white. The tingling moved up my body in sync with the movement of the light. It wrapped around my waist, then flowed up and over my chest and down my arms, flashing as it surrounded my hands.

I held them up, and light flowed between them. So strong, so bright, so powerful. I knew then what it had been trying to tell me. The power in the creek was the same power that was within me.

"Taryn!"

Gideon. I turned and saw him standing on the

bank of Oak Creek, eyes wide with surprise and something close to fear. There was no need to fear, however. The creek meant me no harm, and the energy rippling around me now was only a manifestation of the power I had carried within me all along.

"It's all right," I said, spreading my arms wide. "It can't hurt—"

I'd been about to say, *It can't hurt you.* But then the light flowed out from me and moved to envelop him, and I let out a gasp. He made some sort of exclamation—in his shock, it came out in the Reptilian language—just before his face lit up with wonder.

Because the energy, the light, whatever you wanted to call the manifestation—it was shimmering down his arms, just as it had with me. As if by some unspoken prompt, we both spread our hands toward one another. The energy jumped between them, like two poles on a battery making a connection. I could sense it thrumming in the space between us, vastly more powerful now than it had been just a moment before.

"Do you feel that?" I called out, my voice carrying over the sound of the water and the energy's hum, like the lowest note of a bass that had been plucked and continued to vibrate long after the string had been let go.

"Yes," Gideon replied. He didn't look quite as surprised as he had a few seconds earlier, but under its greenish hue, his face was pale. "How is this possible?"

"I don't know," I said. "The energy—it's in me, just as it's in the creek. And it seems as if it's in you, too."

"I'm not psychic." He glanced down at his outstretched hands, at the sparkling near-white light that surrounded them. "So why is it working for me?"

"Maybe you inherited some latent powers from your father." That seemed the most reasonable explanation to me, although I honestly didn't know for sure. "Or maybe your mother was a little psychic. Did she ever mention anything like that to you?"

"No." Across the several yards that separated us, his eyes met mine. "Perhaps it's the connection we now share. I wouldn't have been able to do this even a day ago."

Could it be that simple? I supposed it could. Gideon and I now shared a physical intimacy, and maybe that was enough to awaken in him the capability to handle this strange energy as well.

Whatever the case, I knew it was time for me to get out of the water. The creek had shown me what I needed to know—that its power was mine, and I would be able to call on it when needed. Besides, I could barely feel my feet, the water was so cold. I made my way to shore, thinking that as soon as I was out of the creek, the energy would dissipate.

But it didn't. If anything, it got stronger the closer I got to Gideon, which seemed to reinforce my earlier theory that the connection between us was the important consideration here. I went to him, barely able to make out his features through the cloud of scintillating energy that surrounded him, surrounded me.

He reached out to touch my face. I felt a surge of power move through my body as the cloud shimmered and shifted, enclosing us in a single brilliant bubble of light. Without stopping to think, I went on my tiptoes so we could kiss.

We seemed to be suspended, floating, sheltered in a perfect quiet place where nothing could touch us, nothing could hurt us. The light glistened all around, within and without.

The kiss could have lasted forever, or only a few seconds. I couldn't tell, and perhaps it really didn't matter. When our mouths lifted from one another, though, the energy evaporated like mist in sunlight, leaving me to wonder if I'd really seen it, really experienced it.

The wonder in Gideon's eyes was all I needed to tell me that I hadn't hallucinated the whole thing. He blinked, then glanced around, as if trying to figure out where it all could have gone.

Yes, the energy had disappeared, but in its place was an unexpected, ravening need. I took his hand and pulled him toward me again, bringing his mouth down to mine so I could kiss him again and again.

It was like setting a match to dry brush. He tasted me, hands moving to cup my face…and then those hands were moving down my body, his arms going around me so he could lift me from the rocky ground, hurry up the path that led to the back door of the cottage.

At another time, I might have marveled at such a casual display of strength. Right then, though, I could only think of how much I needed him, wanted him.

He burst through the back door and moved on to the bedroom. As soon as he set me down, we were all but tearing at one another's clothes, rushing to remove those impediments so we could be flesh to flesh, skin to skin.

Gone was the hesitant, gentle exploration of a few hours earlier. He pushed me down onto the bed, his mouth on my breast, his hand between my legs, even as I reached over to grasp him, to wrap my fingers around his shaft and feel how ready he was.

But that didn't seem to be enough. We shifted around one another, and in the next moment, I'd taken him into my mouth, and his tongue was touching me, sending exquisite shivers of pleasure all through my body, light sparkling around the edges of my vision in an echo of the creek's energy. Suspended in time, we greedily feasted on each other until I shuddered my way through the first orgasm, and I could tell he was close as well.

We moved again, and this time I was on top of him while he filled me, his hands on my breasts, caressing. A wild cry escaped my lips at his touch, but I didn't care. I rocked my hips as we found our rhythm, each one urging the other on, until I came again, the world dissolving in darkness and light while my body shuddered its way through the orgasm and to someplace beyond it. In the next instant, he climaxed as well, a low groan rising from somewhere deep within him, a sound so deep, I could feel it reverberating all through me.

And then it was over, and I was collapsing at his side as he reached out and drew me close, his lips touching my hair as he whispered, "I love you, I love you," over and over again like some kind of invocation. We breathed one another in, until our pulses calmed and our eyes closed.

Spent, we fell asleep in one another's arms.

The lilting *bing-bong* of my phone woke me. I sat up in bed, blinking into the darkness. Beside me, Gideon stirred, then put out a hand to touch my arm. "What is it?" he asked.

"My phone," I replied. "It's still sitting out on the dining room table." The room was pitch-black, so we must have been asleep for some time. I blinked again and glanced over at the clock on the nightstand. Ten minutes after midnight. We really had passed out after our frenzy of lovemaking.

And then there was that whole episode by the creek. I knew I needed time to process what had happened there, to figure out whether Gideon had power of his own or had merely melded with mine because of the bond we shared.

The phone went quiet, and I bit my lip. Phone calls after midnight were pretty much a universal code that something seriously bad had happened. Would whoever it was call back, or was the reason for the call something that could be relegated to voicemail?

Then the *bing-bong* came again, and I knew I had to get up and find out was going on. No time to put on any clothes, so I grabbed my robe off the hook on the back of the door and drew it on as I hurried out to the dining room. Behind me, I heard rustling noises, and guessed that Gideon was getting dressed as well.

After flicking on the chandelier, I reached inside my purse and rummaged around for the phone. As usual, it had slipped out of the side pocket where it was supposed to live and was mixed in with my wallet and my cosmetics bag and all the other miscellaneous junk that floated around in there. At last, my fingers closed around the little rectangular object, and I pulled it out, taking a quick glance at the display as I did so. My house number, the landline my parents had never wanted to get rid of.

Blood running cold, I put the phone to my ear just as Gideon emerged from the hallway outside the bedroom. "Hello?"

"Oh, thank God."

My mother's voice. "What is it?" I asked, my tone sharp. "Are you and Dad okay?"

"Yes, we're fine, but—" She stopped there, her voice hitching a bit.

That was not my mother. She might lose her temper from time to time, but she was not the type to get weepy about things. Not unless something really awful was going on.

"But what? *Mom!*"

A deep, gasping sort of sigh. "It's Kelsey. She's gone."

"Gone?" I repeated, somewhat stupidly. What my mother had just said didn't seem to make any sense, but maybe I wasn't all the way awake yet. I couldn't imagine Kelsey going anywhere. She was hell-bent on hanging around until Michael came to his senses and admitted how he really felt about her.

"It's the Reptilians," my mother said. "They've taken her."

CHAPTER EIGHTEEN

KARA SAT AT HER DINING ROOM TABLE, EYES RED, although it seemed as if she was all cried out by the time Gideon and I got to the house. Kirsten was next to her, holding her hand, while behind her, Lance paced angrily, hands knotted into fists at his side.

"I told her not to go," he growled, frustration and fury spiking out from him in bright, needle-like bursts of crimson and carmine. "Told her it wasn't safe. But she told me I was being silly. Silly!" The last word was more spat than pronounced.

"Go where?" I asked.

Lance stopped pacing. Not that that was much of an improvement; I saw the way his eyes narrowed as they took in Gideon standing next to me. He'd activated his disguise just in case we were stopped by the police or anything like that, but of course Lance knew what was hidden behind the brown eyes and tanned skin. And clearly, he wasn't too happy with the Reptilians right now, even though of course Gideon had absolutely nothing to do with Kelsey's disappearance.

"A party in Cottonwood," Kara said drearily. "A friend of hers from work was throwing it. Kelsey said it wasn't a big deal, that it wasn't as if she was going to be driving up to Flagstaff or something."

"The highway patrol found her car," my father said, his tone quiet but matter-of-fact, as if he knew that Lance didn't need to hear any platitudes right then. Next to him, my mother stirred uneasily in her chair but didn't say anything. "It was on the side of 89A, a little past the turnoff for Page Springs."

"The lights were still on, which is why they stopped," Lance put in. "Classic abduction scenario, when you think about it. Car on the side of the road, lights on, engine running, no one inside. No sign of anyone breaking in, no sign of a struggle. The satellite radio was on, but the clock was frozen. Eleven twenty-two."

A choked little sob escaped Kara's throat right then, and Kirsten squeezed her hand, then said, "We think that was a little fuck-you from the aliens."

"Why?" I asked, mystified. All right, it was clear they wanted all of us to know exactly who had grabbed Kelsey. But I didn't get the significance of the time.

"She was born at eleven twenty-two," Lance replied. His silver-gray eyes narrowed, and he gave the briefest of glances toward Kevin, Kelsey's twin, who sat in one of the spare chairs placed up against the wall next to the sideboard. Farther down the table, on Kara's other side, was Kevin and Kelsey's younger sister, Melissa, who had a robe on over her T-shirt and yoga pants, and who looked very small and frightened.

I didn't bother to ask how the Reptilians had known that small detail. They could know anything they wanted, if it suited their plans.

Gideon spoke up then. "Have you heard anything from them?"

"Nothing," Martin said. He sat on Kirsten's left side, his dark hair rumpled and his chin faintly stubbled. Clearly, the two of them had been asleep when all this went down, just as Gideon and I had been.

I thought of Kelsey, driving along that dark highway, probably not paying too much attention to the road since she'd driven that way a thousand times before. Had a bright light descended from above and plucked her out of her Toyota, or had the aliens gone for something a little more subtle, instead making her car swerve off onto the shoulder so one of their teams could come along and pluck her out of the driver's seat? Lance had said there was no sign of a struggle, so I had a feeling the Reptilians must have used one of their "conveyors," knowing she would be gone in an instant, before the next car came along and spotted anything unusual. At that time of night, there wouldn't have been too many people out on

89A, but it wouldn't have been completely deserted, either.

"I'm sure they want to make us sweat," Lance said. "They've got the upper hand, after all."

"But why?" Melissa asked then. Her voice sounded as small and scared as she looked. Right then, she seemed much younger than nineteen, just a frightened kid. "I mean, Kelsey isn't special like Taryn or Callista, or even Grace. She's just...Kelsey."

Kara shook her head, mouth tightening. I was sure she thought Kelsey was plenty special, but I thought I saw Melissa's point.

"Like Kirsten said, I think it's a fuck-you." My mother's eyes widened at the profanity—I didn't swear much, and certainly not around my parents or the Joneses or the Rineharts—but I just went on, "They're taking all these women, and so they wanted to show us that they could take one of ours, too. It's their way of telling us to back off."

"Back off from what?" Kirsten asked. She looked very tired, smudges in the perfect skin under her eyes. "No offense to anyone here, but we really haven't been doing all that much. A few messages to the right people and a couple of videos that were promptly taken down can't really count as a major offensive."

"True," Gideon said, "but you also have a team working on the device, attempting to see if there's a way to block its energy. If that team is successful, then you will be able to disrupt the Reptilians' abductions, and they can't be very happy about that."

"How would they even know?" My mother looked a little more put together than either Kara or Kirsten, but she'd always been sort of a night owl. I guessed that she and my father hadn't yet gone to bed when the call came in.

"How do they know anything?" Lance replied. "They're surveilling us all the time."

"If that's the case, then why didn't they go into the maker space and take back Gideon's device?" my father asked. "It seems as if that would have been easy enough for them to pull off."

"You don't think I'm stupid enough to leave it there, do you?" Lance crossed his arms, the look he gave my father very close to a glare. "I told Matthew and Lena that they couldn't do anything to the device that couldn't be undone by the end of the day. And I go by and collect it from them when they call and tell me they're about to pack it in. We all know this house is close enough to the creek that it's protected, too. So the device comes home with me and goes in the safe."

"Very resourceful," Gideon said. "I'm actually glad that you have it here, because it makes things that much easier."

"'Easier'?" I echoed, not sure I liked the sound of that.

"Yes," he replied, although I noticed he wouldn't quite meet my eyes, as if he knew I'd care even less for what he was about to say next. "I'll take the device and go to Lir Shalan, and tell him he must release Kelsey."

My body went cold, even though it was fairly warm in the dining room because of all the people packed in there. "He'll never agree to that. Especially not when he knows you've switched sides."

"But does he?" Gideon shifted away from me slightly so he could address the entire room. "It's true that Lir Shalan sent me here to fetch Taryn back, and I have no doubt that he's impatient with me for taking so long to accomplish that task. But most of our interactions have been masked by the creek. He can guess, but he can't know for sure."

"He's guessed enough to call you useless," I replied. "Or had you forgotten about that little exchange I had with him?"

"Exchange?" my mother broke in, her voice sharp. "What exchange?"

"Nothing," I said. "We had an encounter. I got away. End of story."

Her expression seemed to indicate she knew there was more to it than that. But she gave a brief glance around the room before shaking her head. She knew this was not the time to get into it with me, not when I was apparently safe and sound and Kelsey wasn't.

Gideon waited a few seconds, as if making sure my mother and I weren't going to say anything else to each other. Then he said, "Yes, Taryn, he referred to me as 'useless.' But that could have only been a comment about my ineffectiveness in bringing you back to his ship. It doesn't necessarily mean that he knows I've switched sides, so to speak."

"I appreciate the offer," Lance said, the drawl in his voice seeming to indicate he actually felt the exact opposite. But that was Lance for you. "However, what makes you think he'd just hand Kelsey over to you?"

"Because I'd offer him Taryn in exchange."

The room erupted after that, with my parents saying no way would they allow any such a thing, and Kara and Kirsten protesting that it would be far too dangerous, and Martin arguing that you couldn't make any kind of deal with a Reptilian, that they'd always find a way to renege.

For myself, I had another one of those uncomfortable icy tingles go down my back, but I understood what Gideon was saying. Lir Shalan had already admitted that he wanted me. What would be the point in hanging on to Kelsey if he could get what he really wanted instead? She was just another human girl, and to him, they were probably a dime a dozen. He'd only taken her to provoke us, so it seemed the best thing to do was to make him believe we were ready to deal.

Martin did make one very good point, though. I didn't trust Lir Shalan any further than I could throw him, and I doubted that would be very far. The Reptilian leader had to be almost seven feet tall. So there was every chance that he would appear to accept Gideon's offer, and then take steps to make sure he had both me and Kelsey. What he planned to do with her, I had no idea. Hand her off as a prize to one of his lieutenants?

That thought made my stomach churn, so I pushed it aside. We wouldn't allow anything so terrible to happen. After all, Lir Shalan probably thought he had the upper hand, but he couldn't know anything about the experience Gideon and I had shared down at the creek. That had been true power, limitless and stronger than anything I'd ever experienced. The real challenge would be determining whether we'd be able to use it when we were actually away from the creek.

"It's actually a very good idea," I said calmly, once the hubbub had begun to die down.

"You can't mean that," my mother protested. "It's a ridiculous idea. You know Lir Shalan can't be trusted."

"Yes, but…." I looked up at Gideon. His expression was impassive enough, but I could sense the uncertainty in him, his worry that I'd allow my family to sway my decision. "I don't think he knows what Gideon and I working together can do."

"And what's that?" Martin asked, looking frankly curious.

"Well…." I paused then and glanced around. Kara's dining room felt especially crowded because of all the people crammed in there at the moment, but I would have worried about damaging any of the furniture or the paintings on the wall even if a more reasonable number had been occupying the space. "Maybe we should go outside."

My father lifted an eyebrow. "Now?"

"Yes. I know it's almost one o'clock in the morning and it's cold out, but I doubt Kara wants us to wreck her dining room."

For a second, Gideon appeared puzzled, but then he nodded, clearly understanding what I intended to do. "Yes, I think that would be better. And I hope that once everyone sees, they'll realize our cause is not quite as hopeless as they might think."

There were some murmurs and creased brows, but the whole group did follow Gideon and me outside once we started moving toward the front door. Off to the left, opposite the large area that served as overflow parking for the Rinehart household, was an equally open space that in the summer had a large patch of grass, which Lance carefully cultivated so it could be used for picnicking or touch football or simply lying out in the sun. Now, though, it hadn't been reseeded yet, since we could get a hard freeze as late as mid-April in Sedona. The bare dirt seemed like the perfect spot for our demonstration.

I could also sense the creek, and worried that we were too close. But at least it was a hundred yards away, and it wasn't as if Gideon and I were standing in it. We'd just have to see what happened.

It wasn't quite cold enough to see our breath in the air, but I noticed Kara shivering, and saw Lance wrap his arm around her to help keep her warm. Or maybe her shivers had nothing to do with the temperature.

Gideon and I stopped in the center of the open area. His eyes were on mine, glinting in the darkness. There was just enough light coming from the house windows and the lamps on either side of the front door that I could see him clearly enough. His face was calm as he waited for me to take the lead.

I pulled in a deep breath of cool night air. The taste of it was damp and somehow green on my tongue, as if evoking the flavor of the moss that grew on the banks of the creek. And then I recalled that tingling in my limbs, the way the energy had shimmered up and out of the water to surround me. I willed it to do the same thing now, only it would come from within me, rather than from the water.

The night became alive with the same sparkling pale yellow light that had risen out of Oak Creek, this time emanating directly from my body, wrapping me in a veil of shimmering illumination. Distantly, I heard the collective gasp of the people watching, but I couldn't allow myself to be distracted by them.

I held out my hands to Gideon.

He took them, and immediately the energy jumped to him, enveloping his body as well. I nodded, and we raised our hands in unison, feeling that same deep hum, as if it had come from the earth itself.

I didn't want to destroy anything. But I did have

to show everyone what the energy could do. The light arcing between Gideon and me was bright enough to light up the area as if it was daytime, and I gave a quick glance around.

Off to one side was an old tree stump, one so stubborn, even Lance had given up on having it removed. I turned slightly so I was facing it, and Gideon moved with me.

Then I gathered the energy, feeling how it coiled within me, using Gideon's strength as ballast so I could fling the light outward.

It hit the tree stump like a fireball, blowing the remnants of the old oak that had once stood there up and out, showering all of us with chunks of wood, the light searing my retinas. I blinked as I attempted to clear my streaming eyes, and noticed that Gideon was rubbing at his as well.

When I was able to focus again, I saw that the tree stump had disappeared completely. In its place was a black hole in the ground about two feet deep.

"Holy shit," came a man's voice. Since my back was to the group and my ears were still ringing slightly, I couldn't tell for sure who had spoken. I had a feeling it was Martin, though.

In the next instant, everyone was surging past us, going to look at the gaping hole where the tree stump had once stood.

"Well, that's effective," Lance remarked. He still had his arm around Kara, but he reached up with his free hand to rub his jaw. "If you ever want to give up being a psychic, you can always go into stump-clearing."

"How…." My mother this time, her face pale in the semi-gloom. Then she paused, looking away from me and Gideon, and off toward the creek. We couldn't really see it where we stood, but it was close enough that the rustling of its waters was just barely audible. "That's where it came from? The creek?"

"To begin with," I replied. "But I learned something today. The power is in me, too. I don't need the creek to access it. And when I join with Gideon, the way I did just now, it's much, much stronger."

"Lir Shalan won't know what hit him," Martin said grimly. "All right, it seems you do have the power to take him on. What's the plan?"

I glanced over at Gideon. That part was really up to him, since he was the one who would have to reach out to his father, make him believe that he would willingly return.

"I think it's better if we can have him come here to Sedona," Gideon said slowly, as if sorting through possibilities and then discarding them as he decided what would work best. "There's actually a good chance that he's already begun rebuilding the abandoned base. He has the freedom to do so now, since no one with any authority would dare to stop him."

"They're back here?" Kara asked. She burrowed into Lance's side, her blonde hair and stricken face a pale blur in the uncertain light. "Since when?"

"We don't know for sure," I said, wanting only to

comfort her. "But I don't think I would have run into him the way I did last night if he wasn't close. Anyway, it would be better to confront him here. For one thing, he won't be surrounded by so many of his people, and so we won't risk being overrun once we do manage to take him out. Also, the power may be within me, but I'll feel a lot more confident accessing it while I'm here in Sedona. Obviously, Gideon and I haven't tried this trick anywhere else."

"Will he come?" my father asked. For the first time, I noticed how his fingers were knotted with my mother's, although I couldn't say for sure who was seeking reassurance from whom.

Gideon hesitated. Then his gaze fell on me, and I shivered. The expression in his abnormally dark eyes was very bleak. "Oh, yes, he'll come," he said. "We have something he wants."

It was nearly two by the time we got back into my car and headed toward West Sedona and the cottage. Not for the first time, I was very glad of the Honda's self-driving mechanism, because it allowed me to pillow my head on Gideon's shoulder and have him hold me during the drive home.

He was silent for most of the way, no doubt brooding on what seemed to be an inevitable confrontation with his father. As we stopped at a light, I asked, "Can you do this, Gideon?"

"Do what?"

"You know what I mean."

Another long silence. The car lurched forward—I really needed to have its accelerator looked at—but he still didn't speak. At last he said, "I know I can."

"But he's your father."

"Biologically speaking, yes. Otherwise...." Gideon reached for my hand and took it. "If it hadn't been for my mother, I wouldn't have known what a kind word was. Or a hug. Even a smile."

"Reptilians don't smile?" I asked, chilled by what he'd just said. Maybe that was why I'd latched onto something trivial. I didn't want to think about what an emotional wasteland his life must have been after his mother passed away.

"They smile...in a fashion, I suppose. But not from true joy. Instead, they smile at the suffering of others, or when they've gained the upper hand."

"All of them are like that?" I knew I sounded aghast, but I couldn't help myself. I was too tired, and worried, to control my tone. In my mind, I'd always thought of Lir Shalan as a particularly nasty case, and that the other members of his race couldn't be quite as pure evil.

"Most." Gideon hesitated, his fingers playing with mine. He wouldn't quite look at me. "My tutor —Sal Galen—he was as good-natured as one of his kind could manage to be. He did show me some kindness, especially after my mother died. I think he pitied me in a way."

"Why?"

"Because I wasn't human, and I wasn't Reptilian, only something perched in between, trying desperately to be what my father wanted because there was nothing else I could do."

His voice was very calm, but I didn't just hear the pain running through it, I could feel it as well, like tiny cracks making their way across a glass surface. I tightened my fingers against his. "You're both those things, Gideon. But they don't have to define you. What defines you is here." Very gently, I freed my hand so I could place it against his chest and feel the strong, heavy beat of the heart within. "And here." I touched his temple, and he leaned his head against my hand.

"Have I told you how much I love you?"

"You might have mentioned it once or twice."

He chuckled, but it was a rusty sound, not one I found all that convincing. But I wouldn't push it. He was fighting his own inner battles, and all I could do was be there for him and hope he came out of it all unscathed.

But how would that even be possible, when it seemed obvious to me that he planned to kill his own father?

CHAPTER NINETEEN

WHEN GIDEON AND I GOT INTO BED, ALL WE DID WAS hold one another. I was far too exhausted to attempt anything else, and right then, it seemed much more important for us to take comfort this way, in arms holding the other person close and listening to the other person's breathing until we fell asleep, both of us wanting nothing but oblivion.

I woke up too early the next morning, mouth gummy and head aching slightly. If I hadn't known better, I would have said I was suffering from a mild hangover, although I'd never drunk enough to experience one for myself. The symptoms sounded about right, though.

But I'd only had one glass of wine in the afternoon, and it had worn off hours and hours ago. Was this the inevitable aftermath of using that strange power Gideon and I shared? If that was the case, I'd have to make sure I used it as sparingly as possible.

The bed next to me was empty. I put my hand on the place where Gideon had lain, my heart beating a little faster—but then I heard a slight clinking noise from the kitchen and realized he'd probably gone there to make some coffee.

That sounded like a recipe for disaster, so I pushed myself out of bed and got up, grabbing my robe off the hook on the door as I went. I'd crashed the night before while wearing just a T-shirt and my underwear. I didn't much care whether Gideon saw me walking around like that, but the cottage tended to be cold in the morning, and I wanted the extra layer.

Sure enough, he was tending to the coffeemaker when I walked into the kitchen. However, everything seemed to be chugging along just fine, so I decided I wouldn't offend him by checking on the coffee myself.

"Your phone keeps beeping," he said.

I'd dropped my purse on the counter when we got home the night before. Sure enough, I could hear a plaintive little beep from inside, a notification that I'd gotten a text message.

Right before I'd gone to bed, I'd texted Michael. He needed to know about Kelsey, and I honestly didn't know for sure if my parents would have thought to get in contact with him. He was always off in his own orbit, and besides, they hadn't seen the slightly crumpled and much-loved photo he kept hidden in his desk drawer. They didn't know that Michael thought of Kelsey as anything except the daughter of some family friends, a girl with an embarrassing crush on him.

Although I supposed a crush couldn't be all that embarrassing if it happened to be reciprocated.

The text was short: *I'll be down in the morning.*

That was all. Typical Michael. I assumed he would head to our parents' house; there wasn't any space for him here. Actually, I didn't even know if my parents had told him everything that was going on with the Reptilians. He wouldn't have been able to do all that much to help, and they might have figured it was better for him to be safely off in Flagstaff, buried in his studies and far away from the current fray.

Which meant they might not be all that thrilled to have him turn up on their doorstep.

I fought back a sigh and dumped the phone into my purse. When I turned, I saw Gideon watching me with a speculative look on his face. "Bad news?" he asked.

"I don't think so. Just a message from my brother. I told him about Kelsey, and he's coming down to Sedona."

"This is the brother who's studying astronomy?"

"That's right."

"Is he particularly close to her?"

"It's a little more complicated than that." I went

over to the coffeemaker. The light had turned green, indicating the brew was ready. Since Gideon had already put two mugs out on the counter, I went ahead and filled both of them up. Most of the time I would have preferred tea, but that nasty little headache was still pounding away behind my temples. Coffee seemed a surer remedy than tea.

Gideon took the mug I handed to him and sent me a questioning look.

"Kelsey's had a crush on Michael since I can remember. I honestly thought he was indifferent, but that turns out not to be the case. So he's coming down here—not because he can do all that much to help, but because he can't bear to be away when something so awful has happened to her."

"We'll get her back," Gideon said, his tone so firm that it seemed he considered the matter a foregone conclusion.

"I want to think that, but...." I wrapped my hands around the mug I held, glad of its warmth. "I still don't know exactly how you intend to manage the whole thing."

"Simple enough. I'll go to the base and tell Lir Shalan that I'll bring you to him, but only if he releases Kelsey."

"How do you even know he's there?"

For the first time, Gideon looked uncomfortable. "Because I've spoken with him."

The mug almost slipped out of my hands. *"What?"*

"Lance gave me the device last night, so it was easy enough to make contact. I did so a while ago, while you were still asleep."

"And you didn't think to talk to me about it first?"

"We'd already agreed that this would be our course of action. What more was there to discuss?"

I couldn't believe I was hearing this. All right, the night before we had basically laid out more or less what needed to be done. But I'd thought we'd discuss the plan some more before we leapt into action, so to speak.

"And he actually talked to you?" I asked, trying to sound calm. Getting into an argument now wouldn't serve any useful purpose.

"Yes. That was when he confirmed he really was at the base. I told him I would be there in the next few hours."

"Just like that."

"Just like that." Gideon seemed to note the worried look I knew I wore, and set down his mug so he could take my hands in his. "He seemed... pleased. So I think he truly believes that I am ready to come back into the fold."

"He wasn't angry that you're trying to bargain Kelsey away from him?"

"No. If anything, it proves to him that I have learned something about taking what I want. And to be honest, she might be a friend of yours, but she means nothing to him. Just another human woman. He has plenty of those."

Gideon sounded so cold, so matter-of-fact, that a shiver went down my spine. I told myself that he was only being truthful, was trying to make me see the situation the way Lir Shalan saw it, but I couldn't help being uneasy.

"So I'll go with you to the base...."

"No."

"No?" I repeated, sending him a disbelieving look.

"I will go in first and make contact, and determine that Kelsey is safe and that Lir Shalan is willing to make the trade. After that, I will send the signal to have you come meet me."

"Just like that."

"It may take some time to persuade him, but in the end, I am sure he will agree. I know Lir Shalan, Taryn." Gideon let go of my hands and went to pick up his mug of coffee. "He is powerful, but he is not powerful enough to withstand the sort of attack we can mount. It will be over quickly enough. And once he is gone, so also will be his control over those who serve him now. I don't think they will put up much of a defense."

That seemed awfully hopeful, but I didn't protest. Gideon understood Reptilian power structures far better than I did.

I wanted to ask, *And how will you live with yourself,*

if it turns out you'll end up being responsible for the death of your own father?

But somehow, I couldn't find the courage.

I did call my parents to let them know what we were planning. That seemed the best thing; that way they could get the word out to the rest of the group, and they could be standing by.

Just in case.

Michael hadn't turned up yet, since it wasn't quite nine in the morning. My mother seemed to appreciate the warning that he was coming, although my father sounded sort of puzzled as to why Michael would be taking the time out to drive down to Sedona. I didn't bother to enlighten him; I hoped he'd be able to see for himself exactly why my brother was so concerned about Kelsey Rinehart's fate.

I didn't know exactly how I was supposed to prepare myself for this kind of confrontation, but a shower seemed in order. Gideon and I squeezed into the cramped stall, soaping one another, touching each other, body slipping on body as the water rinsed the suds away and his fingers caressed me, bringing me to the verge. And then my back was pressed up against the tiled wall as he held me in place, entering me while I clung to him, losing myself in the way our flesh connected.

Then it was over, and we were rinsing ourselves off. I handed him a towel before wrapping one around myself. Where all that had come from, I didn't know. Maybe we'd both decided we should reaffirm our connection before going to face Lir Shalan. I did feel closer to Gideon, my earlier doubts washed away with the shampoo I'd just rinsed out of my hair.

He pushed the damp mass to one side so he could kiss the back of my neck. Warm, delicious shivers went over me, but I knew we really shouldn't delay any longer.

"So, you'll use the device to go see him?" I asked, once I'd slipped some underwear on and wasn't quite as susceptible to distractions.

"Yes. The vortexes here interfere with their utility somewhat, but not when I can use my device to directly lock on to one at the base."

"Or when you know exactly where the target is."

"Yes." We were standing in front of the bathroom mirror while I combed through my hair. One byproduct of Gideon's Reptilian DNA was that he never seemed to need a shave, so his early morning bathroom rituals didn't take nearly as much time as mine. While I scrunched some product into my hair to tame the frizz, he went on, "The closer you are, the better."

"I know." I wanted to shiver at the thought of being scooped up like that and dropped right into the base, but I told myself that Gideon knew what he was doing. "I've already discussed it with my parents. The whole gang is going to go with me to the Secret Canyon trailhead. Then they'll wait there for us to come back with Kelsey."

"Good." His ruby eyes scanned my face, and he reached up to touch my cheek. "It is going to be all right."

He sounded so confident, I could only nod. I just prayed that his confidence wasn't misplaced.

Not long after we shared a light breakfast—yogurt and toast—he kissed me again, then pressed a button on the device. He vanished at once, leaving me alone in the living room.

His departure was my cue to get moving. I texted my mother's cell, letting her know that the plan had been set in motion. Then all I could do was tidy up a little before retrieving my keys and locking up the cottage. Gideon and I had already decided that it would be better for me not to bring anything along, not a purse, not a backpack. That way, it would look more like I really had been grabbed right in the middle of doing something else. We didn't want Lir Shalan to think that any of this had been planned.

My parents' Range Rover pulled up in front of the house, and I hurried down the front walk and climbed into the back seat. I startled a little when I saw it was already occupied, then realized Michael was the one sitting back there.

"Hey," I said.

"Hey," he replied, and that was about it. We both knew what was at stake here, but since I still didn't have a clue as to whether he'd openly confessed his feelings for Kelsey, I decided it was better not to say anything else.

"Lance and Kara are already on their way," my mother said, turning slightly in her seat so she could look back at my brother and me.

"What about everyone else?"

My father replied, "We all talked it over and decided it would look a little too suspicious to have such a big group loitering around the area. So Martin and Kirsten and Raphael and Callista are staying put. Kirsten wasn't too happy about that, as you can imagine."

Yes, I could. I doubted she wanted to stay on the sidelines while the fate of her niece hung in the balance. And maybe that was a mistake, because if things really did go sideways, having people with powers like Kirsten's and Martin's—or Callista's and Raphael's—around might make the difference.

On the other hand, I understood the need to avoid attracting too much attention by having a huge group descend on the Secret Canyon trailhead. It was a Saturday, and so there probably would be a lot of hikers out and about, but we couldn't count on that as protective camouflage. Also, my parents and the

Rineharts were just ordinary humans, even when you took my mother's psychic powers into account. They wouldn't ping the Reptilians' radar the way having a bunch of Pleiadians loitering around might.

When we pulled up to the trailhead, I saw that Lance and Kara's dark gray Jeep was already parked there, along with several other vehicles. In fact, my parents snagged the last open space, so my hope that the trail would have a decent amount of foot traffic from hikers and tourists seemed to be rewarded.

Like my parents, Kara and Lance were wearing the sort of thing you might expect to see people wearing for a day hike—all-weather pants and T-shirts, hiking shoes. Michael wore jeans and the same nearly destroyed tennis shoes he had on most of the time, but he still didn't look that out of place. A baseball cap with NAU's lumberjack logo on it helped to hide his face.

"So, he's already there?" Kara asked me as my family approached. Her face was strained, shadows prominent under her dark blue eyes. I wondered if she'd slept at all the night before.

"Yes," I said. "He went about twenty minutes ago. So now it's just a waiting game. I have no idea how long it's going to take for him to bring Lir Shalan around, but he made it sound as if it might take a while."

"So I brought some snacks, bottled water, that kind of thing," my mother put in. "Just in case."

Lance nodded in some approval, the slightest

flicker of surprise registering in his expression as he took in Michael's presence. He didn't comment on that, though, but only said, "And your Gideon really thinks Lir Shalan will be willing to make a trade?"

"He's very confident." I hesitated then, not sure what else I should say. Repeating Gideon's remark about how Kelsey really wasn't of that much use because she was just an ordinary human didn't seem very tactful, so I stopped there.

If either Lance or Kara thought I was leaving something out, they didn't show it. Kara shifted so she was staring off to the northeast, in the direction where the alien base was located. "I hate knowing she's so close, and yet there isn't one damn thing we can do about it."

"There is something," my father pointed out. "We're doing it right now. Waiting is never easy, but it's all we can do for the time being. Everything is in Gideon's hands at the moment."

That remark made me swallow nervously. Yes, Gideon had said he could handle this, and of course he knew Lir Shalan better than I or anyone else present did, but still....

My mother murmured in my ear, "Taryn, can I talk to you for a moment?"

"Um, sure."

We stepped away from the group, over to a semi-private little spot guarded by a scrubby manzanita bush and a couple of large boulders. I could see how everyone else sent us a curious look, but no one tried to stop us. After all, it wasn't too terribly strange that my mother would want to talk to me in private.

She wasn't always the easiest person for me to read, mostly because she'd had years of experience in building up her mental barriers and only letting out what she was okay with allowing me to know. Right then, though, she was so stressed that I could feel the pings of worry and anxiety coming from her, the very real fear that she would never see me again.

"It's going to be okay, Mom," I told her. "Gideon will be able to outmaneuver Lir Shalan. And then when we're both there...." I let my words trail off, but I could tell from the flicker in her eyes that she knew what I meant. "You saw our demonstration last night. Lir Shalan won't know what hit him."

"I suppose so. It's just that...." She stopped there and shook her head. For this expedition, she'd pulled back her unruly curls, so like mine, but a few tendrils had escaped the barrette she wore and danced around her face. "Do you trust Gideon?"

I really didn't understand how she could even be asking that. How would I have ever agreed to something like this if I didn't trust him implicitly? "I love him."

"That's not what I asked."

Anger flared in me, but I pushed it back. Getting into an argument now wouldn't help matters at all. "For me, it's one and the same. I trust him because I love him. And I love him because I trust him. Implicitly."

Those facile words didn't seem to reassure her. She crossed her arms, but I didn't see any irritation in her face. Just more worry, naked enough that I would have been able to recognize it even without those little flashes of distress that spiked out from her in all directions, red and orange and dark yellow. "You barely know him."

"How long were you with Dad before you knew you loved him?"

A weary smile touched her lips. "Not all that long. But this isn't the same thing."

"Why? Because Gideon is half Reptilian?"

"Yes, exactly that. And don't bother to bring up Callista and Raphael, because their situation is completely different."

Well, she'd cut me off at the pass there, because that was exactly what I'd been about to do. So I tried another tack. "What, you don't want to have a green-skinned son-in-law?"

My question actually made her chuckle. "That's actually the least of my worries. At least now the general population knows that aliens really do exist, so we've crossed one hurdle. No, it's more that the Reptilians are so very different from us. Not just physically, but the way they think, the way they see the world. Gideon was raised in that world, and he may have a very difficult time adjusting to this one."

"You might have said something about all this earlier," I remarked. "It's a little late to be bringing up any second thoughts."

"When was I supposed to bring it up?" she said simply. "This has all happened at such a breakneck pace that there hasn't been much time to process the possible ramifications. I suppose it was just seeing you standing there, ready but frightened, that brought it all home to me." She paused, the strain clear in her face. "You're my only daughter, Taryn. I don't want anything to happen to you."

I opened my mouth to say, "Nothing is going to happen," but I didn't get quite that far. A strange tingling sensation took over my body, not at all how it felt when the creek's energy was working through me. No, this was more like tiny insects were crawling all over my skin.

The world flickered, my mother's face disappearing even as she reached out toward me, as if in an attempt to prevent me from leaving.

That was impossible, though. Gideon was summoning me to him, and my mother and the surrounding landscape were gone before I even had a chance to blink.

CHAPTER TWENTY

WHEN THE WORLD RESOLVED ITSELF AROUND ME AGAIN, I saw that my surroundings were familiar enough—a room lit by dim reddish fixtures, walls of perfectly planed stone. I blinked, trying to shrug off the last of that creepy-crawly sensation on my skin. Then I realized that, although this had to be the alien base out in Secret Canyon, I'd actually never seen this chamber before.

It was very large and echoing, with a sort of raised dais at one end. On that dais were two large metal chairs, and on those chairs sat Gideon and Lir Shalan.

I stared. When he'd left me at the cottage, Gideon had been wearing jeans and one of the T-shirts I'd bought him. Now, though, he was back in the high-collared flowing robes the Reptilians preferred. What that meant, I didn't know for sure. I only knew that his altered appearance sent a sudden chill through my body. The Gideon I looked at now seemed far too much like the cold-eyed half-alien I'd first met, not the lover who'd caressed me in the shower earlier that morning.

And then I saw Kelsey, standing a foot or so to the left and slightly behind Lir Shalan's chair. Her eyes were glassy, blank, with black smudges of smeared mascara and eyeliner under them. God only knew what Lir Shalan had done to her to make her look so catatonic. I just had to hope that whatever it was, it would wear off quickly once Gideon and I had gotten her away from here.

She was still wearing the tight jeans, high-heeled sandals, and thin-strapped top she must have put on to go to the party the night before. Something about the getup made her look that much more vulnerable, and I wished I could go to her and give her my jacket.

Lir Shalan stood, and Gideon followed suit. I still wasn't all that good at deciphering Reptilian facial expressions, and of course I couldn't "read" the alien leader the way I might a normal human being. However, it really didn't take a psychic to perceive the cloud of triumph that seemed to hang around him.

"Taryn Oliver," he said. "How good of you to join us."

"It's not like I was given much of a choice," I replied, then risked a quick, slanted glance in

Gideon's direction. His expression was blank, his eyes shuttered. I couldn't get anything from him, and another of those cold little tendrils of fear worked its way down my back. I'd known going in that he would have to keep everything tightly tamped down, that he couldn't risk revealing anything of what we had planned, but still, I'd been expecting to see at least a flicker from him, something to tell me that the Gideon I knew and loved was in there somewhere.

"True." Lir Shalan descended from the dais, Gideon a few steps behind. They paused when they were a pace or two away from me. "To be honest, I was not sure whether he would really bring you here. When he disappeared like that, with no word...." The Reptilian leader paused and looked over at his son, then back at me. "I had my doubts. But he assured me the time spent with you was only so he might gain your trust."

"It seems that trust was misplaced," I said then, my throat suddenly dry. "Or he would never have brought me here."

"Perhaps." His gaze flicked toward Kelsey and then back to me, the ruby eyes seeming to glow with a hunger I didn't want to acknowledge. "But he has shown himself to be a true son, because you are here. And here you will stay."

I'd been expecting Lir Shalan to say something along those lines. What I hadn't expected was what he said next.

"In fact, you can keep your friend company, for she will stay as well."

"What?" Even though I'd guessed he might pull something like this, I couldn't keep the shock from my voice. I should have known he would never agree to our bargain. Why give up the one, when he could keep both of us as his captives?

Gideon spoke for the first time. His voice was cold, almost a stranger's. There was nothing in his body language or expression to show that he had any feelings for me at all. "My father welcomed me back. He's always wanted you for me, Taryn...but since I also brought a woman for him, I've proven my trustworthiness."

My brain didn't seem to be properly processing his words. Stammering a little, I asked, "W-what do you mean, you brought a woman for him? She was kidnapped off the highway in the middle of the night!"

Gideon's lips lifted slightly, but I wouldn't have called the expression he wore a smile. "Yes, but it was because of you that I knew she would be there. You don't do a very good job of locking down your phone, Taryn. I saw the text Kelsey sent you, asking you if you wanted to come to the party in Cotton-wood with her. From that text, it was easy enough to extrapolate where she would be last night, and at what approximate time. Because I had access to her text and her number, we were able to tap into her phone as well. She sent a text to her mother at approximately eleven fifteen, saying she was on her way home. After that, it was merely a matter of waiting for her to arrive."

No, that couldn't be true. I did have a habit of leaving my phone lying around, so Gideon could have easily found it. As far as locking it down, well, I used the same standard five-digit security code that anyone else might. Those codes were supposed to be almost impossible to crack—unless you happened to have extraterrestrial technology and tools at your disposal.

I stared at Gideon in horror. He returned my gaze, ruby eyes never looking more alien than they did in that moment. So had the whole thing been a lie? Had he and Lir Shalan been plotting all along, knowing they would have to maneuver me into a place where they could easily snap me up?

My stomach churned, the meager breakfast I'd eaten going sour within. "I don't believe you," I whispered.

His expression didn't change. "Believe what you wish. My father sent me to Sedona to bring you back, and that's precisely what I did. All the rest—that was nothing."

I wanted to ask how he could have faked every-thing—his words of love, the way our energies had meshed. The way he'd stood in Oak Creek and wept as the healing waters washed his sins away.

But then I realized he was half Reptilian, and they were masters of deceit, of manipulation. For all I knew, the legends of Eve and the serpent sprang from humanity's early interactions with the alien race. Yes, I'd gotten twinges of emotion from him, emotions I would have sworn were genuine, but how could I have known for sure? I'd never had interactions with any one of his people before. I didn't know how they were supposed to feel.

All this so he could circle back and bring me to the place where he and his father thought I was intended to be. Just another one of their stolen women, perhaps slightly more important because of my psychic abilities.

Psychic. There was a joke. Those supposed "abilities" sure hadn't done much to help me out here.

Lir Shalan smiled, his lipless mouth lifting in something that seemed more like a grimace. Just looking at him made me want to be sick. "You seem shocked, Taryn Oliver. Did you really think you held such sway over him? Yes, he did show a moment of weakness when he let you go, but it seems he has more than redeemed himself now."

"Damned himself, you mean," I retorted, but my voice shook, and I knew Lir Shalan could see how weak my defiance really was.

"Go ahead and hate him," the Reptilian leader said, the words a silky taunt. "Do you think your hatred matters to any of us?"

"I don't know," I replied. My voice did sound firmer now. Where I'd gotten that strength from, I didn't really know. But now it seemed as if everything was lost, and so it didn't really matter what I said...or how I said it. I crossed my arms and glared at him. "Did Elizabeth hate you?"

"Elizabeth?"

"The woman who bore your son," I told him, hating that he'd even asked the question. "Have you forgotten her name already?"

"It is not that I have forgotten her name, but more that it holds very little importance for me. She was here for a time, and she served her purpose. What she felt or thought of me has no relevance."

Nothing could have driven home to me how alien Lir Shalan was more than the way he spoke of Gideon's mother. She truly had been nothing to him, nothing at all. It didn't matter that she'd given him a healthy child, or ultimately died because she couldn't force her body through one more brutal pregnancy.

But then I remembered how Gideon had said his father had held her that one time, put his arms around her as if to comfort her. Or had that story been a lie, too? That seemed the most plausible explanation; he'd wanted me to see some spark of compassion, of humanity in his father, even though it was clear enough that Lir Shalan possessed none.

I looked from him to Gideon. "Is that how you want it to be between us? Only the ruthless dictates of biology, with no love, no warmth?"

The slightest shudder went through his body. His eyes narrowed as he said, "You are looking at this as a human would. That is understandable. But those sorts of weaknesses are only an impediment when it comes to reestablishing our race."

"It won't even be your race, though, will it?" I asked desperately. I was trying every possible angle of attack in the vain hope that maybe something I said would make him reconsider his course of action. "In a few generations, will you even be able to tell from looking at the offspring of these unions whether they have any Reptilian blood at all?"

Lir Shalan spoke then. "You are human, and so have no understanding of these matters. Appearance is not important. What is important is that our children and our children's children will still carry the seeds of our bloodlines within them. That part of us will still endure. I recognize my son as my son because he carries my blood within him, even though he resembles his mother far more than he does me."

So he remembered that much of her, was able to recognize her features in his son's face. Or was he even looking that closely at all? Maybe all he saw was someone who appeared human, or nearly so.

Gideon came closer, so close that the hem of his long robe brushed against my foot. I shivered but forced myself to stand my ground, even though every instinct was telling me to back away. He must have detected my disgust, because his mouth lifted in a humorless smile, and his eyes took on an unpleasant glint. "So fastidious, Taryn? It wasn't so long ago that you were more than willing to have me touch you. Just a few hours ago, come to think of it."

God, I really was going to be sick. But then I thought of how my mother had stood in this place and let the energy of Sedona work through her, blasting every Reptilian and hybrid within.

Well, almost all of them. One of those hybrids had survived to stagger out into the desert, to find help and love, if only for a little while. If it hadn't been for the man who'd called himself Grayson, Grace Rinehart would never have been born.

I doubted this current scenario would have anything close to that kind of happy ending, but I had to try.

When I reached for it, though, the energy wasn't there. I forced myself to recall how it had felt to have the power surging through me, willed it to come at my command, but it had fled, or had never been there in the first place. Well, at least on its own. I'd shared that energy with Gideon, so I knew it existed. But if it only worked when the two of us were summoning it, then I was in even more trouble than I had thought.

"Take her," Lir Shalan said. "Show her that it is pointless to resist."

Before I could even attempt to flee, Gideon was there, pulling me into his arms. I struggled, trying to free myself from his grip, but I'd noted how strong he was even when he was merely hugging me, and that strength seemed multiplied now that he was intent on preventing me from getting away. Bile rose in my throat, and I shifted my weight, thinking I might at least manage to knee him in the groin even if I couldn't tear my wrists from his grasp.

Then, shockingly clear, his voice came into my mind. *Taryn, my love, don't fight me. This is our moment.*

What the hell are you talking about? I flung at him. Right then, I didn't have the resources to ask how in the world he was able to communicate with me like this. *I'm not going to fall for any more of your lies!*

Those were lies, this is not. I had to put on that act so I could get you close like this. We had to be touching so we could use the energy against him.

There was such conviction in his inner voice that I stopped struggling and stared up into his face, attempting to determine whether this was another trick or whether he truly meant what he'd said. Just past him, I could see Lir Shalan's alien features take on a satisfied leer. He thought I had given in, had finally realized there was no point in trying to resist.

You mean that?

Of course I do, my love. I would never betray you. But I need you now so we can put an end to this.

An end. This conflict had been playing out for longer than I'd been alive. Could we do it? Was our combined strength enough to defeat Lir Shalan and send the Reptilians away from here for good?

Only one way to find out.

I'm here, Gideon.

His fingers interlaced with mine. At once, I could feel the energy begin to surge, seeming to come from the very ground beneath our feet. Maybe the earth truly was its source, flowing up from the vortexes that gave Sedona its particular power. Some people scoffed at the very notion of the vortexes and the energies associated with them, said that there was nothing particularly special about the region except its extreme natural beauty.

I knew better. And so did Gideon.

Brilliant yellow-white light flared, swirling around our limbs and sparking into the cold, still air, the illumination shocking in the dimly lit room. Lir Shalan recoiled, then hissed something in the Reptilian language. A curse, a command for his son to let go of me? I didn't know, and right then I really didn't care. I just wanted him to know what it felt like to be helpless.

The light spilled out in a wave, striking the Reptilian commander in the chest and knocking him to the ground. That sort of blow would have killed a human outright, but of course, Lir Shalan wasn't human. Face contorted with pain, he uttered another incomprehensible phrase, his eyes glaring red death at us. His clawed fingers scrabbled for something at his waist, even as he struggled to pull himself upright. What was he reaching for? A weapon?

I didn't know, but apparently Gideon did. Without even stopping to think, he raised his hands.

Gideon, let me do it, I pleaded. Maybe Lir Shalan wasn't worthy of my pity or compassion, but I still couldn't bear the thought of his son being the person who must kill him.

The briefest of hesitations, and then he shook his head, his jaw set. In that moment, I knew he had to be the one to strike down his father once and for all. Otherwise, Gideon would never be truly free of him.

Brilliant, glowing fire engulfed the alien leader, flowing outward from Gideon's palms. The unearthly illumination surrounded Lir Shalan before knocking him flat once more. His head hit the rocky surface with a sharp *crack,* and black blood began to trickle its way across the floor. Even that wasn't enough, though. Breath hissing from his lipless mouth, he pulled another cylinder from his belt, subtly different in shape from the conveyor/communications device I'd seen Gideon use.

And he pointed it at me.

I raised my hands to summon the energy, but Gideon was too fast for me. The light crackled and flared once again, this time exploding away from him and enveloping Lir Shalan in a glowing cocoon of light. This time, the alien leader collapsed like a balloon that had had the air let out of it, the cylinder falling from his limp fingers and hitting the ground with a clatter.

The light shimmered and pulsed once more, as if making sure he wouldn't move again. Then it disappeared altogether, dissolving into the stony ground beneath our feet. Gideon and I stared at one another for a long moment, and he swallowed once, hard, then hurried over to the prone form of his father and knelt next to him. The alien's red eyes were shut, and

I couldn't tell if he was breathing. His thin slash of a mouth gaped open slightly.

"Is he...?" I began, then stopped. I didn't know what I should say. Yes, I'd wished for Lir Shalan's death, but I worried how Gideon would live with the knowledge that he'd delivered the killing blow, even if he'd all but told me that he needed to be the one to do it.

He looked up, expression bleak, and shook his head. "No. He's still alive...barely."

I didn't know how to feel about that. Relieved? No, not really, because sooner or later, the Reptilian leader would have to wake up. I knew that Gideon and I had better be long gone from the alien base before that happened. And what would happen after that, I really had no idea.

A woman's voice broke in then. "What—where am I?"

Kelsey, putting a hand to her head and blinking around in obvious befuddlement. She took a few tottering steps in her ridiculous high heels, then stopped, obviously staring at Gideon's green skin.

"Who...?"

"It's okay, Kelsey," I said, hurrying over to her. "This is Gideon. He's helping us. Do you remember how you got here?"

She rubbed at her temple. "Not really. There was a bright light, and then there were these horrible faces peering down at me. But I can't remember much more than that." Her gaze shifted to Lir

Shalan's motionless body. "Oh, God, that's one of them!"

"Don't worry," Gideon said grimly as he got to his feet. "He's not going anywhere."

"But we are," I added. "I think it's probably time to get out of here, right?"

"Yes. The sooner the better, I think." He turned toward the door. "Unfortunately, the conveyor device won't work to transport all three of us from the base. We'll have to walk."

I gave Kelsey's heels a dubious glance. "Okay."

"I can go barefoot," she offered, slipping off one sparkly sandal, then the other. They dangled from her hand, incongruous in that strange setting.

Barefoot wouldn't be much of an improvement once we got outside and she had to walk over sharp rocks and weeds, but I decided not to argue. We needed to get out of there.

Even as I went to meet Gideon by the door, Kelsey tagging along behind, it whooshed open. Standing in the hallway immediately outside were at least ten Reptilians, their eyes glaring red fire at us.

Shit.

I raised my hands, even though I really wasn't sure what I could do on my own without being linked to Gideon.

To my surprise, Gideon didn't attack, only stepped out of the way. The Reptilian in the lead, who was a slightly darker gold than Lir Shalan, came into the room, then bent next to his fallen leader. One long-fingered hand rested on the commander's chest, and then the stranger said something in the Reptilian tongue to Gideon, who shook his head and answered in the same language.

"What's going on?" I asked Gideon in an undertone. "Why aren't they trying to capture us or something?"

"This is Sal Galen," Gideon said. "I think I mentioned him to you. He was my tutor. Since that time, however, he was promoted to Lir Shalan's second-in-command. For his service."

"And because I would do as I was told," Sal Galen said in surprisingly good English as he straightened and faced us. "We will take Lir Shalan to the medical bay, but it does not look good. I cannot feel the touch of his mind."

Which meant that his control over the Reptilians under his command was now gone. Was he permanently brain-damaged?

All Gideon did was nod slightly. I couldn't really feel anything from him right then except an overwhelming weariness. "So you are in charge now?"

"It would seem so." Although I hadn't seen him give any commands, the Reptilians accompanying Sal Galen moved past and gathered up the fallen form of their leader, carrying him out of the room briskly and with no apparent show of emotion.

"But...what does that mean?" I asked.

Sal Galen's lipless mouth stretched into a smile. For some reason, though, it didn't give me the creeps in the same way that Lir Shalan's smile had. "It means that a great many things will change."

The Reptilians loaned Kelsey a pair of oversized boots. Where they got them, I wasn't sure, although I guessed they must have come from the uniform cache used to supply their hybrid soldiers. Gideon and Sal Galen exchanged a few words in the Reptilian language, and then we were allowed to make our exit from the narrow little box canyon that hid the "back door" to the base.

Feeling both overwhelmed and confused, I followed Gideon down to a barely perceptible trail that would lead us back to the parking area. Kelsey struggled along behind us in her oversized boots, her own expression nearly as perplexed as the one I knew I wore.

"I still don't understand why they would let us go," I said.

"Sal Galen is not Lir Shalan," Gideon told me.

"Yeah, I kind of gathered that. But still—"

"I told Sal Galen of the power you and I commanded, the power that had struck down his commander. Being a wise man, he decided it was better to allow us our freedom. He will have enough to manage in the coming days, I think."

I could understand that. The incapacitation of Lir

Shalan had to have left an enormous power vacuum. Would Sal Galen be enough to fill it?

"So what does this mean?" I asked then. "Will they leave us alone now? What about the women they've taken?"

Gideon held out a hand to help me over a particularly rough patch of ground, then thoughtfully waited in place so he could do the same for Kelsey. She'd been struggling along bravely, but I knew she had to be suffering in those too-big boots Sal Galen had provided for her.

It wasn't until we'd walked a little further that Gideon finally replied.

"As with most things, we'll just have to see."

CHAPTER TWENTY-ONE

I'D NEVER BEEN SO GLAD TO SEE ANYTHING AS MY parents' SUV when we came over the final rise and began to descend to the parking area at the trailhead. Well, scratch that. I was glad to see everyone gathered there, and smiled tiredly as I watched Kara's hand go to her mouth when she caught sight of Kelsey, safe and sound and trudging along behind us.

That tired smile turned into a grin when I saw my brother Michael surge ahead of everyone else, hurrying up the trail so he could rush past us and gather Kelsey in his arms. She let out a surprised little squeak, then happily allowed him to lift her from the path and carry her down to the parking area. When he set her down, my father raised an eyebrow but didn't say anything. The unspoken question hung in the air.

"Well, I could tell her feet were hurting," Michael said, quite reasonably.

And everyone burst out laughing.

Not wanting to linger, we piled into the cars. Lance had looked at my brother, then at Kelsey, and said, "You can ride with us."

So Gideon and I sat in the back seat of my parents' SUV as my father drove away from the trailhead, following Lance's lead and going a good twenty miles an hour over the speed limit. All I could do was pray that we wouldn't get pulled over. Gideon's long robes might be cause for comment, especially since we were still a long way off from Halloween.

"What happened back there?" my mother finally asked.

"Lir Shalan will no longer be a problem," Gideon replied. He held my hand as we sat close to one another, his fingers wrapped around mine so tightly, I wondered if he ever intended to let go.

Not that I minded.

"He's...." she began, then paused delicately.

"Still alive," I said, "but not a threat. At least, that's what Sal Galen appeared to indicate."

"Who's Sal Galen?"

"My fa—Lir Shalan's second-in-command," Gideon replied.

"He seems like a good guy," I added.

My mother twisted in her seat so she could shoot me a disbelieving look over her shoulder. "Did I hear that right? Did you just call a Reptilian a 'good guy'?"

I shrugged. "He let us go."

She was silent for a moment, digesting that comment. Her gaze flicked to Gideon. "*Is* he a good guy?"

Gideon was silent for a long moment. Then he nodded. "Yes. Better than—well, better than those who came before him."

No one said anything after that. And I didn't mind, because all I wanted to do was lay my head on Gideon's shoulder and know that he hadn't betrayed me, had been there for me when I needed him most —and by doing so, might have saved us all.

My parents dropped us off at the cottage, and, after retrieving the spare key from underneath the hose basket on the side of the house, I hurried Gideon inside. Even in Sedona, his current appearance would be sure to raise eyebrows.

"Kara's in an hour," my mother called out as they drove off.

I gave her the thumbs-up just before I shut the door. As soon as we were alone, Gideon rushed toward me, his arms pulling me close so he could press his lips to mine. I opened my mouth to his, eagerly tasting him, reveling in the sensation of our bodies clinging to one another.

After we pulled apart, though, I gave him a reproving look. "You scared the crap out of me back there."

He pushed a curly lock of hair away from my face. "I am sorry, Taryn. I had to resort to that subterfuge because it was the only means I had of making Lir Shalan believe that I was siding firmly with him. Luckily, he always had a difficult time understanding that the entire galaxy didn't think the same way he did."

"And now?"

"I truly don't know." Gideon's fingers worked at the fastening of the robes he wore, and I wondered exactly what he had planned. If we were supposed to be at Kara's house in less than an hour, that didn't leave much time for falling into bed.

Then again, I didn't think I'd mind being late.

That wasn't what Gideon had in mind, though. Underneath the robes he had on a tight-fitting unitard, which made him look like he was going to participate in the luge at the Olympics or something. With the robes slung over one arm, he went into his borrowed room and began to dig out some clean clothes.

As he stripped out of the unitard, I could see that he still wore the leather wristband that functioned as his mobile camouflage. A little sigh of relief escaped my lips. Yes, I liked him as he was, and never would ask him to disguise himself when we were alone together, but that unobtrusive device would make it much easier for him to function in the regular world.

"So you were able to hang on to that," I said, my gaze moving to the wristband.

Gideon finished pulling a T-shirt over his head and gave me a sideways look. "I thought it might make our lives run a little more smoothly."

Well, I couldn't argue with that. "Probably, yes." An emotion I couldn't quite identify flickered in his eyes, so I hurried to add, "I love you, Gideon. I love everything about you, and that includes the way you look. But I'm not going to lie and tell you that it won't be easier for you to have that protective camouflage whenever we go outside the house."

He came to me then and pulled me close, his arms warm and strong around me. "I can't fault you for that. I understand. It's much better that the world has no idea what I am, that I can blend in as easily as Martin and Raphael do."

I gave a small chuckle. "I hate to break it to you, Gideon, but with your looks, you don't exactly 'blend in.' You're freakin' gorgeous."

Shaking his head, he let go of me then and brought my hand to his lips. Just the brush of his mouth against my skin was enough to send those delicious shivers all through my body, right down to my toes, and again I wished we had the time to reconfirm our connection by doing something a bit more involved than merely kissing.

But still....

I looked up at him, at the sensuous lines of his mouth and the deep-set eyes in their fringe of black lashes. Right then I couldn't see anything in his face except relief, and a low-key kind of joy that we were back together.

I didn't want to destroy that, but I had to know. "Gideon, what about your father?"

He expelled a breath. "Sal Galen will take care of him. If the medical facilities at the base aren't sufficient, Lir Shalan will be taken back to the *Eclipse* to be treated there. He will be kept comfortable."

"That's not what I meant. Can you live with it, even if the worst happens?"

"Taryn, I...." He took a step back so he could gaze down at me. In a way, I wished he would have kept holding my hands, although I thought I understood why he needed to put a little distance between us. "This may be difficult for you to understand, but while Lir Shalan might have contributed to my genetic makeup, he was not what you could call a father, not in the way you think of the relationship. When I was young, I didn't see him very often. After my mother died, when I was older...well, he was somewhat more interested, but only as an asset that could be trained, not because I was his son. All that mattered to him was the continuation of his bloodline, and I served that purpose. But if he should die?" An eloquent lift of his shoulders. "I will feel no guilt. He does not deserve to be mourned."

Harsh words, but I wasn't about to argue with

them. How awful it must be to pass from this world and have no one grieve for you, but Lir Shalan had brought that fate upon himself.

It was those whose lives he'd touched that we needed to worry about now.

I went on my tiptoes and kissed Gideon very gently on the cheek. "Let's go to Kara's."

The extended family was there—even Grace and Logan, who must have hurriedly driven down from Flagstaff. We could all barely fit in Kara and Lance's family room, even though it was the biggest space in the house. Chairs had been stolen from the dining room so everyone would have a place to sit.

I caught sight of Michael and Kelsey snugged into one corner of the couch, his arm around her as she laid her head on his shoulder. That very public display of affection might have surprised me, except I couldn't miss the way she was smiling. She was going to milk this abduction thing for all it was worth, and I couldn't really blame her. After all, she'd waited a good long time for Michael to man up. His expression was a little sheepish, but I just grinned at him as Gideon and I entered the room, hoping he'd understand that he had absolutely nothing to be embarrassed about.

Everyone quieted at the sight of Gideon, and I could feel myself tense. While he'd worn his disguise on the drive over here, I'd asked him to deactivate it once we were standing on the front doorstep. My extended family needed to accept him as he was, even if he would have to use the camouflaging device whenever he was out in public.

We'd walked into the family room hand in hand, and his fingers tightened on mine, even as I sensed a flare of unease coming from him. If they made this difficult, I wasn't sure what I would do. I loved them all—they were my family, whether blood relations or not. But I loved Gideon, too, with an intensity I still was having some difficulty understanding. It would break my heart to have to make a choice between them.

But then my father came up to us, hand outstretched. "Thank you, Gideon," he said. "Thank you for saving our girls."

The darker green of a flush spread across his cheeks. "It was nothing, Mr. Oliver."

"Paul." My father's gaze shifted to me. "That was a very brave thing both of you did."

It was my turn to blush. I hadn't recalled being brave, just doing what had to be done. Actually, I'd mostly been scared shitless. "I'm just glad everyone is safe."

"Well, not everyone," Lance remarked. "There's still the little matter of all those missing women."

"I'm hopeful," Gideon said. "Sal Galen has no reason to carry on as my father did. He is a very different person. My best guess is that he will report the mission here on Earth was a failure, and that his people will need to focus their efforts elsewhere."

Lance raised an eyebrow and appeared remarkably unconvinced. No doubt, he had no reason to think favorably of any Reptilian, no matter what Gideon might have to say on the subject. "That so?"

Raphael spoke up then, before Gideon could reply. He and Callista sat on the love seat, their hands knotted together. Both of them wore worried expressions, which seemed to indicate to me they'd discussed the matter a good bit before coming over here. "You speak of this Sal Galen with a good deal of confidence, Gideon, but I'm not sure we can be that optimistic. Do you truly believe that the Reptilians will not send someone else to pick up where Lir Shalan left off?"

A low murmur swept the room, but Gideon just shook his head. "No, I don't think so. This world is valuable to them, true, but it is not the only one where they are attempting to find a promising genetic match. They've suffered enough defeats now that they'll think twice about trying here on Earth again."

"And this world doesn't want them," I added. "The vortexes are sort of like its immune system, always giving us the boost we need to fight them off. If Sal Galen really is the voice of reason that Gideon says he is, he'll go back to their home world and report that there's no use in wasting any more resources here."

"That sounds overly optimistic," Lance said.

"Just because something is optimistic doesn't mean it's not true," I replied.

"Sal Galen told us that things were about to change," Gideon said. "I can only take such a statement to mean that he doesn't intend to continue Lir Shalan's policies. Even if he's recalled and someone else is sent here—"

"We fight again," Logan broke in. His gray eyes were fierce, and he sat up very straight next to Grace. "As much as we have to, for as long as is necessary."

God, I hoped it wouldn't come to that. Twenty-five years had elapsed between the time Kirsten Jones drove the aliens away and their return this spring. Would we be granted that much of a reprieve? Or would the Reptilians be made even more desperate now that the very future of their race was at stake?

I sent a worried glance up at Gideon, but his expression didn't change. Voice calm, he said, "I don't foresee that happening."

Just as he finished speaking, a small chiming beep came from his pocket. He pulled out the conveyor, which sparkled with little flashing green and yellow lights. "That is Sal Galen. He wants to speak with me."

Was that a good thing or a bad thing? I couldn't begin to guess.

"And you, Taryn," he added.

"It's a trick," Lance said.

My parents looked at each other, some of the light in my mother's eyes beginning to dim.

"It is not a trick," Gideon said. "We will go and talk to him. If that's all right with you, Taryn."

I didn't know if it was all right or not. What I did know was that we couldn't refuse Sal Galen's request, not when we might have a chance of ending all this peacefully.

"It's fine," I replied. "Let's go see what he wants."

We drove farther up the canyon, up to the spot along the ridge line where we emerged from Oak Creek's gorge and were following 89A through the pine forests that surrounded Flagstaff. The alien device would work better up here, away from the influence of the creek, or at least, that was what Gideon told me.

"Why not have us drive out to the base?" I asked as the road wound its way through ponderosa forests. "We could have just parked at the trailhead and walked the rest of the way if the conveyor was having trouble with the vortex energies."

He gave me an enigmatic look. "Because Sal Galen is no longer at the base."

"Oh." I swallowed, and did what I could to push back the little thrill of fear that went over me. I was not particularly looking forward to going back onto the *Eclipse,* but there wasn't much I could do about that now.

We pulled off onto a Forest Service road and followed it for long enough that my Honda wouldn't be visible from the highway. I found a pullout, probably used for people who wanted to leave their vehicles behind as they went hiking, and Gideon and I climbed out of the car.

A quick glance around to make sure we truly were alone, and then Gideon activated the conveyor. The sensation was still unpleasant, but at least this time he held my hand during the process, and I told myself I had nothing to worry about.

I guessed I'd have to see about that.

We materialized in a chamber I'd never seen before, a huge cavernous space that looked as if it might have been intended as a hangar for atmospheric craft. At the moment I didn't see any ships, though.

What I did see was a very large crowd of people, at least several hundred of them. I blinked, realizing that I was staring at a group of human women of various races and ethnicities, each with her Reptilian companion. What the hell?

My body tensed. Gideon didn't release his hold on my hand, even as Sal Galen approached. Next to him was a young woman maybe a few years older than I, pretty, with long fawn-brown hair and striking green eyes.

She looked calm enough. Nothing about the way

she stood there in her long dress seemed to indicate she was being held here against her will. In fact, she even smiled when Sal Galen looked down at her before addressing Gideon and me.

"Thank you for coming," he said.

Gideon inclined his head, and I managed a half-hearted smile. What in the world was going on here?

"I wanted to tell you about your father," Sal Galen said then. "He has been made comfortable, but we have determined that the damage to his mind cannot be reversed."

I felt Gideon tense, but he just nodded again, while I could only feel a flood of relief. It was horrible to be happy that someone had suffered permanent brain damage. However, at least this meant that we wouldn't have to worry about Lir Shalan ever again. And maybe this was Sedona's way of finding justice. The alien leader might have found something noble in dying for a cause, but I doubted he would have been pleased by a fate that involved being a mindless invalid for the rest of his life.

"We are about to leave," Sal Galen went on. "And we will be leaving for good."

His words should have relieved me, but I could only think about the woman who stood next to him, and the hundreds more who looked on silently, each with her Reptilian guard.

"What about them?" I asked, lifting my chin in the direction of the watching women.

"They are coming with us."

Gideon shook his head. "You know that is not acceptable."

Sal Galen offered us one of those lipless Reptilian smiles. In this case, though, it wasn't condescending, or cruel. Rather, he seemed amused, as if he was in on a joke we couldn't understand. "The rest have been sent home. These are the ones who wanted to stay."

I must not have been hearing correctly. He couldn't possibly mean that all those women had chosen to remain with their Reptilian captors...could he?

Frowning slightly, Gideon said, "I don't understand."

The woman standing next to Sal Galen spoke then. She had a soft, barely noticeable Southern accent. "I know this all must seem strange to you. But we were offered the choice. We want to go with them."

"But why?" Maybe it had been rude of me to ask the question, but I couldn't keep myself from doing so.

Her hand slipped down to cup her belly. Only for a second or two, but in that moment, I knew she must be carrying Sal Galen's child. "They're not all like Lir Shalan," she said. "Many...but not all. Not all the Reptilians are monsters, just as not all men are good people. A lot of us have nowhere to go, or at least nowhere we want to go back to. We're being offered a chance to make a difference. They need us."

Sal Galen looked down at her, and his expression softened. I'd never been able to read a Reptilian before, but I could feel it then, a soft pulse of affection, of…

…of love.

Was it possible? Gideon had made it sound as if the Reptilians were incapable of love, but he could have only been speaking of his experiences with his own father. And maybe, just maybe, that strange alien race did have it within their hearts to love…if that love was able to find its true object.

"I see," Gideon said. He looked past Sal Galen to the assembled group of Reptilians and humans. Most of them stood very close to one another; some of them were actually holding hands. With so many clustered together, I couldn't get anything except a very general impression, but I didn't sense any fear. Nervousness, excitement, but nothing to tell me that these women didn't want to go with the aliens who had claimed them. "And I have your assurances that the others have already been sent back?"

"Yes. It took some time, but they will all awake in their beds, with perhaps a memory of a bad dream."

"But surely they'll be told that they were abducted," Gideon said. "And what if any of them were with child?"

"Some were," Sal Galen said. His tone sounded subdued, but he looked directly at us without blinking. "They did not want those children, but of course the embryos they carried were precious to us. So they were taken in the usual manner, and will be sustained until they can survive on their own. It is not optimal, of course, but I would not force an unwanted child on anyone. Parents will be found for them when the time comes."

Probably the best solution to a very difficult situation. And the situation wasn't even completely unheard-of; abduction stories were full of phantom pregnancies, of accounts from women who swore they were pregnant, but who then awoke from their abduction experiences with absolutely no evidence that they'd ever been carrying a child. In this situation, it was probably a mercy that they'd escaped so unscathed.

"It is the best I could manage," Sal Galen went on. "But it has been determined that we have enough candidates here to provide some hope, and so we are going home."

I didn't know enough about biology and genetics to know whether a few hundred-odd women and the children they might produce would be enough to salvage an entire race. Maybe, especially if the embryos taken from the women who didn't want them were added to that number. Better minds than mine must have made that determination.

Gideon nodded. "The wisest course. I think this world has shown that it does not respond well to interference."

"True enough." Sal Galen paused then, his gaze sharpening as he looked at Gideon. "But you, Lir Gideon—you are staying?"

Without hesitation, Gideon replied, "Oh, yes. This is my home now." And his fingers tightened on mine, warm and welcome and reassuring.

So the Reptilians were gone, their not-so-captive brides leaving with them. I wondered about those women, about what it was in their lives that made them think a future on an alien planet with an alien mate would be better than what they were leaving behind. But then I recalled the haunted look in that nameless woman's eyes as she'd stood close to Sal Galen and told me that not all Reptilians were monsters. Maybe she was leaving the real monster behind somewhere on good old planet Earth.

Earth. Yes, the Reptilians had gone back to their home world, but they'd still left a mess behind them. When several thousand women reappear at the same time with nearly identical stories about being kidnapped by aliens, it's the sort of thing that's pretty hard to sweep under the rug.

There were hearings, lawsuits, mutters about a possible impeachment. That didn't go anywhere, mostly because there was no real evidence connecting the President to the people who'd brokered the original deal with Lir Shalan. She even took a lie detector test to prove her innocence, but many people believed she must have been in on the scheme, regardless of what the lie detector said. With the aliens gone, there was no one around to either corroborate her story or deny it.

For myself, I was fairly certain her hands were clean in this matter. Maybe I was giving too much credit to my sex, but I just didn't want to think that a woman would sell out other women in such a way. At any rate, she managed to hang on to her office while a flurry of house-cleaning went on around her, although everyone knew she'd only be a one-term commander-in-chief. No reelection efforts could survive that kind of scandal.

The same sort of soul-searching and house-cleaning went on around the globe. Several leaders, including the president of Venezuela, were actually removed from their posts.

As for the tech the Reptilians were supposed to have handed over...well, its fate was much more mysterious. Maybe they'd stalled and hadn't actually provided anything concrete yet. I could see Lir Shalan doing just that, making promises while women were being systematically scooped up from around the globe, hoping he could hedge and obfuscate long enough that he would meet his quota and then disappear, leaving those gullible humans empty-handed.

Or maybe it had all been removed to the deepest, darkest, most secret lab facilities money could buy.

Lance and Martin and Raphael and my father had several lengthy discussions on the topic, trying to decide whether the tech actually existed, and, if so, where it had gone and who had taken it. True to his usual jaundiced outlook on the world, Lance insisted that the remnants of the oil companies, trying to hang on to the market share they had left, had spirited it away somewhere to prevent anyone from having access to truly renewable energy. My father thought it must be in a secret base, while Martin and Raphael —who did have far more experience dealing with the Reptilians—guessed it had never been in human hands at all.

And Gideon had just shaken his head and smiled. When I asked him for his thoughts on the matter, he'd only shrugged and said that if the World Space Agency came out and announced its new ships had been equipped with faster-than-light drive, then he'd know where the technology had ended up. Until then, he didn't want to hazard a guess.

We were still living in the cottage, trying to figure out what to do with ourselves. Kara had said we could stay there as long as we needed, giving us a much-appreciated refuge, but I knew that couldn't last forever. Lance knew people who knew people, and so it hadn't been too difficult to provide Gideon with a false identity, one that made him seem like just another American citizen, same as the rest of us. I went back to work doing readings at Crystal Visions because we needed to have some money coming in, even though Kara wasn't charging us any rent.

And then Gideon saw me staring at the computer one morning, gazing at the page where I was supposed to start registering for classes. "You seem troubled," he said.

"Oh, well...." I lifted my shoulders. "I was supposed to transfer to NAU for the fall semester, and I need to sign up for classes soon if I want to get anything good. But now...."

At once, he bent and kissed me on the cheek. "My love, nothing has changed. You should go."

I blinked at him. "But what about you?"

"Well," he said reasonably, "I suppose I should go, too."

And he did. I still wasn't sure how Lance and his secret army of hackers managed it, but somehow they manufactured an academic record for Gideon and sent it off. It must have been something pretty stellar, because he was accepted within the week, even though transfers for the fall semester were officially closed.

So we would be moving to Flagstaff and going to college together, and even though that fate seemed a little mundane for the son of a former Reptilian leader, Gideon was happy about the changes coming in our future. "I need to fit in, don't I?" he asked. "How better than as just another college student?"

I couldn't really argue with that. He even managed to line up a job at the Starbucks at the mall, working as a barista. Well, I couldn't deny that he did make a good cup of coffee. For myself, there weren't a lot of openings for psychics in Flagstaff, but I found a part-time position at a crystal shop in the old town district, so I wouldn't be going too far afield. Between those two jobs—and because Michael had said we could take over his inexpensive apartment when the lease was up—we felt we were pretty well set.

On the Fourth of July, Kara had everyone over to the house for their traditional barbecue. The big oaks and sycamores that shaded the property made it fairly safe for Gideon to leave off his disguise, so we were able to relax and enjoy being with the family. By that point, everyone was so used to his appearance that it really didn't merit a second glance.

The sun was hot, but under the trees the breeze was pleasant. Lance and Kevin had brought out the long picnic tables they kept in storage for much of the year, and we all gathered around, trying to decide what to eat next—another hot dog, or some of Kara's famous barbecue beans, or maybe it was time to move on to strawberry shortcake. Beer bottles cooled in several plastic tubs, and sangria sat in a glass dispenser full of bits of lemon and lime and orange.

I sipped sangria and leaned my head against Gideon's shoulder, watching as Melissa and Grace and Logan played Frisbee out on the lawn. My father and Lance were wrapped up in another of their ongoing conspiracy discussions, while Martin, Kirsten, Kara, and my mother seemed content to listen and just shake their heads every once in a while. Raphael and Callista had wandered off to wade in the creek. And Michael sat at the end of the table, Kelsey next to him, as they were immersed in a conversation about the condo they'd just rented, and were figuring out the logistics of getting moved in before he started his new job at Lowell Observatory in late August, now that his dissertation had been accepted.

"Happy?" Gideon asked, his voice warm and low at my ear.

I looked around at all of us, at this strange family that had endured the test of time, alien invasions, and personal triumphs and tragedies. There had been moments in my life when I'd desperately wanted to be normal, when I didn't want the gifts I'd inherited, but the girl who'd wished she could be just like everyone else had long since fled. It was my very differences that had brought me to where I was now, to the man who sat beside me and woke up next to me every day. I knew I wouldn't have wanted it any other way.

"Oh, yes, Gideon," I said, then covered his hand with mine. The contrast between his green skin and my lightly tanned fingers was almost shocking in the bright sunlight, but I didn't mind. His alien coloring was part of who he was, part of who he would always be, and I wouldn't ever do anything to change it. I took in a deep breath of the warm air, the light wind scented with the perfumes of a thousand flowers and the deeper, mossier notes of the creek. Sedona's energy slept within me, its task now done.

My fingers tightened on Gideon's, feeling the strength in him, the courage to face a new and different future on a world he was still coming to know.

"I'm very happy, my love."

The End

AUTHOR'S NOTE

Coming Full Circle

When I first sat down to write *Bad Vibrations* back in 2011, I really had no intention of creating anything except a fun paranormal romance adventure story that would indulge my lifelong interest in UFOs and the supernatural. Self-publishing at Amazon was fairly new back then, and I didn't give much thought to turning the book into a series.

My research brought me to Sedona, and I fell in love with the wild natural beauty of the place, from the soaring red rocks to the clear waters and cascades of Oak Creek. Fast-forward a few years, and my writing career was taking off to the point where I could create my stories full time. *Desert Hearts* and *Angel Fire* joined *Bad Vibrations* as I realized there was a much bigger story to tell. In the interim, my husband and I relocated to Sedona for several years, where I found more inspiration among the red rocks. The Sedona Files saga grew and grew, and came to include the second generation of UFO hunters in *Star Crossed, Falling Angels,* and *Enemy Mine.*

Bad Vibrations was set in the early spring, as is *Enemy Mine.* That decision wasn't anything conscious on my part, but I realize now that moving through the seasons and the years has allowed these books to come full circle, to arrive at a place of growth and renewal, even as the series winds down to its end.

Blessings,
Christine Pope

ALSO BY CHRISTINE POPE

PROJECT DEMON HUNTERS

(Paranormal Romance)

Unquiet Souls

Unbound Spirits

Unholy Ground

THE WITCHES OF CANYON ROAD

(Paranormal Romance)

Hidden Gifts

Darker Paths

Mysterious Ways

A Canyon Road Christmas

Demon Born

An Ill Wind

Higher Ground

THE WITCHES OF CLEOPATRA HILL*

(Paranormal Romance)

Darkangel

Darknight

Darkmoon

Sympathetic Magic

Protector

Spellbound

A Cleopatra Hill Christmas

Impractical Magic

Strange Magic

The Arrangement

Defender

Bad Blood

Deep Magic

Darktide

Books 1-3 and Books 4-6 of this series are also available in two separate omnibus editions at special boxed set prices. Chronicles of Cleopatra Hill includes the series' two "back in time" novellas, *Bad Blood* and *The Arrangement*.

Or get the entire series in one enormous, specially priced boxed set! (Not available on Amazon.)

THE DJINN WARS

(Paranormal Romance)

Chosen

Taken

Fallen

Broken

Forsaken

Forbidden

Awoken

Illuminated

Stolen

Forgotten

Driven

Unspoken (June 2019)

Books 1-3 and Books 4-6 of this series are also available in two separate omnibus editions at special boxed set prices!

THE WATCHERS TRILOGY*

(Paranormal Romance)

Falling Dark

Dead of Night

Rising Dawn

The Watchers Trilogy is also available in a specially priced boxed set!

THE SEDONA FILES*

(Paranormal Romance)

Bad Vibrations

Desert Hearts

Angel Fire

Star Crossed

Falling Angels

Enemy Mine

Get the first three books of this series in an omnibus edition, or read the complete six-book series in one super-low-priced boxed set!

TALES OF THE LATTER KINGDOMS

(Fantasy Romance)

All Fall Down

Dragon Rose

Binding Spell

Ashes of Roses

One Thousand Nights

Threads of Gold

The Wolf of Harrow Hall

Moon Dance

The Song of the Thrush

Books 1-3 and Books 4-6 of this series are also available in two separate omnibus editions at special boxed set prices.

THE GAIAN CONSORTIUM SERIES*

(Science Fiction Romance)

Beast (free prequel novella)

Blood Will Tell

Breath of Life

The Gaia Gambit

The Mandala Maneuver

The Titan Trap

The Zhore Deception

The Refugee Ruse

Books 1-3 of this series are also available in an omnibus edition at a special boxed set price!

STANDALONE TITLES

Hearts on Fire

Sympathy for the Devil

Taking Dictation

Night Music

Golden Heart

* Indicates a completed series

ABOUT THE AUTHOR

USA Today bestselling author Christine Pope has been writing stories ever since she commandeered her family's Smith-Corona typewriter back in grade school. Her work includes paranormal romance, fantasy romance, and science fiction/space opera romance. She makes her home in Arizona.

Don't miss out on any of Christine's new releases — sign up for her newsletter today!

Christine Pope on the Web:
www.christinepope.com

facebook.com/ChristinePopeAuthor
twitter.com/ChristineJPope